"They're Here..." Invasion of the BODY SNATCHERS

A Tribute

Kevin McCarthy

"They're Here..."
Invasion of the BODY SNATCHERS

A Tribute

Edited by Kevin McCarthy and Ed Gorman

BERKLEY BOULEVARD BOOKS, NEW YORK

"THEY'RE HERE . . .": *INVASION OF THE BODY SNATCHERS:* A TRIBUTE

A Berkley Boulevard Book / published by arrangement with the authors

PRINTING HISTORY
Berkley Boulevard trade paperback edition / January 1999

Book design by Lisa Stokes

Cover photographs by Motion Picture and Television Archive

For information address: The Berkley Publishing Group, a member of Penguin Putnam Inc., 375 Hudson Street, New York, New York 10014.

The Penguin Putnam Inc. World Wide Web site address is
http://www.penguinputnam.com

ISBN: 0-425-16527-2

BERKLEY BOULEVARD
Berkley Boulevard Books are published by The Berkley Publishing Group,
a member of Penguin Putnam Inc., 375 Hudson Street, New York, New York 10014.
BERKLEY BOULEVARD and its logo
are trademarks belonging to Berkley Publishing Corporation.

PRINTED IN THE UNITED STATES OF AMERICA

10 9 8 7 6 5 4 3 2 1

CONTENTS

Introduction
These Immigrants Don't Need No Stinkin' Green Cards!

Dean Koontz

WHEN I SAW THE FIRST VERSION OF *INVASION OF the Body Snatchers,* directed by Don Siegel, I was only a kid, but I knew it contained more truth than any movie I had ever seen before.

I don't mean that I suddenly suspected the neighbors of having gone to high school in another galaxy or that I expected to find a giant pod tucked in the back of my closet. Well, okay, I *did* expect to find a giant pod in my closet, but the worst thing I ever turned up, after countless panicky searches night after night, was an old sneaker with an aromatic touch of mildew in it. And that was just last week.

When I say the movie brims with truth, I am not saying that the story line is literally true. Rather, it expresses profound truths through a compelling metaphor. Some critics have suggested that the film plays on fears of communism and is perhaps the most effective of the red-scare movies, but that's an inadequate interpretation. In the twentieth century, so *many* powerful forces have reshaped society so rapidly, compared to the more measured pace of change in previous centuries, that it's no surprise when we feel besieged and in danger of losing our humanity. Communism and fascism are the obvious examples of ideologies that not merely devalued the individual but denied legitimacy to the very idea that the masses exist for any purposes other than to serve an elite and to die for the philosophies of that elite. Yet an honest evaluation of most political movements that have followed the collapse of fascism and communism will reveal utopian fantasies of one stripe or another, each of which would sacrifice individuals to some imagined greater good and would result in hive societies that allow no freedom and no joy, except the psychotic joy of the true believer swept away by messianic rapture.

Even many basically nonpolitical movements with admirable intentions have embraced the antihuman attitudes and methodology of totalitarian ideologies. For example, though it is imperative that the environmental movement function rationally and successfully, if we are to have an ecologically healthy world to give to future generations, it seems as though half of the various organizations under the environmentalism umbrella have been co-opted by fanatics who want to use ecological concerns to effect social engineering that was tried and failed under both fascist and communist regimes; many actually argue that human beings are "unnatural," an infection that is destroying the planet, and that we have no right to be here.

The furious pace of technological change is another dehumanizing force. Labor-saving technology was supposed to give us more leisure time, but a greater percentage of our waking hours is spent in work or work-related tasks than ever before, as we spin like squirrels in exercise cages, desperate to keep current with change and, therefore, employable. This leaves less time for mothers and fathers to spend with their families and virtually no time at all to interact with their neighbors, to function as an integral part of their communities. A sense of isolation grows.

We were told that the information revolution would solve all the problems that previous technological change had wrought. The personal computer is indeed liberating, and the day may actually come when it saves us time rather than merely enabling us to do more work than ever before. Many claim to have found a sense of community through the Internet; but this can be little more than an illusion if few of these long-distance friendships result in the communicants meeting face-to-face and meaningfully interacting with one another beyond cyberspace. Relationship-building at a distance, through the filter of a computer, is ultimately ineffective for the sincere friend-seeker, but it is ideally suited to the sociopath whose powers of manipulation are enhanced when he can operate not merely behind his usual masks but behind an electronic mask as well. Many of us spend the evening hours online, staring at a screen rather than at human faces, communicating without the profound nuances of human voices and facial expressions, seeking sympathy and tenderness without the need to touch.

All the while, through our bones creeps the persistent feeling that we are losing our humanity. No wonder we *still* respond to Don Siegel's *Invasion of the Body Snatchers* so powerfully, even more than forty years after its initial release. Increasingly alienated from community, family, and friends, we feel an uneasiness that at times borders on paranoia.

When modern men and women lost religious faith, they lost the associated belief that human beings are special, that we were created with purpose to undertake a life with meaning. Science, technology, and politics have not yet filled that void and probably never will be able to do so, especially not if they continue to be powered by the ideologies that have thus far informed them. If we believe that we are just animals, without immortal souls, we are already but one step removed from pod people.

The original *Invasion of the Body Snatchers* has at its center this fundamental truth of modern life, which is why year by year its power as art grows rather than diminishes. Aware of how rarely the products of Hollywood contain any truth, I resisted seeing Philip Kaufman's—and W. D. Richter's—remake when it hit theaters. I assumed that it would not measure up to the original, that it would be packed with bogus and unnecessary special effects, that Hollywood once again would have succeeded in turning a silk purse into a sow's ear. When I finally watched it on laser disc, I was astonished and delighted to discover that it was a superb piece of work. By moving the setting from a small town to a metropolis, the director and screenwriter brought new power to the dual themes of alienation and dehumanization. The scenes near the end, in which packs of shadowy pod people rush through city streets in pursuit of the unconverted, bring instantly to mind images of Nazis chasing down Jews and evoke the terrors of every genocide, pogrom, and political repression that has made this such a century of shame.

I had thought that the inimitable Kevin McCarthy's superb, understated performance in the original couldn't be equalled. Although there is no entirely parallel role in the remake, Donald Sutherland's Matthew Bennell is as compelling as McCarthy's small-town doctor. The performances of Veronica Cartwright, Brooke Adams, and Jeff Goldblum help this version of the story to achieve immediacy and poignancy.

No films would have existed, of course, without Jack Finney's classic science-fiction novel, *The Body Snatchers*. I have a long list of writers whose work I admire, and the reasons for admiring them are varied. I find Ray Bradbury's fiction exceptional because of his bold use of language, his willingness to take chances with wildly colorful metaphors and striking imagery, and his ebullience and contagious love of life. I can reread the best of James M. Cain, because his economical prose, his risky use of pulp conventions in a mainstream context, and his unblinking fascination with the dark side of the human heart are bracing. Few writers handle characterization, pace, and milieu a fraction as well as John D. MacDonald. I don't read Jack Finney for his style, which is clean and engaging but not as strongly personal as that of Bradbury. I don't read Finney for his narrative pace, which is compelling enough but which is certainly not marked by breathless suspense. To me, one of the greatest strengths of Jack Finney's work is his ability to describe and explore complex emotions in an admirably low-key fashion that nevertheless leaves the reader saying, "Yes, I know exactly how that feels." This is a considerable achievement. Dickens could do it. Comparatively few are good at it. Even writers whose novels scintillate with ideas, atmosphere, and mood are often emotionally dead on the page. In some, this may result from inadequate empathy; others may produce emotionally barren work because they mistakenly equate genuine sentiment with sentimentality and fear being pilloried by sarcastic critics. Finney's two most famous novels—*The Body Snatchers* and *Time and Again*—make us *feel*, and that is why they have such lasting power, though each tale evokes a rather different set of emotions. This is also why Finney's work is well suited to film adaptation: film is fundamentally an emotional rather than intellectual medium. Which is not to say that Finney's books lack intellectual content; indeed, we feel what these characters feel precisely because they are people who *think*, people of some charm and wit. Fear, joy, loneliness, longing—Finney had a way with this material, and that was a gift of gold to Don Siegel, Daniel Mainwaring, Philip Kaufman, and W. D. Richter.

It's a gift of gold to all of us, in fact, and tonight I'm going to treat myself to a double feature: the Siegel and Kaufman versions. First, of course, I'll inspect the back of my closet. And look under the bed. And see if there's anything odd in the garage cabinets. I ought to do a quick search of the attic, too, and make sure there's nothing but a spare tire in the trunk of the car. And, hey, with all the companies dealing in house alarms and personal-security these days, why hasn't *someone* invented a device that can warn you if the person to whom you're talking is composed of a significant percentage of vegetable matter? We really *need* a gadget like that. We really, really do.

"They're Here..." Invasion of the BODY SNATCHERS

A Tribute

Photo from *Invasion of the Body Snatchers* courtesy of Republic Entertainment, Inc.

INVASION OF THE BODY SNATCHERS

Stephen King

LET ME SUGGEST THAT ONE OF THE FILMS OF THE last thirty years to find a pressure point with great accuracy was Don Siegel's *Invasion of the Body Snatchers*. Further along, we'll discuss the novel—and Jack Finney, the author, will also have a few things to say—but for now, let's look briefly at the film.

There is nothing really physically horrible in the Siegel version of *Invasion of the Body Snatchers;** no gnarled and evil star travelers here, no twisted, mutated shape under the facade of normality. The pod people are just a little different, that's all. A little vague. A little messy. Although Finney never puts this fine a point on it in his book, he certainly suggests that the most horrible thing about "them" is that they lack even the most common and easily attainable sense of aesthetics. Never mind, Finney suggests, that these usurping aliens from outer space can't appreciate *La Traviata* or *Moby Dick* or even a good Norman Rockwell cover on the *Saturday Evening Post*. That's bad enough, but—my God!—they don't mow their lawns or replace the pane of garage

---

*There is in the Philip Kaufman remake, though. There is a moment in that film which is repulsively horrible. It comes when Donald Sutherland uses a rake to smash in the face of a mostly formed pod. This "person's" face breaks in with sickening ease, like a rotted piece of fruit, and lets out an explosion of the most realistic stage blood that I have ever seen in a color film. When that moment came, I winced, clapped a hand over my mouth . . . and wondered how in the hell the movie had ever gotten its PG rating.

glass that got broken when the kid down the street batted a baseball through it. They don't repaint their houses when they get flaky. The roads leading into Santa Mira, we're told, are so full of potholes and washouts that pretty soon the salesmen who service the town—who aerate its municipal lungs with the life-giving atmosphere of capitalism, you might say—will no longer bother to come.

The gross-out level is one thing, but it is on that second level of horror that we often experience that low sense of anxiety which we call "the creeps." Over the years, *Invasion of the Body Snatchers* has given a lot of people the creeps, and all sorts of high-flown ideas have been imputed to Siegel's film version. It was seen as an anti-McCarthy film until someone pointed out the fact that Don Siegel's political views could hardly be called leftish. Then people began seeing it as a "better dead than Red" picture. Of the two ideas, I think that second one better fits the film that Siegel made, the picture that ends with Kevin McCarthy in the middle of a freeway, screaming "They're here already! You're next!" to cars which rush heedlessly by him. But in my heart, I don't really believe that Siegel was wearing a political hat at all when he made the movie (and you will see later that Jack Finney has never believed it, either); I believe he was simply having fun and that the undertones . . . just happened.

This doesn't invalidate the idea that there is an allegorical element in *Invasion of the Body Snatchers*; it is simply to suggest that sometimes these pressure points, these terminals of fear, are so deeply buried and yet so vital that we may tap them like artesian wells—saying one thing out loud while we express something else in a whisper. The Philip Kaufman version of Finney's novel is fun (although, to be fair, not quite as much fun as Siegel's), but that whisper has changed into something entirely different: the subtext of Kaufman's picture seems to satirize the whole I'm-okay-you're-okay-so-let's-get-in-the-hot-tub-and-massage-our-precious-consciousness movement of the egocentric seventies. Which is to suggest that, although the uneasy dreams of the mass subconscious may change from decade to decade, the pipeline into that well of dreams remains constant and vital.

This is the real danse macabre, I suspect: those remarkable moments when the creator of a horror story is able to unite the conscious and subconscious mind with one potent idea. I believe it happened to a greater degree with the Siegel version of *Invasion of the Body Snatchers*, but of course both Siegel and Kaufman were able to proceed courtesy of Jack Finney, who sank the original well.

From urban paranoia to small-town paranoia: Jack Finney's *The Body Snatchers*.* Finney himself has the following things to say about his book, which was originally published as a Dell paperback original in 1955:

"The book . . . was written in the early 1950s, and I don't really remember a lot about it. I do recall that I simply felt in the mood to write something about a strange event or a series of them in a small town; something inexplicable. And that my first thought was that a dog would be injured or killed by a car, and it would be discovered that a part of the animal's skeleton was of stainless steel; bone and steel intermingled, that is, a thread of steel running into bone and bone into steel so that it was clear the two had grown together. But this idea led to nothing in my mind. . . . I remember that I wrote the first chapter—pretty much as it appeared, if I am recalling correctly—in which people complained that someone close to them was in actuality an imposter. But I didn't know where this was to lead, either. However, during the course of fooling around with this, trying to make it work out, I came across a reputable scientific theory that objects might in fact be pushed through space by the pressure of light, and that dormant life of some sort might conceivably drift through space . . . and [this] eventually worked the book out.

"I was never satisfied with my own explanation of how these

---

*As previously noted, the late-seventies remake of the Finney novel resets the story in San Francisco, opting for an urban paranoia which results in a number of sequences strikingly like those which open Polanski's film version of *Rosemary's Baby*. But Philip Kaufman lost more than he gained, I think, by taking Finney's story out of its natural small-town-with-a-bandstand-in-the-park setting.

dry leaflike objects came to resemble the people they imitated; it seemed, and seems, weak, but it was the best I could do.

"I have read explanations of the 'meaning' of this story, which amuse me, because there is no meaning at all; it was just a story meant to entertain, and with no more meaning than that. The first movie version of the book followed the book with great faithfulness, except for the foolish ending; and I've always been amused by the contentions of people connected with the picture that they had a message of some sort in mind. If so, it's a lot more than I ever did, and since they followed my story very closely, it's hard to see how this message crept in. And when the message has been defined, it has always sounded a little simple-minded to me. The idea of writing a whole book in order to say that it's not really a good thing for us all to be alike, and that individuality is a good thing, makes me laugh."

Nevertheless, Jack Finney has written a great deal of fiction about the idea that individuality is a good thing and that conformity can start to get pretty scary after it passes a certain point.

His comments (in a letter to me dated December 24, 1979) about the first film version of *The Body Snatchers* raised a grin on my own face as well. As Pauline Kael, Penelope Gilliatt, and all of those sober-sided film critics so often prove, no one is so humorless as a big-time film critic or so apt to read deep meanings into simple doings ("In *The Fury*," Pauline Kael intoned, apparently in all seriousness, "Brian De Palma has found the junk heart of America.")—it is as if these critics feel it necessary to prove and re-prove their own literacy; they are like teenage boys who feel obliged to demonstrate and redemonstrate their macho . . . perhaps most of all to themselves. This may be because they are working on the fringes of a field which deals entirely with pictures and the spoken word; they must surely be aware that while it requires at least a high-school education to understand and appreciate all the facets of even such an accessible book as *The Body Snatchers*, any illiterate with four dollars in his or her pocket can go to a movie and find the junk heart of America. Movies are merely picture books that talk, and this seems to have left many literate movie critics with acute feelings of inferiority. Filmmakers themselves are often happy to participate in this grotesque critical overkill, and I applauded Sam Peckinpah in my heart when he made this laconic reply to a critic who asked him why he had *really* made such a violent picture as *The Wild Bunch:* "I like shoot-em-ups." Or so he was reputed to have said, and if it ain't true, gang, it oughtta be.

The Don Siegel version of *The Body Snatchers* is an amusing case where the film critics tried to have it both ways. They began by saying that both Finney's novel and Siegel's film were allegories about the witch-hunt atmosphere that accompanied the McCarthy hearings. Then Siegel himself spoke up and said that this film was really about the Red Menace. He did not go so far as to say that there was a Commie under every American's bed, but there can be little doubt that Siegel at least believed he was making a movie about a creeping fifth column. It is the ultimate in paranoia, we might say: they're out there *and they look just like us!*

In the end it's Finney who comes away sounding the most right; *The Body Snatchers* is just a good story, one to be read and savored for its own unique satisfactions. In the quarter-century since its original publication as a humble paperback original (a shorter version appeared in *Collier's*, one of those good old magazines that fell by the wayside in order to make space on the newsstands of America for such intellectual publications as *Hustler, Screw,* and *Big Butts*), the book has been rarely out of print. It reached its nadir as a Fotonovel in the wake of the Philip Kaufman remake; if there is a lower, slimier, more antibook concept than the Fotonovel, I don't know what it would be. I think I'd rather see my kids reading a stack of Beeline Books than one of those photo-comics.

It reached its zenith as a Gregg Press hardcover in 1976. Gregg Press is a small company which has re-issued some fifty or sixty science fiction and fantasy books—novels, collections, and anthologies—originally published as paperbacks, in hardcover. The editors of the Gregg series (David Hartwell and L. W. Currey) have chosen wisely and well, and in the library of any reader who cares honestly about science fiction—and about books themselves as lovely artifacts—you're apt to find one or more of these distinctive green volumes with the red-gold stamping on the spines.

Oh dear God, we're off on another tangent. Well, never mind;

I believe that what I started to say was simply that I think Finney's contention that *The Body Snatchers* is just a story is both right and wrong. My own belief about fiction, long and deeply held, is that story *must* be paramount over all other considerations in fiction; that story *defines* fiction, and that all other considerations—theme, mood, tone, symbol, style, even characterization—are expendable. There are critics who take the strongest possible exception to this view of fiction, and I really believe that they are the critics who would feel vastly more comfortable if *Moby Dick* were a doctoral thesis on cetology rather than an account of what happened on the *Pequod*'s final voyage. A doctoral thesis is what a million student papers have reduced this tale to, but the story still remains—"This is what happened to Ishmael." As story still remains in *Macbeth, The Faerie Queen, Pride and Prejudice, Jude the Obscure, The Great Gatsby* . . . and Jack Finney's *The Body Snatchers*. And story, thank God, after a certain point becomes irreducible, mysterious, impervious to analysis. You will find no English master's thesis in any college library titled "The Story-Elements of Melville's *Moby Dick*." And if you do find such a thesis, send it to me. I'll eat it. With A-1 Steak Sauce.

All very fine. And yet I don't think Finney would argue with the idea that story values are determined by the mind through which they are filtered, and that the mind of any writer is a product of his outer world and inner temper. It is just the fact of this filter that has set the table for all those would-be English M.A.'s, and I certainly would not want you to think that I begrudge them their degrees—God knows that as an English major I slung enough bullshit to fertilize most of east Texas—but a great number of the people who are sitting at the long and groaning table of Graduate Studies in English are cutting a lot of invisible steaks and roasts . . . not to mention trading the Emperor's new clothes briskly back and forth in what may be the largest academic yard sale the world has ever seen.

Still, what we have here is a Jack Finney novel, and we can say certain things about it simply because it is a Jack Finney novel. First, we can say that it will be grounded in absolute reality—a prosy reality that is almost humdrum, at least to begin with. When we first meet the book's hero (and here I think Finney probably would object if I used the more formal word *protagonist* . . . so I won't), Dr. Miles Bennell, he is letting his last patient of the day out; a sprained thumb. Becky Driscoll enters—and how is that for the perfect all-American name?—with the first off-key note: her cousin Wilma has somehow gotten the idea that her uncle Ira really isn't her uncle anymore. But this note is faint and barely audible under the simple melodies of small-town life that Finney plays so well in the book's opening chapters . . . and Finney's rendering of the small-town archetype in this book may be the best to come out of the 1950s.

The keynote that Finney sounds again and again in these first few chapters is so low-key pleasant that in less sure hands it would become insipid: nice. Again and again Finney returns to that word; things in Santa Mira, he tells us, are not great, not wild and crazy, not terrible, not boring. Things in Santa Mira are nice. No one here is laboring under that old Chinese curse "May you live in interesting times."

"For the first time I really saw her face again. I saw it was the same nice face . . ." This from page nine. A few pages later: "It was nice out, temperature around sixty-five, and the light was good; . . . still plenty of sun."

Cousin Wilma is also nice, if rather plain. Miles thinks she would have made a good wife and mother, but she just never married. "That's how it goes," Miles philosophizes, innocently unaware of any banality. He tells us he wouldn't have believed her the type of woman to have mental problems, "but still, you never know."

This stuff shouldn't work, and yet somehow it does; we feel that Miles has somehow stepped through the first-person convention and is actually talking to us, just as it seems that Tom Sawyer is actually talking to us in the Twain novel . . . and Santa Mira, California, as Finney presents it to us, is exactly the sort of town where we would almost expect to see Tom whitewashing a fence (there would be no Huck around, sleeping in a hogshead, though; not in Santa Mira).

The Body Snatchers is the only Finney book which can rightly be called a horror novel, but Santa Mira—which is a typical "nice" Finney setting—is the perfect locale for such a tale. Perhaps one horror novel is all that Finney had to write; certainly it was enough to set the mold for what we now call "the modern horror novel." If there is such a thing, there can be no doubt at all that Finney had a large hand in inventing it. I have used the phrase "off-key note" earlier on, and that is Finney's actual method in *The Body Snatchers,* I think; one off-key note, then two, then a ripple, then a run of them. Finally the jagged, discordant music of horror overwhelms the melody entirely. But Finney understands that there is no horror without beauty; no discord without a prior sense of melody; no nasty without nice.

There are no Plains of Leng here; no Cyclopean ruins under the earth; no shambling monsters in the subway tunnels under New York. At about the same time Jack Finney was writing *The Body Snatchers,* Richard Matheson was writing his classic short story "Born of Man and Woman," the story that begins: "today my mother called me retch. you retch she said." Between the two of them, they made the break from the Lovecraftian fantasy that had held sway over serious American writers of horror for two decades or more. Matheson's short story was published well before *Weird Tales* went broke; Finney's novel was published by Dell a year after. Although Matheson published two early short stories in *Weird Tales,* neither writer is associated with this icon of American fantasy-horror magazines; they represent the birth of an almost entirely new breed of American fantasist, just as, in the years 1977–1980, the emergence of Ramsey Campbell and Robert Aickman in England may represent another significant turn of the wheel.*

I have mentioned that Finney's short story "The Third Level"

---

*At the same time Finney and Matheson began administering their own particular brands of shock treatment to the American imagination, Ray Bradbury began to be noticed in the fantasy community, and during the fifties and sixties, Bradbury's name would become the one most readily identified with the genre in the mind of the general reading public. But for me, Bradbury lives and works alone in his own country, and his remarkable, iconoclastic style has never been successfully imitated. Vulgarly put, when God made Ray Bradbury He broke the mold.

predates Rod Serling's *The Twilight Zone* series; in exactly the same fashion, Finney's little town of Santa Mira predates and points the way toward Peter Straub's fictional town of Milburn, New York; Thomas Tryon's Cornwall Coombe, Connecticut; and my own little town of Salem's Lot, Maine. It is even possible to see Finney's influence in Blatty's *The Exorcist,* where foul doings become fouler when set against the backdrop of Georgetown, a suburb which is quiet, graciously rich . . . and nice.

Finney concentrates on sewing a seam between the prosaic reality of his little you-can-see-it-before-your-eyes town and the outright fantasy of the pods which will follow. He sews the seam with such fine stitchwork that when we cross over from the world that really is and into a world of utter make-believe, we are hardly aware of any change. This is a major feat, and like the magician who can make the cards walk effortlessly over the tips of his fingers in apparent defiance of gravity, it looks so easy that you'd be tempted to believe anyone could do it. You see the trick, but not the long hours of practice that went into creating the effect.

We have spoken briefly of paranoia in *Rosemary's Baby*; in *The Body Snatchers,* the paranoia becomes full, rounded, and complete. If we are all incipient paranoids—if we all take a quick glance down at ourselves when laughter erupts at the cocktail party, just to make sure we're zipped up and it isn't *us* they're laughing at—then I'd suggest that Finney uses this incipient paranoia quite deliberately to manipulate our emotions in favor of Miles, Becky, and Miles's friends, the Belicecs.

Wilma, for instance, can present no proof that her uncle Ira is no longer her uncle Ira, but she impresses us with her strong conviction and with a deep, free-floating anxiety as pervasive as a migraine headache. Here is a kind of paranoid dream, as seamless and as perfect as anything out of a Paul Bowles novel or a Joyce Carol Oates tale of the uncanny:

> *Wilma sat staring at me, eyes intense. "I've been waiting for today," she whispered. "Waiting till he'd get a haircut, and he finally did." Again she leaned toward me, eyes big, her voice a hissing whisper. "There's a little scar on the back of Ira's neck; he had a boil there once, and your*

father lanced it. You can't see the scar," she whispered, "when he needs a haircut. But when his neck is shaved, you can. Well, today—I've been waiting for this!—today he got a haircut—"

I sat forward, suddenly excited. "And the scar's gone? *You mean—"*

"No!" she said, almost indignantly, eyes flashing. "It's there*—the scar—exactly like Uncle Ira's!"*

So Finney serves notice that we are working here in a world of utter subjectivity . . . and utter paranoia. Of course *we* believe Wilma at once, even though we have no real proof; if for no other reason, we know from the title of the book that the "body snatchers" are out there somewhere.

By putting us on Wilma's side from the start, Finney has turned us into equivalents of John the Baptist, crying in the wilderness. It is easy enough to see why the book was eagerly seized upon by those who felt, in the early fifties, that there was either a communist conspiracy afoot, or perhaps a fascist conspiracy that was operating in the name of anti-communism. Because, either way or neither way, this is a book about conspiracy with strong paranoid overtones . . . in other words, exactly the sort of story to be claimed as political allegory by political loonies of every stripe.

Earlier on, I mentioned the idea that perfect paranoia is perfect awareness. To that we could add that paranoia may be the last defense of the overstrained mind. Much of the literature of the twentieth century, from such diverse sources as Bertolt Brecht, Jean-Paul Sartre, Edward Albee, Thomas Hardy, even F. Scott Fitzgerald, has suggested that we live in an existential sort of world, a planless insane asylum where things just happen. IS GOD DEAD? asks the *Time* magazine cover in the waiting room of Rosemary Woodhouse's Satanic obstetrician. In such a world it is perfectly credible that a mental defective should sit on the upper floor of a little-used building, wearing a Hanes T-shirt, eating take-out chicken, and waiting to use his mail-order rifle to blow out the brains of an American president; perfectly possible that another mental defective should be able to stand around in a hotel kitchen a few years later waiting to do exactly the same thing to that defunct president's younger brother; perfectly understandable that nice American boys from Iowa and California and Delaware should have spent their tours in Vietnam collecting ears, many of them extremely tiny; that the world should begin to move once more toward the brink of an apocalyptic war because of the preachings of an eighty-year-old Moslem holy man who is probably foggy on what he had for breakfast by the time sunset rolls around.

All of these things are mentally acceptable if we accept the idea that God has abdicated for a long vacation, or has perchance really expired. They are mentally acceptable, but our emotions, our spirits, and most of all our passion for order—these powerful elements of our human makeup—all rebel. If we suggest that there was no reason for the deaths of six million Jews in the camps during World War II, no reason for poets bludgeoned, old women raped, children turned into soap, that it just happened and nobody was really responsible—things just got a little out of control here, ha-ha, so sorry—then the mind begins to totter.

I saw this happen at first-hand in the sixties, at the height of the generational shudder that began with our involvement in Vietnam and went on to encompass everything from parietal hours on college campuses and the voting franchise at eighteen to corporate responsibility for environmental pollution.

I was in college at the time, attending the University of Maine, and while I began college with political leanings too far to the right to actually become radicalized, by 1968 my mind had been changed forever about a number of fundamental questions. The hero of Jack Finney's later novel, *Time and Again*, says it better than I could:

> *"I was . . . an ordinary person who long after he was grown retained the childhood assumption that the people who largely control our lives are somehow better informed than, and have judgment superior to, the rest of us; that they are more intelligent. Not until Vietnam did I finally realize that some of the most important decisions of all time can be made by men knowing really no more than most of the rest of us."*

For me, it was a nearly overwhelming discovery—one that really began to happen, perhaps, on that day in the Stratford Theater when the announcement that the Russians had orbited a space satellite was made to me and my contemporaries by a theater manager who looked like he had been gutshot at close range.

But for all of that, I found it impossible to embrace the mushrooming paranoia of the last four years of the sixties completely. In 1968, during my junior year at college, three Black Panthers from Boston came to my school and talked (under the auspices of the Public Lecture Series) about how the American business establishment, mostly under the guidance of the Rockefellers and AT&T, was responsible for creating the neofascist political state of Amerika, encouraging the war in Vietnam because it was good for business, and also encouraging an ever more virulent climate of racism, stateism, and sexism. Johnson was their puppet; Humphrey and Nixon were also their puppets; it was a case of "meet the new boss, same as the old boss," as the Who would say a year or two later; the only solution was to take it into the streets. They finished with the Panther slogan, "All power comes out of the barrel of a gun," and adjured us to remember Fred Hampton.

Now, I did not and do not believe that the hands of the Rockefellers were utterly clean during that period, nor those of AT&T; I did and do believe that companies like Sikorsky and Douglas Aircraft and Dow Chemical and even the Bank of America subscribed more or less to the idea that war is good business (but never invest your son as long as you can slug the draft board in favor of the right kind of people; when at all possible, feed the war machine the spics and the niggers and the poor white trash from Appalachia, but not our boys, oh no, never *our* boys!); I did and do believe that the death of Fred Hampton was a case of police manslaughter at the very least. But these Black Panthers were suggesting a huge umbrella of conscious conspiracy that was laughable . . . except the audience wasn't laughing. During the Q-and-A period, they were asking sober, concerned questions about just how the conspiracy was working, who was in charge, how they got their orders out, et cetera.

Finally I got up and said something like, "Are you really suggesting that there is an actual Board of Fascist Conspiracy in this country? That the conspirators—the presidents of GM and Esso, plus David and Nelson Rockefeller—are maybe meeting in a big underground chamber beneath the Bonneville Salt Flats with agendas containing items on how more blacks can be drafted and the war in Southeast Asia prolonged?" I was finishing with the suggestion that perhaps these executives were arriving at their underground fortress in flying saucers—thus handily accounting for the upswing in UFO sightings as well as for the war in Vietnam—when the audience began to shout angrily for me to sit down and shut up. Which I did posthaste, blushing furiously, knowing how those eccentrics who mount their soapboxes in Hyde Park on Sunday afternoons must feel. I did not much relish the feeling.

The Panther who spoke did not respond to my question (which, to be fair, wasn't a question at all, really); he merely said softly, "*You* got a surprise, didn't you, man?" This was greeted with a burst of applause and laughter from the audience.

I *did* get a surprise—and a pretty unpleasant one, at that. But some thought has convinced me that it was impossible for those of my generation, propelled harum-scarum through the sixties, hair flying back from our foreheads, eyes bugging out with a mixture of delight and terror, from the Kingsmen doing "Louie Louie" to the blasting fuzztones of the Jefferson Airplane, to get from point A to point Z without a belief that someone—even Nelson Rockefeller—was pulling the strings.

In various ways throughout this book I've tried to suggest that the horror story is in many ways an optimistic, upbeat experience; that it is often the tough mind's way of coping with terrible problems which may not be supernatural at all but perfectly real. Paranoia may be the last and strongest bastion of such an optimistic view—it is the mind crying out, "*Something* rational and understandable is going on here! These things *do not just happen!*"

So we look at a shadow and say there was a man on the grassy knoll at Dallas; we say that James Earl Ray was in the pay of certain big Southern business interests, or maybe the CIA; we ignore the fact that American business interests exist in complex circles of power, often revolving in direct opposition to one another, and suggest that our stupid but mostly well-meant involvement in Vietnam was a conspiracy hatched by the military-industrial complex; or that, as a recent rash of badly spelled and printed posters in

New York suggested, that the Ayatollah Khomeini is a puppet of—yeah, you guessed it—David Rockefeller. We suggest, in our endless inventiveness, that Captain Mantell did not die of oxygen starvation back there in 1947 while chasing that odd daytime reflection of Venus which veteran pilots call a sundog; no, he was chasing a ship from another world which exploded his plane with a death ray when he got too close.

It would be wrong of me to leave you with any impression that I am inviting the two of us to have a good laugh at these things together; I am not. These things are not the beliefs of madmen but the beliefs of sane men and women trying desperately, not to preserve the status quo, but just to find the fucking thing. And when Becky Driscoll's cousin Wilma says her uncle Ira isn't her uncle Ira, we believe her instinctively and immediately. If we don't believe her, all we've got is a spinster going quietly dotty in a small California town. The idea does not appeal; in a sane world, nice middle-aged ladies like Wilma aren't s'posed to go bonkers. It isn't right. There's a whisper of chaos in it that's somehow more scary than believing she might be right about Uncle Ira. We believe because belief affirms the lady's sanity. We believe her because . . . because . . . *because something is going on!* All those paranoid fantasies are really not fantasies at all. We—and Cousin Wilma—are right; it's the *world* that's gone haywire. The idea that the world has gone haywire is pretty bad, but as we can cope with Bill Nolan's fifty-foot bug once we see what it really is, so we can cope with a haywire world if we just know where our feet are planted. Bob Dylan speaks to the existentialist in us when he tells us that "Something is going on here/But you don't know what it is/Do you, Mr. Jones?" Finney—in the guise of Miles Bennell—takes us firmly by the arm and tells us that he knows exactly what's going on here: it's those goddamn pods from space! *They're* responsible!

It's fun to trace the classic threads of paranoia Finney weaves into his story. While Miles and Becky are at a movie, Miles's writer friend Jack Belicec asks Miles to come and take a look at something he's found in his basement. The something turns out to be the body of a naked man on a pool table, a body which seems to Miles, Becky, Jack, and Jack's wife, Theodora, somehow unformed—not yet quite shaped. It's a pod, of course, and the shape it is taking is Jack's own. Shortly we have concrete proof that something is terribly wrong:

> *Becky actually moaned when we saw the [finger] prints, and I think we all felt sick. Because it's one thing to speculate about a body that's never been alive, a blank. But it's something very different, something that touches whatever is primitive deep in your brain, to have that speculation proved. There were no prints; there were five absolutely smooth, solidly black circles.*

These four—now aware of the pod conspiracy—agree not to call the police immediately but to see how the pods develop. Miles takes Becky home and then goes home himself, leaving the Belicecs to stand watch over the thing on the pool table. But in the middle of the night Theodora Belicec freaks out and the two of them show up on Miles's doorstep. Miles calls a psychiatrist friend, Mannie Kaufman (a shrink? we are immediately suspicious; we don't need a shrink here, we want to shout at Miles; call out the army!), to come and sit with the Belicecs while he goes after Becky . . . who earlier has confessed to feeling that her father is no longer her father.

On the bottom shelf of a cupboard in the Driscoll basement, Miles finds a blank which is developing into a pseudo-Becky. Finney does a brilliant job of describing what this coming-to-being would look like. He compares it to fine-stamping medallions; to developing a photograph; and later to those eerie, lifelike South American dolls. But in our current state of high nervousness, what really impresses us is how neatly the thing has been tucked away, hidden behind a closed door in a dusty basement, biding its time.

Becky has been drugged by her "father," and in a scene simply charged with romance, Miles spirits her out of the house and carries her through the sleeping streets of Santa Mira in his arms; it is no trick to imagine the gauzy stuff of her nightgown nearly glowing in the moonlight.

And the fallout of all this? When Mannie Kaufman arrives, the men return to the Belicec house to investigate the basement:

There was no body on the table. Under the bright, shadowless light from the overhead lay the brilliant green felt, and on the felt, except at the corners and along the sides, lay a sort of thick gray fluff that might have fallen, or been jarred loose, I supposed, from the open rafters.

For an instant, his mouth hanging open, Jack stared at the table. Then he swung to Mannie, and his voice protesting, asking for belief, he said, "It was there on the table! Mannie, it was!"

Mannie smiled, nodding quickly. "I believe you, Jack . . ."

But we know that's what all of these shrinks say . . . just before they call for the men in the white coats. *We* know that fluff isn't just fluff from the overhead rafters; the damned thing has gone to seed. But nobody else knows it, and Jack is quickly reduced to the final plea of the helpless paranoiac: You gotta believe me, doc!

Mannie Kaufman's rationalization for the increasing number of people in Santa Mira who no longer believe their relatives are their relatives is that Santa Mirans are undergoing a case of low-key mass hysteria, the sort of thing that may have been behind the Salem witch trials, the mass suicides in Guyana, even the dancing sickness of the middle ages. But below this rationalistic approach, existentialism lurks unpleasantly. These things happen, he seems to suggest, just because they happen. Sooner or later they will work themselves out.

They do, too. Mrs. Seeley, who believed her husband wasn't her husband, comes in to tell Miles that everything is fine now. Ditto the girls who were scared of their English instructor for a while. And ditto Cousin Wilma, who calls up Miles to tell him how embarrassed she is at having caused such a fuss; of *course* Uncle Ira is Uncle Ira. And in every case, one other fact—a name—stands out: Mannie Kaufman was there, helping them all. Something is wrong here, all right, but we know very well what it is, thank you, Mr. Jones. We have noticed the way Kaufman's name keeps cropping up. We're not stupid, right? Damn right we're not! And it's pretty obvious that Mannie Kaufman is now playing for the visiting team.

And one more thing. At Jack Belicec's insistence, Miles finally decides to call a friend in the Pentagon and spill the whole incredible story. About his long distance call to Washington, Miles tells us:

> *It isn't easy explaining a long, complicated story over the telephone. . . . And we had bad luck with the connection. At first I heard Ben and he heard me, as clearly as though we were next door to each other. But when I began telling him what had been happening here, the connection faded. Ben had to keep asking me to repeat, and I almost had to shout to make him understand me. You can't talk well, you can't even think properly, when you have to repeat every other phrase, and I signaled the operator and asked for a better connection . . . I'd hardly resumed when a sort of buzzing sound started in the receiver in my ear, and then I had to try to talk over that . . .*

"They," of course, are now in charge of communications coming into and going out of Santa Mira ("We are controlling transmission," that somehow frightening voice which introduced *The Outer Limits* each week used to say; "*We* will control the horizontal . . . *we* will control the vertical . . . we can roll the image, make it flutter . . . we can change the focus . . ."). Such a passage will also strike a responsive chord in any old antiwar protester, SDS member, or activist who ever believed his or her home phone was tapped or that the guy with the Nikon on the edge of the demonstration was taking his or her picture for a dossier someplace. *They* are everywhere; *they* are watching; *they* are listening. Surely it is no wonder that Siegel believed that Finney's novel was about a-Red-under-every-bed or that others believed it was about the creeping fascist menace. As we descend deeper and deeper into the whirlpool of this nightmare it might even become possible to believe it was the pod people who were on the grassy knoll in Dallas, or that it was the pod people who obediently swallowed their poisoned Kool-Aid at Jonestown and then spritzed it down the throats of their squalling infants. It would be such a relief to be able to believe that.

Miles's conversation with his army friend is the book's clearest delineation of the paranoid mind at work. Even when you know the whole story, you aren't allowed to communicate it to those in authority . . . and it's hard to think with that buzzing in your head!

Linked to this is the strong sense of xenophobia Finney's major characters feel. The pods really are "a threat to our way of life," as Joe McCarthy used to say. "They'll have to declare martial law," Jack tells Miles, "a state of siege, or something—anything! And then do whatever has to be done. Root this thing out, smash it, crush it, kill it."

Later, during their brief flight from Santa Mira, Miles and Jack discover two pods in the trunk of the car. This is how Miles describes what happens next:

> *And there they lay, in the advancing, retreating waves of flickering red light: two enormous pods already burst open in one or two places, and I reached in with both hands, and tumbled them out onto the dirt. They were weightless as children's balloons, harsh and dry on my palms and fingers. At the feel of them on my skin, I lost my mind completely, and then I was trampling them, smashing and crushing them under my plunging feet and legs, not even knowing that I was uttering a sort of hoarse, meaningless cry—"Unhh! Unhh! Unhh!"—of fright and animal disgust.*

No friendly old men holding up signs reading STOP AND BE FRIENDLY here; here we have Miles and Jack, mostly out of their minds, doing the funky chicken over these weird and insensate invaders from space. There is no discussion (vis-à-vis *The Thing*) of what we could learn from these things to the benefit of modern science. There is no white flag here, no parley; Finney's aliens are as strange and as ugly as those bloated leeches you sometimes find clinging to your skin after swimming in still ponds. There is no reasoning here, nor any effort to reason; only Miles's blind and primitive reaction to the alien outsider.

The book which most closely resembles Finney's is Robert A. Heinlein's *The Puppet Masters*; like Finney's novel, it is perhaps nominally SF but is in fact a horror novel. In this one invaders from Saturn's largest moon, Titan, arrive on Earth, ready, willing, and able to do business. Heinlein's creatures are not pods; they are the leeches in actuality. They are sluglike creatures that ride on the backs of their hosts' necks the way that you or I might ride a horse. The two books are similar—strikingly so—in many ways. Heinlein's narrator begins by wondering aloud if "they" were truly intelligent. He ends after the menace has been defeated. The narrator is one of those building and manning rocketships aimed at Titan; now that the tree has been chopped down, they will burn the roots. "Death and destruction!" the narrator exults, thus ending the book.

But what exactly is the threat which the pods in Finney's novel pose? For Finney, the fact that they will mean the end of the human race seems almost secondary (pod people have no interest in what an old acquaintance of mine likes to refer to as "doing the trick"). The real horror, for Jack Finney, seems to be that they threaten all that "nice"—and I think this is where we came in. On his way to his office not too long after the pod invasion is well launched, Miles describes the scenery this way:

> *. . . the look of Throckmorton Street depressed me. It seemed littered and shabby in the morning sun, a city trash basket stood heaped and unemptied from the day before, the globe of an overhead streetlight was broken, and a few doors down . . . a shop stood empty. The windows were whitened, and a clumsily painted* For Rent *sign stood leaning against the glass. It didn't say where to apply, though, and I had a feeling no one cared whether the store was ever rented again. A smashed wine bottle lay in the entranceway of my building, and the brass nameplate set in the gray stone of the building was mottled and unpolished.*

From Jack Finney's fiercely individualistic point of view, the worst thing about the Body Snatchers is that they will allow the nice little town of Santa Mira to turn into something resembling a subway station on Forty-second Street in New York. Humans, Finney asserts, have a natural drive to create order out of chaos (which fits well enough with the book's paranoid themes). Humans want to improve the universe. These are old-fashioned ideas, perhaps, but Finney is a traditionalist, as Richard Gid Powers points out in his introduction to the Gregg Press edition of the novel. From where Finney stands, the scariest thing about the pod people is that chaos doesn't bother them a bit and they have absolutely no sense of aesthetics: this is not an invasion of roses from outer space but rather an infestation of ragweed. The pod people are going to mow their lawns for a while and then give it up. They don't give a shit about the crabgrass. They aren't going to be making any trips down to the Santa Mira True Value Hardware so they can turn that musty old basement annex into a rec room in the best do-it-yourself tradition. A salesman who blows into town complains about the state of the roads. If they aren't patched soon, he says, Santa Mira will be cut off from the world. But do you think the pod people are going to lose any sleep over a little thing like that? Here's what Richard Gid Powers says in his introduction about Finney's outlook:

> *With the hindsight afforded by Finney's later books, it is easy to see what the critics overlooked [when they] interpreted both the book and the movie . . . simply as products of the anti-Communist hysteria of the McCarthyite fifties, a know-nothing outburst against "alien ways of life" . . . that threatened the American way. Miles Bennell is a precursor of all the other traditionalist heroes of Jack Finney's later books, but in* The Body Snatchers, *Miles's town of Santa Mira, Marin County, California still is the unspoiled mythical* gemeinschaft *community that later heroes have had to travel through time to recapture. When Miles begins to suspect that his neighbors are no longer real human beings and are no longer capable of sincere human feelings, he is encountering the beginning of the insidious modernization and dehumanization that faces later Finney heroes as an accomplished fact.*
>
> *Miles Bennell's victory over the pods is fully consistent with the adventurers of subsequent Finney characters: his resistance to depersonalization is so fierce that the pods finally give up on their plans for planetary colonization and mosey off to another planet where the inhabitants' hold on their self-integrity is not so strong.*

Further on, Powers has this to say about the archetypical Finney hero in general and the purposes of this book in particular:

> *Finney's heroes, particularly Miles Bennell, are all inner-directed individualists in an increasingly other-directed world. Their adventures*

> *could be used as classroom illustrations of Tocqueville's theory about the plight of a free individual in a mass democracy. . . .* The Body Snatchers *is a raw and direct mass-market version of the despair over cultural dehumanization that fills T. S. Eliot's* Wasteland *and William Faulkner's* The Sound and the Fury. *Finney adroitly uses the classic science fiction situation of an invasion from outer space to symbolize the annihilation of the free personality in contemporary society . . . he succeeded in creating the most memorable of all pop cultural images of what Jean Sheperd was describing on late-night radio as "creeping meatballism": fields of pods that hatch into identical, spiritless, emotional vacuous zombies—who look so damned much just like you and me!*

Finally, when we examine *The Body Snatchers* in light of the Tarot hand we have dealt ourselves, we find in Finney's novel almost every damned card. There is the Vampire, for surely those whom the pods have attacked and drained of life have become a modern, cultural version of the undead, as Richard Gid Powers points out; there is the Werewolf, for certainly these people are not really people at all, and have undergone a terrible sea change; the pods from space, a totally alien invasion of creatures who need no spaceships, can certainly also fit under the heading of the Thing Without a Name . . . and you might even say (if you wanted to stretch a point, and why the hell not?) that citizens of Santa Mira are no more than Ghosts of their former selves these days.

Not bad legs for a book which is "just a story."

THE FICTION OF JACK FINNEY

◎ ◎ ◎

Jon L. Breen

MILWAUKEE-BORN WALTER BRADEN FINNEY (1911–1995), professionally known as Jack, was one of the best and most successful writers of popular fiction in the second half of the twentieth century. That may sound like hyperbole—certainly many writers have written more bestsellers and made their names more familiar to the public—but it's an easy statement to defend.

Consider this: each of Finney's four novels of the fifties was serialized in a high-paying slick magazine; each of them was actually filmed successfully; and at least one of the films is considered a classic of its genre. His fifth novel, written with a particular star in mind, was adapted to film with that star in place. A later novel, though never filmed at least partly because of the expense that would be required to do it justice, has become a beloved modern classic.

Does this record of success mean Finney had a rare affinity with the popular taste of his times? Yes. Does it mean he wrote his books with one eye on the possibility of a screen adaptation? Yes, he readily admitted it. Does it mean he was a hack who pandered to his audience, adjusting his viewpoint to coincide with theirs? No. Does it mean he hit on a workable formula and repeated it from book to book? Anything but. Does it mean he wrote screen treatments and published them disguised as novels?

Decidedly not. Few writers could have it both ways, attaining outstanding commercial success while being true to a consistent artistic vision, as completely as Jack Finney.

Finney might be likened to Earl Derr Biggers, a popular writer earlier in the century who also had a sensibility uncannily attuned to what the public wanted and the ability to deliver it in a natural, uncontrived way. Unlike Biggers, who is best remembered for his creation of detective Charlie Chan, Finney almost never returned to the same cast of characters. He did, however, have a recurring theme that turned up even in the most unexpected corners of his work: that American life is gradually, sometimes subtly, sometimes dramatically, changing for the worse; that only a few years ago, times were simpler but richer; people were more innocent, more optimistic, more joyful; lives had more purpose and were more fully lived; things were just, well, better all around, not just when *we* were younger but when the country and the world were younger. Finney's protagonists are afflicted with a sweet but painful nostalgia, a longing for a time or a place or a mood other than their own. (Continuing for a moment the comparison with Biggers, consider the nostalgic view conveyed in *The House Without a Key* of Honolulu, now [in 1925] ruined by tourism and commercialism but a paradise in the relatively recent 1880s.)

While Finney's two most famous works are undoubtedly *The Body Snatchers* (1955), thanks to the two successful film versions, and *Time and Again* (1970), for the richness of his time-travel plot, he produced in his half-century career a wide variety of crime, fantasy, mainstream fiction, and science fiction in which he often returned to his familiar theme of wistful nostalgia but, in subject matter and approach, almost never repeated himself.

Finney's first published story, "The Widow's Walk," appeared in *Ellery Queen's Mystery Magazine* in July 1947. According to the introduction by editor Queen (Frederic Dannay):

> *Mr. Finney is thirty-five years old, married, has no children, and lives in Manhattan. At present he is a copywriter in the advertising agency of Dancer-Fitzgerald-Sample—he has been writing advertising*

> *copy for the past twelve years. The* EQMM *Annual Contest spurred him to write fiction, almost the only writing he has done outside of his work since he finished college in 1934. . . . [N]ow he is tilting his typewriter at the windmill of radio. His first attempt at radio ratiocination is, in his own words, "quite a bloody script—two killings in less than fifteen minutes" (which is certainly par for the course).*

I'm not sure how much radio writing Finney actually did—probably not very much, since it didn't take him long to establish himself in the far more lucrative slick magazine market.

In a concluding note, EQ credits "The Widow's Walk," a domestic crime short story of the type later dramatized on Alfred Hitchcock's TV program, with "two of the most important elements in a detective story": a clue and fair play to the reader. The story is the first-person account of a young woman named Annie contemplating the murder of her invalid mother-in-law. Its wickedly clever surprise twist makes it a classic of the type, and editor Queen's claim of fair play is borne out.

Finney appeared only twice more in *EQMM*. In introducing a November 1951 reprint of the 1948 *Collier's* story "It Wouldn't Be Fair," EQ describes the story as a parody of classical detective fiction. Again, the main character is named Annie, but quite a different Annie. The mystery-obsessed girlfriend of New York cop Charley, she "often solves cases a full forty-eight pages before Perry Mason," and her disdain for the intelligence of real-life police puts a crimp in their romance. While showing its author a knowledgeable devotee of the kind of pure detective fiction he seldom ventured to write, the story also demonstrates the qualities Queen's introduction claims for Finney's fiction: "Jack Finney has developed a slick, sophisticated, streamlined style; his dialogue is bright; his situations are genuinely amusing; his characters combine warmth and gaiety—and who can resist those qualities these cold and gloomy days?"

Finney's continuing theme of longing for a world outside one's present reality is manifest in both stories: the first Annie's for her happy premother-in-law married life, the second Annie's for the comforting (and *fair*) world of classical detective fiction. For one

Annie, a reasonable compromise solution presents itself; for the other, there is only despair.

Finney's third and last *EQMM* appearance is "The Other Arrow," a January 1956 reprint of a 1952 story written with F. M. Barratt and originally published in *Collier's* as "Diagnosis Completed." Described as a medical mystery in the Dr. Thorndyke/Dr. Coffee mode, it also includes a Queenian dying message from the murder victim, a pharmacist's diabetic wife. The relationship of retiring Dr. Lerner and his young replacement Dr. Knapp is in the great tradition of medical fiction and drama. Dr. Lerner's old-fashioned view of general medical practice, complete with house calls, even more remote now than at the time the story was first published, carries the theme of longing for a better time.

The fact that *EQMM* never published a second Finney original is accounted for by his remarkable record of success selling to the major American slick magazines. Between 1947 and 1962, he contributed (by my quick count) fifty-three short stories and three serialized novels to those slicks indexed in *Reader's Guide to Periodical Literature*. Initially *Collier's* was his major market; after that publication's mid-fifties demise, he became a regular first in *Good Housekeeping* and finally in *McCall's*, with scattered contributions to *Ladies' Home Journal*, *Cosmopolitan*, and *Saturday Evening Post*. At least one of his later stories, "Hey, Look at Me!", would appear in *Playboy*, equally well-paying but not indexed by the conservative *Reader's Guide*. While his *genre* stories—crime, fantasy, and science fiction—often had a later life, his unreprinted works of general fiction—with tantalizing titles like "Breakfast in Bed" (*Collier's*, May 15, 1948), "My Cigarette Loves Your Cigarette" (*Collier's*, September 30, 1950), and "Husband at Home" (*LHJ*, April, 1951)—illustrate the impermanence of most magazine fiction.

In Finney's most famous short stories, the science fiction and fantasy tales collected in *The Third Level* (Rinehart, 1957) and *I Love Galesburg in the Springtime* (Simon and Schuster, 1963), the nostalgia for a past better and happier than the present is usually conveyed through time-travel situations that foreshadow his definitive treatment of that device in *Time and Again*. In the first volume's title story, the 1950s narrator happens upon a third level of Grand Central Station where the year is 1894—unable to buy a ticket to idyllic

Galesburg, Illinois, with his odd-looking new-style money, he returns to the present and ends the story searching for the third level and failing to find it. The final twist is a tribute to Finney's storytelling savvy and a note especially appropriate to the fifties. (How ironic that the period Finney's heroes so often want to escape from is the one that many of today's nostalgics would like to go back to!)

Finney continues his romanticization of Galesburg, where he had attended Knox College, at greater length in the title tale of the second volume of short stories. Beginning with a businessman telling the reporter/narrator about his decision *not* to build a factory in Galesburg following his encounter with a ghost streetcar, the story concerns the efforts of the past city to resist encroachments of the present.

Brilliant as he is in the short story form, Finney may be even better as a novelist. As Marcia Muller writes in *1001 Midnights* (Arbor, 1986), Finney "has the unusual ability to create edge-of-the-chair tension and sustain it throughout a long narrative." This knack is well-demonstrated in his first novel, *Five Against the House*, serialized in *Good Housekeeping* in 1953, and published in book form by Doubleday the following year.

Nineteen-year-old narrator Al Mercer, like his creator at an earlier time, is a small-college student in Illinois. Beginning on one boring rainy day, he joins three at-loose-ends fraternity brothers to plot a crime. At first, it is to be a Brinks truck robbery, but after an embarrassing encounter with the police while following such a truck, they decide instead to return to Reno, where they had all worked the previous summer, to knock over Harold's Club. They are helped in their planning by Al's waitress girlfriend Tina Greyleg.

Five Against the House is a big caper novel, but it's an amateur caper, generally more interesting (to this reader at least) than a professional one. Most of the conspirators, especially Al and Tina, are presented sympathetically. Al offers Tina this rather strained rationalization for the robbery:

> *"I think gambling is wrong. People have learned that everywhere, and gambling's been outlawed nearly everywhere in all civilizations.*

> *Now, just because a handful of men in the state of Nevada make it technically legal, doesn't make it right. Hell, gambling's* wrong *and you know it. A few people profit, giving nothing and doing nothing in exchange. And I think everyone concerned is harmed by it. . . .*
>
> *"So I say they're fair prey. . . . I feel I'm honest, and wouldn't steal. But to me this isn't stealing; by any standard I respect, that money doesn't belong to Harold's Club, and I'll take it if I can, and it will never bother my conscience for a moment."* (Doubleday, page 52)

Finney's technique, repeated in later caper novels, is to hint at the group's method but withhold details until the crime itself is carried out. The author's nostalgic bent is displayed in an imprecation to value the ordinary, as when the Reno conspirators are crossing the country imprisoned in a trailer and value their rare nighttime forays outside, as well as the turns at the wheel that permit them to see ordinary things with fresh eyes.

While a big caper novel about knocking over a gambling casino sounds like pure fiction noir, Finney's slick-paper style somewhat lightens the mood. As in most of his later books, the view of sexuality is very restrained by contemporary standards, reflecting (in common with most of his happy endings) a fifties movie sensibility. But one of the darkest moments in Finney's work comes when a policeman offers the boys a harrowing description of the future he sees for them in prison.

Finney's second novel, *The Body Snatchers*, was serialized in *Collier's* (November 26–December 24, 1954) and published in expanded form as a Dell paperback original in 1955. In many ways, the novel is closely followed in Don Siegel's 1956 film *Invasion of the Body Snatchers*. In fact, quite a bit of Finney's dialogue was transferred directly into Daniel Mainwaring's script, and of course the central situation is unchanged. But in some very important ways, the two versions differ. Both are classics, but not necessarily for the same reasons.

The Body Snatchers includes the familiar Finney paean to small-town America and old-fashioned doctoring, the latter in the person of Santa Mira general practitioner Miles Bennell, a character even more given to kidding and wisecracks on the page than as played on the screen by Kevin McCarthy. Miles is asked by old girlfriend, now fellow divorcée, Becky Driscoll to look into her cousin Wilma's claims that her beloved uncle Ira is not really her uncle, though no change in his manner, appearance, or memory is apparent. Miles finds similar cases are epidemic in the little town. Gradually the truth is revealed: extraterrestrials have come to earth in the form of giant seed pods and taken over the bodies of the townspeople, turning them into emotionless automatons whose mimicking of human memory, appearance, and mannerisms is not quite good enough to fool sensitive friends and relatives.

While the film is rightly credited with reflecting the anticommunist paranoia of the fifties, the novel's mood is different. It is more a cerebral science-fictional mystery, the greater space afforded by print allowing for speculation and theorizing about the problem at hand that the film has no time for. When a partially formed pod creature is found in the basement of Miles's writer friend Jack Belicec, there is more consideration and discussion of what the phenomenon means and what to do about it. When psychiatrist Mannie Kaufman (Dan in the film) presents his theory of mass hysteria, he offers several historical cases to support his claim.

Some of the most striking scenes in the book are not in the film at all. When Miles and Becky are trapped in his office, with pods waiting to replicate them when they fall asleep, he concocts an ingenious way to misdirect the pods through the use of his two office skeletons. A particularly chilling scene finds Miles and Becky visiting the public library to research newspaper references to the giant seed pods, only to find that the beloved town librarian Miss Wyandotte is among those who have been snatched. One astonishing passage offers a harsh snapshot of American race relations, as Miles compares the changes in the snatched townspeople to an unexpected view of a black shoeshine man's bitter reality.

Introducing the 1976 Gregg Press reprint of *The Body Snatchers*, Richard Gid Powers describes Miles Bennell and other Finney heroes as "inner-directed individuals in an increasingly other-directed world . . . [whose] adventures could be used as classroom illustrations of Tocqueville's theory about the plight of the free individual in mass democracy." He goes on to sum up the achievement of

Finney's first novel as "a raw and direct mass-market version of the despair over cultural dehumanization that fills T. S. Eliot's *Wasteland* and William Faulkner's *The Sound and the Fury*. Finney adroitly uses the classic science fiction situation of an invasion from outer space to symbolize the annihilation of the free personality in contemporary society" (page xi).

Finney's third novel and second paperback original, *The House of Numbers* (Dell, 1957), was the expanded version of a magazine short story (*Cosmopolitan*, July 1956). The first-person narrator this time is twenty-six-year-old Benjamin Harrison Jarvis, who finds himself in the surprising position of assisting his brother Arnie's escape from San Quentin. Thus, it's the second of the author's three big caper novels, and like the other two is based on in-depth research into its background. As Marcia Muller writes in *1001 Midnights*, "Finney knows San Quentin, although his view of it is colored by his association with then-warden Harley O. Teets, a humanitarian administrator to whom the book is dedicated. (In fact, the dialogue of the fictional warden reads a lot like a public relations release.)"

The third of the big caper books, *Assault on a Queen* (Simon and Schuster, 1959), was serialized in the *Saturday Evening Post* (August 22–September 26, 1959) as "U-19's Last Kill." It begins with a third-person prologue in which Frank Lauffnauer, formerly a German submarine crewman in World War I, rediscovers his old ship sunk off Fire Island. But most of the story is told by a typical Finney narrator, twenty-six-year-old network publicist Hugh Brittain, whose pervasive dissatisfaction with his empty life leads him to quit his job and join some other navy veterans in an elaborate crime: refurbishing the old submarine and using it to rob the Queen Mary. Once again, Finney's amateur criminals try to show they aren't really evil people by offering justification for an *almost* victimless crime. Vic DeRossier, the old navy buddy who is trying to bring Hugh into the caper, likens the caper to knocking over a house party of the very rich:

> *"[E]very last person there is either out-and-out wealthy, very well off, or making a slug of money. Every one of them, Hugh, or they wouldn't be there. Would you take a few hundred dollars from each of*

them, if you could? It'd be illegal, all right; a crime, and yet—every single one of them could easily afford it. It'd mean no more to them than losing fifty cents to you. . . . To you, though, it would make all the difference in the world; you'd be closer to rich, to having the kind of life you want than you ever will be otherwise." (pages 38–39)

As the conspirators, including of course one beautiful woman, take on the job of getting the submarine back in working order, Finney drives home his customary theme in a passage that may also explain the rarity of sports references in his nostalgic reveries:

There is an enormous loss we all of us suffer, growing up—we stop playing. The things adults call play very seldom are. With hardly an exception they're competitions, even hunting or fishing, even golf, all alone. Rarely ever again do we experience pure play, doing something for its own sake completely, utterly absorbed and lost in it, nothing else mattering. (page 104)

The main character of *Good Neighbor Sam* (Simon and Schuster, 1963) was created with Jack Lemmon in mind. In case anyone missed the envisioned casting, the jacket copy unsubtly compares Finney's comic novel to *Some Like It Hot* and *The Apartment*. Sam Bissell is a twenty-nine-year-old copywriter for the San Francisco advertising firm of Burke & Hare. He is married to Minerva (Min), a twenty-five-year-old brunette who, in the manner of Finney heroines, thinks she is too heavy but really isn't. Their sexy neighbor Janet needs a husband in order to inherit her grandfather's fortune. Since her divorce is pending, her lawyer argues she is still married under strict interpretation of the will, though the other legatees could argue she was not married according to the *spirit* of the will. When Janet's cousins come to visit, Jack (his wife ever understanding) is pressed into service as the neighbor's husband. Finney handles the farcical events to follow with a flawless comic touch and along the way presents some pointed satire on his former profession of advertising, having much fun with campaigns on behalf of Nesfresh eggs and a nostrum called "BELS for the belly." One slogan on behalf of a client's product is wisely rejected at the source:

"SCIENTIFIC TESTS PROVE! THE ONLY CIGARETTE THAT PRODUCES BENIGN TUMORS!" (page 144).

Good Neighbor Sam is pure comedy and the first Finney book that can't be easily pigeonholed in the crime, fantasy, or SF genres. However, a comic turn by an inept private eye and the con game aspect of the plot *almost* nudge it into the crime fiction category.

Finney continued in a farcical vein in *The Woodrow Wilson Dime* (Simon and Schuster, 1968), expanded from the short story "The Coin Collector," originally published in the *Saturday Evening Post* (January 30, 1960) as "The Other Wife" and included in Finney's second collection, *I Love Galesburg in the Springtime.* The hero is another advertising copywriter, New Yorker Ben Bennell (note the last name), whose discovery of the titular coin allows him to cross over into a recognizable but somewhat altered parallel universe.

His next novel, the illustrated *Time and Again* (Simon and Schuster, 1970), is Finney's finest achievement. Narrator Simon Morley, an advertising illustrator, is recruited by a top secret government project created to test Einstein's theory of time. The evocation of Einstein means the events of the novel, outrageous as they may seem, can arguably be classified as science fiction rather than pure fantasy. As project director Dr. Danziger, a Harvard theoretical physicist, explains it:

> *"[W]e're mistaken in our conception of what the past, present and future really are. We think the past is gone, the future hasn't yet happened, and that only the present exists. Because the present is all we can see. . . . [W]e're like people in a boat without oars drifting along a winding river. Around us we see only the present. We can't see the past, back in the bends and curves behind us. But it's there. . . . [A] man ought to be able to step out of that boat onto the shore. And walk back to one of the bends behind us." (page 52)*

The means to achieve this turning backward in time consists of finding a place unaltered since the period you want to visit and surrounding yourself with objects and information from that time. Thus, Si Morley is set up in an apartment in the Dakota, an old New York apartment building on the edge of Central Park, where he steeps himself in New York of the 1880s, reading contemporary newspapers and magazines; using furniture and household appliances, growing whiskers and wearing clothes appropriate to the period; determinedly thinking himself into the targeted place and time. And eventually, he carries his camera and sketch pad into the wonderland of New York in 1882.

In this novel, Finney's rare ability to describe rooms and their contents, and street scenes in all their detail, achieves its ultimate application. Period photographs and drawings are reproduced to help the process, but the magic of the writing does most of the work. A passage describing a walk along Fifth Avenue captures the scene and the time traveler's sense of wonder:

> *The cross streets slipped by—Forty-ninth, Forty-eighth, Forty-seventy, Forty-sixth—all strange unfamiliar identical streets of uninterrupted row after row of high-stooped brownstones precisely like blocks still existing on the West Side. As we'd moved down toward the thick of the city, the street became more and more alive. There they were now, moving along the walks, crossing the street—the people. And I looked out at them, at first with awe, then with delight; at the bearded, cane-swinging men in tall shiny silk hats, fur caps like mine, high-crowned derbies like the man's across the aisle, and—younger men—in very shallow low-crowned derbies. Almost all of them wore ankle-length great coats or topcoats, half the men seemed to wear pince-nez glasses, and when the older men, the silk-hatted men, passed an acquaintance, each touched his hat brim in salute with the head of his cane. The women were wearing head scarfs or hats ribbon-tied under the chin; wearing short, tight-waisted cutaway winter coats, or capes or brooch-pinned shawls; some carried muffs and some wore gloves; all wore button shoes darting out from and disappearing under long skirts.*
>
> *There—well, there they* were, *the people of the stiff old woodcuts, only . . . these moved. The swaying coats and dresses there on the walks and crossing the streets before and behind us were of new-dyed cloth—maroon, bottle-green, blue, strong brown, unfaded blacks—and I saw the shimmer of light and shadow in the appearing and disappearing long folds. And the leather and rubber they walked in pressed into and marked the slush of the street crossings; and their breaths puffed out into the*

winter air, momentarily visible. And through the trembling, rattling glass panes of the bus we heard their living voices, and heard a girl laugh aloud. Looking out at their winter-flushed faces, I felt like shouting for joy. (page 121; ellipses Finney's)

Half of Finney's writing life remained after *Time and Again*, but he would be considerably less prolific. He would produce four more books at widening intervals in the quarter century remaining to him. All have their attractions, but they are inevitably somewhat anticlimactic after his masterpiece.

Marion's Wall (Simon and Schuster, 1973) returns to the young, married suburban ambiance of *Good Neighbor Sam*. Thirty-year-old narrator Nick Cheyney, an employee of Crown Zellerbach, and wife Jan are peeling wallpaper in their new apartment in an old San Francisco house when they unearth a 1926 message from a former tenant: silent film actress Marion Marsh, once the lover of Nick's father when he lived in the same building. A public TV viewing of Marion's silent film appearance causes the ghost of the actress, who died in a car crash in the roaring twenties when her film career had only just begun, to materialize. She inhabits the body of Jan to attempt a movie comeback, and later Nick is himself possessed by the shade of Rudolph Valentino. The novel is a valentine (no pun intended) to silent movies and movie collectors—for Nick, a prime mcguffin is the lost reels of Erich Von Stroheim's famous film *Greed*. The novel depicts an earlier era for film buffs, a pre-video period when viewing was often tied to one-shot TV showings and the only chance to own a film was to buy comparatively expensive eight-millimeter prints from a Blackhawk catalog. (When the novel was reprinted along with *The Woodrow Wilson Dime* and *The Night People* in the 1987 omnibus *Three by Finney*, the action was misguidedly updated to 1985, making total nonsense of the chronology and the film-collecting references.)

The Night People (Doubleday, 1977) also involves Northern California suburbanites. Lew Joliffe, an apartment-dwelling San Francisco lawyer, is a transplanted midwesterner nostalgic for snow. At night, he takes solitary walks and does odd things (like lying down in the lanes of a freeway or acting out pitching on a Little League mound) without the knowledge of his girlfriend Jo Dunne. With Harry and Shirley Levy—he's another lawyer attracted to daredevil stunts and generally harmless pranks—Lew and Jo form the titular Night People, whose final stunt, involving scaling the superstructure of the Golden Gate Bridge, is a lulu. For some reason, though, these characters, four slow-rising yuppies who need to get a life, are less endearing than the author's usual. It may be that Finney's decision (otherwise unprecedented in the novels) to write in the third person damaged the kind of tenuous reader identification needed to render his central characters likeable.

By this time, Finney was taking more and more time between books. His penultimate work, *Forgotten News: The Crime of the Century and Other Lost Stories* (Doubleday, 1983), is his only nonfiction book, a volume that had its roots in the research for *Time and Again*. Beginning with an appreciation of the woodcut illustrations in *Frank Leslie's Weekly*, Finney goes on to recount at length the 1857 murder case of dentist Harvey Burdell, culminating in the trial of Emma Cunningham for the crime, and slightly more briefly the sinking of the steamship *Central America* in the same year. As in most of his fiction, Finney employs the first person, describing the way he did his research and his reactions to what he found in the 1857 files of the *New York Times* and *Leslie's*. The book is extensively illustrated in a style similar to *Time and Again*.

From Time to Time (Simon and Schuster, 1995) makes Simon Morley a series character, the only one in Finney's canon. Morley, who stayed in New York of the 1880s at the end of *Time and Again*, now visits 1912 in an effort to prevent World War I. The *Titanic* is also involved in the plot. In reviewing the novel in *EQMM* (September 1995), I remarked, "The sequel isn't quite up to the original—the contrivances that set the story in motion are somewhat strained, and the plot seems an excuse for the musings on time and social history—but Finney's unique touch disarms criticism. Like its predecessor, the novel makes an effective use of period photographs and drawings. The glimpse into the life of vaudeville performers, though only slightly related to the story, is especially memorable."

Why has Finney the writer been so much less well-known than

the books and stories he wrote? For one thing, he was somewhat reclusive, rarely giving interviews and never (at least to my knowledge) appearing at fan conventions. While not quite a popular fiction equivalent of Thomas Pynchon or J. D. Salinger, he clearly believed the work should speak for itself. Secondly, he had a disdain for being pigeonholed in a genre. His attempt to reach a wider slick-magazine readership with adaptations of science fictional concepts developed over the years in the pulps and digests did not endear him to the SF community, which often disdains such efforts. And accomplished as he was in the crime fiction field, he effectively left it after *Assault on a Queen* to produce works that often drew on several popular genres—romance, fantasy, mystery, science fiction, comedy—at once. Such mixing of categories, now routine in the works of best-selling writers like Stephen King and Dean Koontz, was far less common in the sixties and seventies and certainly militated against brand-name identification.

One supposes all of this mattered little to Finney, who apparently made enough money to write what he wanted to and take as much time as he needed to do it. Any writer offered the chance to make a financial killing *and* write a couple of modern classics along the way would probably take it, even if (maybe, in Finney's case, *especially* if) relative personal anonymity was part of the package.

THE *INVASION OF THE BODY SNATCHERS* OUVRE: THREE MOVIES AND A NOVEL

James Combs

REMEMBER THE FIRST TIME YOU SAW A CLOWN? How your breath dropped to a whisper. How you stared stunned, eyes frosted, while your body evaporated and your mind drifted slowly away and left your sense of reality fractured forever.

Or maybe it was your first mannequin. Your heart and lungs shut down and you waited for "it" to do something, but at the same time, hoping desperately that it wouldn't, because you couldn't possibly decide which was worse: a chilling, frozen, unmoving unreality, or an equally unbelievable indication that it was somehow "real" after all. You feared either possibility. Deep down you knew that you didn't want to see it do anything. If it did nothing, you could stand there, merely frightened; but if it did something, now the most terrifying of all possibilities, you would let out a horrendous scream and it would *come and get you!* So you did nothing as your imagination flickered back and forth like a strobe light in the darkness of your mind. *Finally* that dreaded moment came when you feared you might do something in your underwear and have yet another burden to bear.

Perhaps it was when you woke in the darkness with eyes yet dulled by sleep, and saw an unknown life form, some kind of "thing" lurking in the fog of gathered shadows at the foot of your bed. Your head went wild. You could hear the hairs on your head sizzle at the roots and your heart leapt up into the dry cavern of your mouth, until you feared you might bite into it and die. Suddenly, you knew that it (a demon?) knew you were there. Run. Hide. Where? No! Don't move! Worst thing you can do. Freeze. Don't let it hear you breathe.

Suddenly there is a thump. Thump. Thump. A drumming. Loud drumming. *It knows I'm here.* Utter panic flushes through your body until you realize that the drumming is the sound of your own terrified heart throbbing in your ears.

Maybe you were the kid who prayed every night:

Now I lay me down to sleep
I pray the Lord my soul to keep
If I should die before I wake—
IF I SHOULD DIE BEFORE I WAKE!!!

Wait a minute. If I die before I wake . . . and now you have a brand-new fear: dying in your sleep.

Add this to your (clown/mannequin, demon-in-the-darkness) memory and you have the two basic childhood memories that Jack Finney preys on in *Invasion of the Body Snatchers*: simulacra/doppelganger (is it mom or memorex?) and sleep/death (if I should die before I wake?). After all, it was the Bard himself who described death as that "little sleep."

Ma Bell wants you to reach out and touch someone. *Invasion of the Body Snatchers* reaches out and taps you on your most fragile memories with an icy finger, then, when you turn around, grabs you by the childhood, and won't let go.

Fans of *Invasion of the Body Snatchers* are legion and the plot is too well-known to repeat here. The Jack Finney novel was made into three movies (1956, 1978, 1993) and referenced in at least ten other movies, featured in two others, and spoofed in at least one movie (http://us.imdb.com/cache/title-exact/ 57620 [57620, 57621, and 19366]). The 1956 black-and-white version of *Invasion of the Body Snatchers* is recognized by the majority of fans as the best of the three versions. It has not only been placed on the National

Register of Films, but also, deservedly, turns up on almost everyone's list of top ten horror films of all time *and* top ten SF films of all time. Hard-core fans will know that Sam Peckinpah, who played the bit part of Charlie the meter reader, was the dialogue director for the first movie (1956) and that most of his reported humor was removed from the final script. Also, his original bleak ending (pods are being shipped all over the state, but no one believes the hero) was changed into a happy ending by the addition of both a prologue and an epilogue (authorities notify the FBI to stop all trucks containing pods).

The star of the 1956 movie (Kevin McCarthy) also turns up in the 1978 movie in a wry reprise of his famous scene on the crowded highway, at the end of the movie: "They're coming. Listen to me. You're next. They are already here. They're coming." The director of the original (Don Siegel) is also featured in the 1978 version as the taxi driver who reports on his radio that he has "two type H fares" in his cab. Also reprised is a touch of the Finney and the rumored Peckinpah humor: in explaining how a husband could have changed ("he is not my husband"), Leonard Nimoy (the psychiatrist) suggests that the husband could be having an affair, could be gay, contracted a social disease, or become a Republican.

The 1978 movie stars Donald Sutherland, who brings so little energy to the plot that the viewer might begin to suspect that he is already one of the pod people, merely pretending to be an actor playing the part of a human. When he is called to view the first "pod body," he suddenly races off to save his lady friend from a similar fate with nary a plot element to indicate that this should be his next move. There is simply no reason given in the movie that might allow him to suspect possible danger to his friend.

The setting moves from the tiny village of Santa Mira to the metropolis of San Francisco, and like the original version, the pods seem to be well on their way to successful domination of the planet by the end of the movie. Two sinister additions are made to the plot. First, the viewer sees several scenes of garbage trucks stopping to pick up tiny garbage bags from pod people, and as the apparent human remains are added to the load, a fine dust fills the air and drifts away. Second, the pod people also have a unique alarm system when they encounter humans. They point and scream. The scream is an otherworldly, quasi-electronic shriek, which gets the immediate attention of those fine little hairs on the back of your neck.

The third and so far final version (1993), while the least critically acclaimed, is, in some ways, the most effective of the three. It is not surprising to meet fans who have not only not seen this version—some have never even heard of it. It seems to have come and gone with little fanfare.

This time the setting is an army base somewhere in the South (filmed in Selma, Alabama). Toxic material is stored here, and an EPA scientist has been sent to check it out. The implication is that the toxic material somehow "triggers" the pods. The scientist brings his wife and two children—a teenage girl and a preschool boy—with him. No sooner are they settled in when the boy runs away from day school because the kids all draw the same picture and want him to take a nap. He is picked up by a young helicopter pilot and taken home, where the pilot meets the teen and the romantic interest is introduced. The boy sees his mom disintegrate and the "new" pod mom appear. He won't go to her because "Mommy is dead; she's not my mommy." The special effects are well done: the pod takes over by tendrils that slither into *all* the orifices in your head. The teen is nearly taken over by a pod while snoozing in the bathtub. The duplicate falls through the ceiling on top of her and she wakes and escapes, only to find Dad in the same process and very nearly taken over. She awakens him just in time. The pod is under the bed and grabs her by the leg, but they both escape. The father grabs the boy and runs to Mom, shouting, "We've got to get out of here." Mom then delivers these lines, in an eerie, compelling scene, which is easily the best the movie has to offer:

> *Go where?*
> *Steve, this is important.*
> *Steve, this is important.*
> *That's right, go where?*
> *What happened is not an isolated incident.*
> *It is something that is happening to everyone, everywhere.*

So . . .
Where you gonna go?
Where you gonna run?
Where you gonna hide?
Nowhere, cause there's no one like you, left.

They run anyway, but the camp is overrun by pod people. Long lines of trucks full of pods are being dispatched to other military bases all over the county. Only the teen and the helicopter pilot escape, in a helicopter, of course. The movie ends most ambiguously. As the two wonder aloud whether anyone will believe them, there follows scene after scene of pod trucks being blasted to bits by rockets from helicopters. The final scene shows the teen in the cockpit with radio gear as a voice intones, "Welcome to Atlanta, you are cleared to land." The movie ends as Mom's "Where you gonna go? Where you gonna run? Where you gonna hide?" refrain is repeated in an electronic, distorted, nearly slowed-down-to-stop version. The screen and the viewer's mind go into an ambiguous blank. Did the teen convince the authorities to blow their own people to smithereens based on her word? Hard to believe, especially given the repeated electronic refrain. What's an audience to think? Is it a deliberately ambiguous ending? If so, in this respect, and in at least two others, the 1993 movie has come easily and most faithfully back to the book itself. And when the book is compared to the movies, it is clear that the real *Invasion of the Body Snatchers* has yet to be faithfully brought to the screen.

The problem may be that interpreters are stymied by the various endings or suggested outcomes that Finney gives the reader to ponder. First there's the powerful "suggested" bleak ending. Not only will the pods take over and destroy mankind, they will also destroy all life forms on the planet. And all this within a half a dozen years or so. Then Finney, like those involved in the 1956 *Invasion of the Body Snatchers* seems to have decided to give readers/audiences a positive, hopeful ending. Unfortunately, it's so lame ("they shoot horses, don't they?") it's quadriplegic. The pods leave their vast pod nursery, abandon Earth, and rise up into the sky "and the spaces beyond it." Apparently, as Finney later describes it, to drift for eons and eons on waves of light through intergallactic space until they find another sentient planet to descend upon to devour and destroy. And all because Doc and his gal have rolled a few barrels (six) of burning gasoline into the vast pod nursery. As Doc describes it: "Quite simply, the great pods were leaving a fierce and inhospitable planet . . . and I understood that nothing in the whole vast universe could ever defeat us." (*Invasion of the Body Snatchers,* Award Books, 1965, pg. 189) Sorry, but Finney's ending deserves the euthanasia that all the films gave it.

Finally, Finney quibbles by allowing his hero to ponder, in the final two paragraphs of the novel, if he has really understood everything. Maybe he hasn't the right interpretation to what happened. The novel ends with maybes. Maybe, like the mysteries of spontaneous combustion or reported rains of frogs, we will never know or understand. In the end, the hero of the novel knows only that it happened, never quite sure *why* or *how* or *what* it all means. . . .

The uncommitted ending seems so familiar that the reader is led back to the opening paragraph:

> *I warn you that what you're starting to read is full of loose ends and unanswered questions. It will not be neatly tied up at the end, everything resolved and satisfactorily explained.*

And that's that. The novel's disclaimers, like bookends, begin and end the novel. It is little wonder that Hollywood seemed always at a loss as to how to handle the possibilities of the ending or "endings," as we later learn.

There are other minor elements in the novel missing from the movies. First, there is the Finney whimsy/humor: the pods touch down in a trash heap on a farm and duplicate the puddle of juice at the bottom of a can of Del Monte peaches, then a broken ax handle and possibly a farm animal or two before they get it right.

Another element is the dark-for-its-day humor of Doc Bennell, which may or may not have been in the original script: "We have a special on appendectomies this week . . . better stock up. . . ." "I drink all day as everyone knows. On operating days, especially." Doc keeps his hat on a skeleton named Fred (which later gets replicated by a pod). His response to Uncle Ira's remark, "How's business, Miles? Kill many today?" is "Bagged the limit." Doc refers to the ever-increasing number of patients who claim their loved ones are *not* their loved ones: "It's a new hobby over our way. A cinch to replace weaving and ceramics." Doc suggests a cure to his friend, Mannie, the psychiatrist: "Maybe we ought to try a little bloodletting." He jokes that he is giving up his practice to "join an abortion ring."

If we, the audience, are attracted to horror in an attempt to exorcize the demons, the images of death and violence we see in everyday life, in the global newspapers, the TV, the gorefest of our movies *(Faces of Death I, II, III, IV)*, on the streets of our cities, and in our villages—the pedophile next door—and if our demons have come out into the daylight, we need powerful images indeed, to provide our near-millennium populace with a proper catharsis. But what do the makers of *Invasion of the Body Snatchers* I, II, and III provide us with? Monsters too bland to be evil, monsters slick and persuasive who try to convince us that podhood is not all that bad, in fact there are some advantages.

Were you scared by the scenes where the pods try to persuade people to go to sleep? Monsters of this ilk are not really evil, merely repulsive, merely icky, not threatening in their mild mannered Clark Kent zombieness: These doppelgangers are Alfred E. Neuman (Who cares?) monsters. Time to get some popcorn or visit-the-can monsters.

The subtle evil of the Finney scene lurks and crawls, slinks by peripherally; it's way out there somewhere; it waits for you. ("You're next. It's coming for you.") It is an ever so slow, but sure arrival, a long languid coming. It may even allow you a false free breath, but like sleep, in the end, as inexorable as destiny, it will get you.

It even relishes your false sense of security, but in the end this evil will come for you—it's just in no special hurry, like the pod people, a plodding nonchalance. It chuckles at your sense of security, plays upon your avoidance of reality, your inability to think on things like death or eternity. This evil has a sense of humor. It is born of the necessity of drifting eon-endlessly yet sanely on waves of light as it moves infinitely slowly through the vast and utter darkness of the universe on its journey home to your soul.

The movies desperately need to draw a line between the good guys and the bad guys. The bad guys are not a mean, horrible, mucus-dripping, slimy monsters big enough to break you, stomp you, crush you—not a nightmare, but a vegetable, and a baby vegetable at that. The only apparent difference between the hero and the villains in the *Invasion of the Body Snatchers* movies is a short nap.

But that's not all the movies lack. They lack, believe it or not, an even more intriguing possibility in the first of the "suggested" endings, the bleak ending. This bleak "implied outcome" requires a rather long quote, but it is necessary to see fully where the ending *seemed* to be headed.

Synopsis: Mannie the pod person, once a psychiatrist, along with several other pod people, have the hero, Dr. Miles Bennell, and the heroine and lover, Becky Driscoll, trapped in the doc's office. Miles and Becky are exhausted and can hardly stay awake. The pod people are simply going to place the pods nearby, lock the humans in the office, and let nature take its course: let pod and person do what comes naturally: sleep and duplicate:

> *"All right, Miles," he said quietly, "so you know. We tried to make it easy on you, that's all; because after it was over, it wouldn't have mattered, you just wouldn't have cared. Miles, I mean it"—his brows raised persuasively—"it's not so bad. Ambition, excitement—what's so good about them?" he said, and I could tell he meant it. "And do you mean to say you'll miss the strain and worry that goes along with them? It's not bad, Miles, and I mean that. It's peaceful, it's quiet. And the food still tastes good, books are still good to read—"*

"But not to write," I said quietly. "Not the labor, hope, and struggle of writing them. That's all gone, isn't it, Mannie?"

He shrugged. "I won't argue with you, Miles. You seem to have guessed pretty well how things are."

"No emotion." I said it aloud, but wonderingly, speaking to myself. "Mannie," I said, as it occurred to me, "can you make love, have children?"

He looked at me for a moment. "I think you know that we can't, Miles. Hell," he said then, and it was as close to anger as he was capable of coming," you might as well know the truth: you're insisting on it. The duplication isn't *perfect. And can't be. It's like the artificial compounds nuclear physicists are fooling with: unstable, unable to hold their form. (pg. 158)*

This has been a common theme since Frankenstein (1818): scientists messing where they ought not mess, with the handiwork of God.

"We can't live, Miles. The last of us will be dead"—he gestured with a hand, as though it didn't matter—"in five years at the most."

The idea that the pods themselves will die in a few years was never picked up by any of the movies.

Budlong (first to find the spores) said it: parasites. Parasites of the universe, and they will be the last and final survivors in it. (pg. 159)

It's a fascinating concept that none of the movies have approached: the pods have not only destroyed our solar system, but, if not stopped, will eventually, some light-eons from now, *destroy the universe.* But wait, folks, there's more, as Budlong, the pod person professor, picks up the narrative:

Doctor, the function of life is to live if it can, *and no other motive can ever be allowed to interfere with that. There is no malice involved; did you hate the buffalo? We must continue because we must; can't you understand that?" He smiled at me pleasantly. "It's the nature of the beast." (pgs. 159–160)*

To paraphrase Pogo, we have met the beast and he is us. Who will win the race to be the first to destroy the universe? Will it be pod or will it be people? Will it matter to an empty universe? As Stephen Crane once wrote:

"Sir, I exist," cried the man to the universe.

"However," replied the universe, "the fact creates in me no sense of obligation."

Is this how the universe ends, in the manner of T. S. Eliot: not with a big bang but with a final whimper of the last sentient (emotional) being? Or will it be the last pod? And who will be left to know . . . or care?

Go where?
That's right, go where?
It is something that is happening to everyone, everywhere
So . . .
Where you gonna go?
Where you gonna run?
Where you gonna hide?
Nowhere, cause there's no one like you left.

So, for all its flaws, *Invasion of the Body Snatchers* 1993, with its ambiguous ending, its ecological theme (toxins), and its brilliant echoing refrain of Finney's "bleak" ending follows the novel more closely than any of the other movies: the closest, so far. The *Invasion of the Body Snatchers* ouvre is early black humor, early ecological concern, not to mention being close to, if not the original, granddaddy of horror noire.

So what's the score so far: a happy-ending movie, humans win; a bleak ending movie, the pods win; a seemingly deliberate who knows—ambiguous ending movie. Finally, there's the novel itself, which supplies, with its bookend disclaimers, all of the above and more: the possible pod/humankind death of the universe, the rich black humor, and the horror of the absurd. All of which suggests that the complete story has yet to be told. The *Invasion of the Body Snatchers* ouvre isn't over yet. The challenge to film the final chapter, the ultimate *Invasion of the Body Snatchers* awaits.

OF TIME AND PODS: THE FANTASTIC WORLD OF JACK FINNEY

Fred Blosser

IN JACK FINNEY'S UNIVERSE, THE EXTRAORDINARY and the mundane are not two separate and mutually exclusive conditions of existence.

The first consistently erupts into the second. One merges with the other.

Miles Bennell from *The Body Snatchers* can vouch for that. So can Si Morley, Nick Cheyney, Ben Jarvis, Lew Jollife, and all of Finney's other protagonists.

In Finney's universe, you discover that space aliens have overrun your sleepy hometown, and they look just like—hell, they *are*—your sweetheart, your best friend, the kindly old retiree down the street. You travel back in time to the New York City of the 1880s to solve the mystery of a peculiar carving on a gravestone. You realize that your wife has been possessed by the ghost of a flamboyant silent movie actress. You break *into* San Quentin Penitentiary. . . .

One of the characters in *The Body Snatchers* says: "We all prefer the weird and thrilling to the dull and commonplace. . . ." Recognizing this basic fact of human nature, Finney was a genius in conveying the emotional jolt that comes when the commonplace suddenly turns into the bizarre.

For some, like Si Morley and Lew Jollife, embracing the extraordinary is a matter of choice. Others, like Miles Bennell and Nick Cheyney, simply have no say in the matter.

Of Finney, Ed Gorman wrote: "To my generation

of fantasy and suspense writers, he will always be one of the most important of literary gods." Born Walter Braden Finney in Milwaukee in 1911, this master of the strange and the ordinary sold his first short story to *Ellery Queen's Mystery Magazine* in 1946. His first novel, *5 Against the House*, followed in 1954.

The five of the title are four bored college students—Al, Jerry, Guy, and Brick—and Al's girlfriend, Tina, who together plan and pull a heist at a Reno gambling casino. The scheme is worked out with the ingenuity and attention to realistic detail that were consistent hallmarks of Finney's writing.

Big heist novels were a popular genre in the fifties, but they mostly dealt with hard-boiled professional thieves who approach robbery as a business. Finney pioneered a new subgenre in which everyday amateurs team to pull off a big job as a kick or an intellectual challenge. Others would follow Finney's lead in the late fifties and sixties with movies and books like *The Thomas Crown Affair* (Avon, 1968), *Ocean's 11* (Cardinal, 1960), *Gambit* (Viking Press, 1962), and many more.

In *The Body Snatchers* (1955; revised version, 1978), Finney turns from crime to science fiction. Small-town doctor Miles Bennell discovers that Santa Mira, California (Mill Valley, in the 1978 revision) has been overrun by creatures from outer space that sprout from oversized pods. These invaders replicate the forms and superficial personalities—but not the souls—of the humans with whom they come into contact. And what else can you say about this classic that hasn't already been said better—for example, by Ed Gorman and others elsewhere in this very book? Nothing, probably.

Some critics at the time saw the novel as a McCarthy-era warning about the insidious spread of godless communism. Others interpreted it as a criticism about mindless McCarthyism. Maybe the tale mirrors our fear that the frantic expediencies of modern life are already turning us all into real-life pod people, possessing no more warmth or substance than the images we see on a TV set. "Sometimes," Miles reflects early in the story, "I think we're refining all humanity out of our lives."

Finney himself claimed that the story was meant as entertainment, nothing more. But a later generation of writers would find inspiration for a uniquely twentieth-century school of horror fiction rooted in the quiet terrors of small-town life. It was a lesson taught by Finney, Matheson, Bradbury, and Bloch, and taken to heart by King, Koontz, and Gorman. No longer could you evade monsters by staying clear of Dracula's Transylvania or Lovecraft's decaying New England backwaters. The monsters were coming to *you*, and they were as close as the corner gas station, the local high school, your own backyard.

The House of Numbers (1957) was an inventive return to crime fiction with the patented Finney touch of approaching a familiar genre (in this case, the prison-break story) in a new and different way. When San Quentin inmate Arnie Jarvis faces a possible death sentence in an attack on a guard, he convinces his brother Ben to mount a rescue. To do so, Ben himself must sneak into the prison, take Arnie's place for a day—long enough for the latter to rig an escape route for himself—and then go back over the wall before somebody discovers the deception.

As usual, Finney's setting is impeccably researched, his characters incisively drawn, his stratagems cleverly developed. Who but Finney would have pegged a prison escape on a confusion of identities? When Ben successfully passes himself off as Arnie to a prison guard who has already met him in the outside world as Ben, one is reminded of the chilling impostures of *The Body Snatchers*: "Of course to this man I could only be Arnold Jarvis, the man he knew was an inmate here; naturally Arnold Jarvis would resemble his brother."

Finney was also busy in the 1950s as a writer of short stories for the *Saturday Evening Post, Collier's*, and other popular slicks. These tales were eventually collected in two volumes—*The Third Level* (1957) and *I Love Galesburg in the Springtime* (1963). To single out only a few of these gems, "Contents of a Dead Man's Pockets" is a tense little chiller worthy of de Maupassant and John Collier. "The Third Level," "Of Missing Persons," and "I'm Scared" are fantasy classics, the veritable forerunners of Rod Serling's *Twilight Zone*.

In fact, one wonders. Debuting as it did in the prosaic era of Ike and Norman Vincent Peale, would Serling's TV series have found a receptive audience if Finney hadn't already cultivated millions of readers with his compact parables about time travel, strange disappearances, and doorways to idyllic alien worlds? I think the question is open for discussion.

Ironically, Serling himself would later write the script for the 1966 movie version of Finney's last novel of the fifties. In *Assault on a Queen* (1959), another team of amateurs assembles. Their immediate goal: to raise a German U-boat lost off Long Island in the closing days of World War I. Next step: to use the sub as their vehicle for a raid on the Queen Mary as the luxury liner returns to port with a full complement of wealthy passengers.

Once again, Finney reveals his talent for exploring an arcane subject in fascinating detail while unreeling a tense, fast-paced crime plot. How does a World War I sub operate, and how do you restore it to working order after it's lain untended on the ocean floor after forty years? Finney tells you, and the particulars are worth the price of admission all by themselves.

On top of that, Finney delivers a story line that continually takes the reader by surprise. As Hugh Brittain and his cohorts board the Queen Mary, as rivalry mounts between Hugh and his coconspirator Ed Marino over the attention of their gorgeous partner Rosa, events never go in quite the direction you expect them to go. Finney never settles for the easy cliché, the familiar plot device.

Finney wrote two novels in the sixties, both dealing with marital crises. But don't expect the suburban angst of John Updike or John Cheever. In *Good Neighbor Sam* (1963), amiable adman Sam agrees to pose as his wife's best friend's husband to help the friend secure an inheritance. The deception spirals hilariously out of control when one of Sam's clients decides to showcase the fraudulent pair as America's perfect couple in a national ad campaign.

The Woodrow Wilson Dime (1968; revised version, 1987) expands upon an earlier short story, "The Coin Collector" (or "The Other Wife," its original title). Benjamin Bennell (Miles's less ambitious younger brother?) is an unfulfilled New York ad writer who has grown bored with his dead-end job and his wife Hetty. One day, a way out of his bind presents itself. A dime stamped with the profile of Woodrow Wilson pays Ben's admission into an alternate universe.

In this world next door, Ben is wealthy, the owner of his own agency, and married to the voluptuous Tessie. It should be paradise, but Finney sardonically points out a basic fact of life for the wistful Ben Bennells of the world, whatever that particular world may be: What you don't have is always what you most desire.

What Ben now wants is his original wife, Hetty. But the alternate-universe Hetty is already engaged to slick patent attorney Custer Huppfelt. The quest to win her back leads Ben to yet another parallel world—one in which he's flat broke and divorced from Hetty, and Custer again stands in the way of romantic bliss—and to a wacky scam that recalls the comedy capers of Donald E. Westlake.

Another unfulfilled adman is the hero of *Time and Again* (1970). "There wasn't anything really wrong with my life," Simon (Si) Morley ponders. "Except that, like most everyone else's I knew about, it had a big gaping hole in it, an enormous emptiness, and I didn't know how to fill it."

Government operative Rube Prine suggests an answer. Scientists have discovered a simple technique for time travel, and Prine offers Si the chance to step back to the New York City of 1882 as a test subject.

The Feds look at time travel strictly as a military device, a way to change the past advantageously for present-day national security. For Si, the Project offers a way to answer a question that has puzzled his lady friend Kate for years: Why did the mailing of a certain letter on January 23, 1882, result years later in the suicide of a New York financier named Andrew Carmody, whose son became Kate's adopted father?

Arguably rivaling *The Body Snatchers* as Finney's most popular work, *Time and Again* is many things, all of them quite wonderful. It's perhaps the most impressive historical novel ever written about everyday urban life in nineteenth-century America. It's an absorbing mystery that turns on Si's pursuit of Andrew Carmody. It's a clever examination of the mechanics and paradoxes of time travel that made mainstream SF safe for moviemakers like Nicholas

Meyer with *Time After Time* (1978) and Spielberg and Zemeckis with *Back to the Future* (1985). It's also an appealing love story about Si's romance with Julia, a woman of 1882, and about Finney's own infatuation with a quieter, simpler age of wintry sleigh rides on Fifth Avenue, before the "first of the terrible corrupting wars" of the twentieth century.

There's also a thoughtful subtext that gives the novel an added emotional charge. As Si compares the 1880s with the 1970s and measures the social and technological changes in between, he realizes that society often does terrible things in the name of progress. Too often, the public accepts the self-serving dictates of politicians and corporations without reckoning the consequences. By the time we comprehend our mistakes, it's too late.

As Si meditates, "I was, and I knew it, an ordinary person who long after he was grown retained the childhood assumption that the people who largely control our lives are better informed than, and have judgment superior to, the rest of us. . . . Not until Vietnam did I finally realize that some of the most important decisions of all time can be made by men knowing really no more than, and who are not more intelligent than, most of the rest of us."

It's a dilemma that resonated with Finney's audience in 1970, the year when National Guardsmen fired on students at Kent State, when disgust over America's befouled lakes, rivers, and air led to historic environmental reforms. It still resonates today, maybe more so than ever—hence the satisfaction the reader feels when Si returns to 1882 to marry Julia and to change the past in one small, critical way that prevents the Project from ever coming into existence. . . .

Marion's Wall (Simon & Schuster, 1973) was Finney's loving tribute to another golden age, the heyday of 1920s Hollywood and silent movies. When Nick and Jan Cheyney move into an old Victorian in San Francisco, they discover a message scrawled on a wall in lipstick under an old layer of wallpaper—"Marion Marsh lived here. Read it and weep." Marion was an aspiring actress who died in an automobile accident in 1927 just after landing her breakthrough movie role. Her ghost still inhabits the house, and it begins to inhabit Jan's body, too.

This development makes life uncertain for Nick. Whenever he

begins to make love to Jan, he can't be sure whether it's actually her or the flamboyant Marion. One expects Finney to play this Thorne Smith situation for risqué humor, and he does. The novel provides some delightful laughs, along with Finney's charming meditations about the glamorous Hollywood of Valentino, Swanson, and Theda Bara. But there's also an echo of Miles Bennell's dilemma in *The Body Snatchers*:

> *"This was Jan's face, her dark hair, her arms, hands and body, but . . . there was a recklessness in the eyes, a fullness to the smiling lips, a tension and excitement in every line of that familiar body, that I'd never seen before. . . . This was another woman. . . ."*

In *The Night People* (1977), four affluent but bored suburbanites in Mill Valley embark on a progressively more outlandish and dangerous series of nighttime pranks. They are counterparts of the restless college students of *5 Against the House* two decades later, rebelling against the complacency of a well-paid, comfortable, and rootless existence. As the main character, Lew Jollife, reflects: "He liked his job—liked it all right, that is, but could give it up. Liked where they lived, but could leave. Could give up anything, it seemed."

The book's big set piece is one of Finney's most gripping: a nighttime climb by Lew and his friend Harry to the top of the Golden Gate Bridge. But *The Night People* may be most remarkable as a parable of anomie and angst in the comfortable white-collar middle class during the Ford and Carter era, comparable to the free-flowing, absurdist seventies movies of Paul Mazursky and Robert Altman.

Forgotten News (1983) was a nonfiction entertainment about sensational but now-forgotten events of the 1800s, based on Finney's extensive research in period newspapers for *Time and Again*. Along with *About Time* (1986), a volume of time-travel tales from Finney's earlier short story collections, the book revived popular interest in *Time and Again*. Fans began wondering: Did Simon Morley really give up time travel? Was the Project truly defunct? Finney finally answered those questions twelve years later in his final book.

As *From Time to Time* (1995) opens, we learn that Si Morley wasn't completely sucessful in altering the past. Scientists piece together evidence that twentieth-century history has unrolled in at least two different but sometimes contiguous tracks. Meanwhile, Rube Prien and others stubbornly pursue subliminal memories of an alternate 1970 in which they launched a time travel experiment called the Project. . . .

Ingeniously, Rube and his colleagues reverse Si's tampering with time and convince Morley to make another foray into the past. The destination is 1912; the mission, to safeguard a shadowy government agent known to history only as "Z." There is a chance to avert World War I if Si can locate Z and keep him from sailing on an ill-fated voyage to Europe—or failing that, if Si can prevent the sinking of the liner on which Z booked his return passage: the *Titanic.*

If the sequel isn't as satisfying as the original, it may be simply that the reader misses the greater profusion of detail that crowded *Time After Time.* Still, there is much charm in Finney's description of the old, majestic ocean liners, and when Si explores the culture of vaudeville and goes to see a performance by Al Jolson in the flesh, the reader has the sense of being in a world a little closer to our own time, a little more familiar than the horse-drawn-cart setting of the earlier book.

The denouement, as Si desperately tries to alter the course of the *Titanic,* again points out the perplexing dilemmas of time travel. If you could do something to prevent a monstrous event from happening, would you do it, even if the other consequences are unguessable? And how do you know that the action you take won't in fact lead to the occurrence that you want to avert?

As the book concludes, Si returns for good to the 1880s, determined never to venture into time again but hopeful of making small changes to protect his immediate family from the bad things the future holds in store.

It's a poignant ending, as if Finney, in a personal way, were saying his own farewell to a full career of exploring the mundane and the marvellous. Shortly after *From Time to Time* was published, Jack Finney died, on November 16, 1995.

THEY CAME FROM ANOTHER WORLD!

Billie Sue Mosiman

THE MOVIE THEATER POSTERS FOR JACK FINNEY'S story-turned-into-film, *Invasion of the Body Snatchers*, was a screamer of an advertisement that helped pack the seats. Blood-red lettering proclaimed the title. Yellow spotlights poured out of the dark night heavens, highlighting the stars in the movie, Kevin McCarthy and Dana Wynter, as they ran from a city under invasion. Overhead hovered thousands of menacing spaceships. "Something is happening. Send your men of science quick!" was lettered in the top corner of the poster.

Americans, puzzled and intrigued by this marketing ploy that played on their growing public uneasiness and paranoia, stood in front of the theaters featuring these posters, eagerly reached for their wallets, and bought tickets.

It was 1956 and I was a little kid sitting in the back seat of a fairly new Ford, my parents in the front seat, at a drive-in theater somewhere in Texas. The lot was filled with cars. Already the dripping buttered popcorn, monster dill pickles, hot dogs, and cold drinks were being consumed from the refreshment stand. Some families hauled out folding chairs or blankets to spread on the grassy spaces between the speakers. Older children were called away from the swing sets and slides set up in front of the massive white outdoor screen. Smaller children, brought to the drive-in dressed in their pajamas, were settled down for the night. This was not a movie for the very little ones, everyone knew that.

Then the screen filled with the opening title screen of *Invasion of the Body Snatchers.* I don't know about the other viewers of the film in 1956, but that night one little girl in the backseat of her parents' car was so frightened she had nightmares for months afterward. And the influence of the film left its mark on her as much as a cattle brand would have left a fleshy pink scar.

If there is a national legacy (and there is) of the original version of *Invasion of the Body Snatchers,* it's the creepy undeniable gut-level fear that *something might be out there.* Many film reviewers of note and movie pundits who love to look for psychological connections have pointed out that the reason *Invasion of the Body Snatchers* became a cult movie and fondly remembered is because at the time, in 1956, the story reflected the worry the American society harbored for the communist bloc of Russia and the threat of nuclear war.

I wouldn't deny that that may have been part of how the film got under the skin of audiences, but the real reason it had such an impact, the *real* reason it gave the nation nightmares and the trembling shakes in the middle of the night was because . . . what if the story's scenario might come true? What if one day aliens might really appear and, by some magical, chemical, or mechanical means, look *just like us*? How could we tell them apart from our own kind? How could we defeat lookalikes?

In one scene in the film, McCarthy says, "In my practice I've seen how people have allowed their humanity to drain away. Only it happened slowly instead of all at once. They didn't seem to mind. . . . All of us—a little bit—we harden our hearts, grow callous. Only when we have to fight to stay human do we realize how precious it is to us, how dear." In another scene, when he states, "I'd hate to wake up some morning and find out that you weren't you," we really understand deep down in the dark places of our souls what kind of terror this story holds for the human race. If aliens *don't* show up and take over human bodies, there are other, perhaps even more horrifying threats waiting for mankind. The wife may wake to find her husband is not the man she thought he was. Or the husband may come home from work and discover his wife has left him, that she's taken on a whole new life without him. Children may mature and become adults their parents don't know at all. If none of that comes to pass and we live to ripe old ages, surely the darkness will creep over our minds toward the end and render us incapable of recognizing our closest and dearest kin.

In other words, alien invasion and infiltration is one thought the story frightens us with, but there's also the underlying and boldly stated possibility of one day turning around to find either you or your loved ones are entirely new beings, people you don't know anymore, people who may not love you. Or for some unfathomable reason, you may not love them. You could be all alone. It's this psychological factor of aloneness and alienation from those one trusted and loved that works its simple position on the minds of the viewers.

Audiences today might believe that *The X-Files* invented the idea that something is out there, but they're only borrowing the idea from Jack Finney's brilliant novel and Don Siegel's incredible movie.

The X-Files, Dark Skies, and various other television shows are just the latest of a long line of entertainments that borrow from Finney's idea.

Thin Air (1969) was one of the first films borrowing liberally from the idea of alien invasion and human body snatching. A British military paratrooper disappears in midair during a jump from an army plane. Two investigators, Patrick Allen and Neil Connery, try to unravel how this happened. What they uncover is an alien plot to steal the bodies of earthlings by snatching them out of the air.

In 1978, the first remake of *Invasion of the Body Snatchers* was made. Donald Sutherland played a health inspector who stumbles onto the alien pods. His girlfriend—Brooke Adams—Leonard Nimoy, and Jeff Goldblum, all help Sutherland uncover the alien plot. Sutherland destroys a large greenhouse full of incubating pods, but later, when he encounters his girlfriend, it turns out *he's* a pod person, too. Of course! (What you fear most, you become, is the subtle message here.)

One of the more interesting aspects of this remake version are the cameo roles of Kevin McCarthy, the star in the original, and Don Siegel, the director of the original. Also, Robert Duvall appears in a bit part.

In 1983, along came *Strange Invaders*, starring Paul LeMat, Diana

Scarwid, Nancy Allen, Louise Fletcher, Michael Lerner, Kenneth Tobey, Wallace Shawn, June Lockhart, and Michael Laughlin. A New York college professor returns to his hometown of Centerville, Illinois, in search of his missing wife, only to find himself embroiled in an alien invasion. Nancy Allen plays a tabloid newspaper reporter who teams up with LeMat. The scenes with the mother ship are particularly chilling.

In this film it's 1958 when aliens visit the town of Centerville, Illinois. Twenty-five years later, LeMat, now a professor at Columbia University, can't reach his ex-wife in Centerville. When he arrives in town, no one's ever heard of her before! Returning to New York, he teams up with the newspaper reporter who has written about alien encounters. There is an abduction of LeMat's daughter by aliens; a confrontation in Centerville, and the professor and newspaper writer are captured by aliens and taken aboard the huge mother ship. Only the ex-wife gets whisked off with the ship in the end.

In 1993, *Invasion of the Body Snatchers* was remade again, and called simply, *The Body Snatchers*. One of the most chilling scenes is when Meg Tilly asks, "Where ya gonna go? Where ya gonna run? Where ya gonna hide?" She asks these questions and we stop and wonder: yes, where is there sanctuary from such an invasion as this? The story was changed from the original, and this time our lead male isn't a doctor, but an Environmental Protection Agency official who brings his family with him to a military base. Meg Tilly is a young wife and mother who becomes a pod person. Gabrielle Anwar plays the standard alienated teen who finds a friend in a wild local girl.

Once alien pods have taken over nearly all of the military base, the daughter and a young military man escape in a helicopter. They blow up the base, a convoy of pod-filled trucks headed for military bases around the country, then finally land at an airport in Atlanta, Georgia. It might be overrun with pod people too . . . who knows?

It wasn't that this was such a bad retelling of the original 1956 version, but people who had seen the original and were affected by it might have felt how lukewarm this effort turned out to be. Another reason why this latest remake might not have held the same terror is the fact that military training has much to do with erasing individual desires and replacing them with discipline to officers and allegiance to country. How can it be so frightening to see a man whose individualism is partially obscured lose it altogether as a pod person? Psychologically, the setting and the group of people involved were completely wrong for the story being told. It defused the uneasiness and fear of viewers. There wasn't enough contrast, except for the mother's loss to the aliens, to make the film work on the subconscious level where it really does its feral, bone-chilling job.

What remake could compare with the original? Who could show the fear in his eyes the way Kevin McCarthy did when on the run through the city, flagging down cars on the freeway for help? Or when he realized his girlfriend, Becky, had fallen asleep in the cave, and she was lost to him forever? In the original, with pods for Miles and Becky placed in the doctor's waiting room, Dr. Kaufman says to Miles, trying to convince him to give in and sleep:

> *"Less than a month ago, Santa Mira was like any other town. People with nothing but problems. Then, out of the sky came a solution. Seeds drifting through space for years took root in a farmer's field. From the seeds came pods which had the power to reproduce themselves in the exact likeness of any form of life. Your new bodies are growing in there. They're taking you over cell for cell, atom for atom. There is no pain. Suddenly, while you're asleep, they'll absorb your minds, your memories and you're reborn into an untroubled world. Tomorrow you'll be one of us. There's no need for love. Love, desire, ambition, faith—without them life is so simple, believe me."*

The problem with this promise is that human beings know that their minds and their memories—that love, desire, ambition, and faith—are all they have to make them human. Yes, they walk upright, but sometimes so do the great apes. Yes, they laugh and no other creature can do that, but even dogs smile.

It's the rational, thinking, decision-making mind that separates man from beast, that makes him a god on his planet, and it is his memories that guide him into the future. It's his love that causes him to sacrifice himself and behave with gentility. It's his desire and ambition to be better than he is that drives him to invent, create, and manufacture. It's his faith that he is on a *safe* journey into the unknown that keeps him going forward each and every day.

Take it all away and man loses not only himself and his hope for redemption, but he loses his place with the gods, he loses the world and everything in it. For without these human attributes, he loses himself.

No matter how many books or stories or films try to improve on or imitate *Invasion of the Body Snatchers,* it can't be done. Not with the force and paranoia and fear produced by the very first, the original, the best. A whole generation of imaginations were influenced by Finney's book and Siegel's 1956 movie.

I say this with the authority of a middle-aged woman from that very generation, who as a little girl sat in the backseat of a darkened Ford in a Texas drive-in and was never the same again.

From here it's fair to ask of moviemakers or novelists who wish to borrow, steal, or otherwise try to play off one of the most intriguing and effective stories of our age: Where you gonna go? Where you gonna run? Where you gonna hide?

A NICE PLACE TO VISIT, BUT . . .

William Relling, Jr.

AS FANS OF *INVASION OF THE BODY SNATCHERS* IN its various incarnations—and if you weren't fans, you wouldn't be reading this book, would you?—many if not most of you may be already aware of some of the backstory information I'm about to impart. Stick with me for the sake of those not yet in the know, and you'll be (I hope) rewarded for your patience.

So. Just after New Year's Day in 1955, director Don Siegel, producer Walter Wanger, and screenwriter Daniel Mainwaring hied themselves up from Los Angeles to Mill Valley, California, to visit author Jack Finney. Their purpose: to discuss with Finney their upcoming movie version of his serialized novel that was at the time completing its run in *Collier's* magazine. Mill Valley, Finney's home, lies (then as now) some ten or so miles north of San Francisco, in Marin County; to get there (then as now) you drive across the Golden Gate Bridge and then up along Highway 101. The filmmakers not only wanted to meet with Finney to talk over the movie's story line, but they also wanted to scope out the town itself as a location for their film shoot—Mill Valley being Jack Finney's model for the fictional community of Santa Mira, the setting for his story.

After checking out the town, Siegel, Wanger, and Mainwaring agreed that it would be swell to shoot their movie there, but for one thing: Allied Artists, the studio putting up the money to make *Body*

Snatchers, had given them a budget of only $350,000. Which was, even by Hollywood standards of that era, a teeny amount of dough, and certainly not enough to allow an entire film crew to relocate from L.A. Consequently, Siegel and his location scouts would have to make do with southern California exteriors doubling for northern California ones.

Their two primary locations ended up being in Beachwood Canyon (not far from the Hollywood Reservoir) and Sierra Madre, a bedroom community that lies just east of Pasadena (home of the Rose Bowl) and just west of Arcadia (home of the Santa Anita racetrack), in the foothills of the San Gabriel Mountains. Siegel probably chose Sierra Madre for what critic Pauline Kael has suggested is its "realistic atmosphere . . . a drab, isolated small town that seems to close in on its characters." Not the most charitable assessment of what the place was (and still is) like, but also not an inaccurate one.

I know, because I resided in Sierra Madre for a time, when I first moved to southern California in 1978. Because I was such a fan of *Body Snatchers*, I was, of course, aware that Sierra Madre had been Santa Mira in a movie that remains not just a big favorite, but one of the scariest I've ever seen.

Twenty years ago it struck me that Sierra Madre didn't seem much changed from the way Don Siegel et al had presented it in the 1950s. And today, another two decades along, Sierra Madre still hasn't changed much. If this very day you were taking a stroll along Sierra Madre Boulevard, the town's main drag, and if you didn't know better, you'd have no idea you were less than a mile from a twelve-lane superhighway that would carry you right into the heart of the second largest megalopolis in the United States. Sierra Madre remains as sleepy and sedate and benignly if blandly pleasant now as it was when Dwight and Mamie Eisenhower occupied the White House.

Kind of an eerie thought, isn't it? If you start to wonder why that is?

It's actually a very nice town, as L.A. bedroom communities go. Founded in 1881 as the jumping-off point for several camp trails (the most significant being the seven-mile-long trail leading to the summit of Mount Wilson, the region's highest point), by the turn of this century, Sierra Madre was a bustling little burg of about seven hundred residents, most of whom worked either in the local orange groves or at the town's main manufacturing enterprise, a cigar factory. By the 1920s, it had evolved into a resort community, the supply center for a number of mountain summer camps that had sprung up around the area, once people figured out that it was usually much cooler during the day up there in the heavily wooded San Gabriel foothills in July and August than it was down in the Los Angeles basin. In 1938, however, a flood wiped out many of the camps, none of which anyone seems to have bothered to rebuild. Though to this day, there are a few residents who still live in small cabins dotting the mountain trails.

That's one of Sierra Madre's more interesting aspects—that so many of the people who live there seem to have done so for a long time. And lots of them recall the spring of 1955, when all those crazy people trucked up from Hollywood to make what was hyped to the locals as a big-time movie studio production.

My friend John Delgatto has been a Sierra Madre resident since his family moved there from Wisconsin in 1954, when he was seven years old. John, who is president of Sierra Records, Books, and Home Video (an independent music label that specializes mostly in high-quality folk, country, and bluegrass acts) maintains Sierra Records's offices about five hundred yards from the very spot where forty-odd years ago, dozens of Sierra Madre residents worked as extras, posing as Santa Mirans. They unloaded truckfuls of malevolent seed pods, while an exhausted Kevin McCarthy and Dana Wynter hid nearby, observing in terror.

"Actually," says John, "the first movie I remember anyone doing around here was Bob Hope's *The Seven Little Foys*. They used a house that's still there called the Piney House, up on Lima Street. And it was a big deal to the town, because it was *Bob Hope*. I remember people going by and looking at the set, and that was the first time I realized that, 'Oh, they use my town for movies.' But they only used it for the opening shot of Bob Hope's house, then they left and we never saw 'em again.

"*Invasion of the Body Snatchers* was a much bigger deal. They closed off the entire town. I was going to grade school at the time, and they let everybody out early one day because some film crew was shooting this 'major motion picture,' and we could all go take a look.

"I remember walking down the street with my little satchel of books, and the first thing I noticed were these gigantic arc lamps lined up along the street—all these weird-looking lights just strung up and down the street. When I got to the set, they were shooting what turned out to be material for the trailer. They'd gathered a bunch of people from the town, local people, and had them all running down the street. Just townspeople—my dad was one of them. I remember people running, guys with change in their pockets falling out, all supposed to be running from . . . we didn't know *what*. Some kind of a monster. *Invasion of the Body Snatchers*? At the time, we didn't know what the story was about. We had no concept of it, we only knew the title.

"Everything that said 'Sierra Madre' on it had been changed to 'Santa Mira,' that was obvious. There's a part where Kevin McCarthy walks across the street, and he goes past a bank that was and still *is* there, called the Sierra Madre Bank. They'd changed it to the Santa Mira Bank, so it stuck in my mind that this was supposed to be happening in some town called Santa Mira, and not actually where I lived.

"There's another famous shot that's also from the town, near the beginning of the movie, where McCarthy goes to visit Virginia Christine. When she's saying there was something wrong with her uncle? Later we see her at her little store, which was just south of Baldwin Avenue. [The other of Sierra Madre's two primary thoroughfares.] "And the siren that goes off when McCarthy and Dana Wynter are trying to escape? That was on top of the firehouse. Until they stopped using it, in the 1970s, it was the emergency signal here in town—that horn they recorded is actually the horn that's still on top of the firehouse building. Everyone knows it around here, because it had such a distinctive sound. So when you'd hear it in the movie, you'd right away go, 'Aha! Sierra Madre!' "

It's also interesting to note the degree to which, over these past four decades, *Body Snatchers* has integrated itself into Sierra Madre's local history and folklore. John Delgatto recalls: "In the late sixties there was this disc jockey, Jazzbo Collins, who was mainly known up in the San Francisco area, but he was also down here in L.A. There was an incident where someone discovered these poisonous violin spiders in Sierra Madre Park. Suddenly there was a very big deal about this bizarre 'infestation,' and Jazzbo started getting involved with it, after somebody said to him, 'You know, Sierra Madre, that's where they did the movie *Invasion of the Body Snatchers*.' Jazzbo ran with that, and it got reinforced again, about Sierra Madre and the movie."

Another incident occurred a few years later, after John's father, a local businessman, was elected to Sierra Madre's city council. "There was a dispute over something," John recounts. "I don't even remember what the reason was, but somebody in town didn't like something that was going on. Somebody who got mad at the whole council. Well, right then, at that same identical time, one of the L.A. TV stations, I don't know if it was Channel 9 or Channel 11 or what, they would rerun movies. They'd show the same movie every day, over and over again. As it happens, at the time, they were running *that* movie, and apparently somebody got it in their head: *This is supposed to be Sierra Madre*. One morning, a few days later, my dad gets a phone call from the chief of police who says, 'I wanted to tell you before you hear it from anybody else, but somebody's played a prank on you. There's a bunch of seed pods, just like in the movie. And one of 'em has your name on it, along with the other council members.'

"They'd been left right in the middle of Kersting Square. The newspaper took pictures of these pods sitting there, and at the next council meeting, the chief of police presented one to each of the council members, as a sort of gift. Somebody'd seen the movie and tried to recreate the pods out of papier-mâché, stuffed with newspaper and stapled around the edges. Then they drew little vines on 'em, the way it was in the movie, and put the name of each councilman on each one. The idea was that the councilmen weren't the real councilmen because they were screwing up so badly, they must have been replaced by pod people. My dad got a big laugh out of it."

• • •

Truth to tell, I doubt that Don Siegel and Walter Wanger and Daniel Mainwaring really saw Sierra Madre as little more than an acceptable manifestation of their vision of Santa Mira. Evidence for this would include their use of several other southern California exterior locations to represent portions of their fictional town—not just Beachwood Canyon, but places like Chatsworth, Glendale, and Los Feliz as well. In fact, if you watch the film carefully, you'll notice that—except for the landscape looking vaguely more southern than northern California—you really can't tell in what part of the state Santa Mira is supposed to be.

There aren't many clues; for example, when Kevin McCarthy dials the local operator and insists on speaking to the FBI, he asks to be connected to the Los Angeles office—("On your call to Los Angeles, Doctor, they don't answer. All the Los Angeles circuits are dead.")—the implication being that L.A. is the closest big city to Santa Mira. Later, however, when McCarthy and Dana Wynter are surreptitiously observing truckloads of pods being prepared for shipment out of Santa Mira, the police officer-turned-pod-person directing distribution calls out the name of Crescent City, the northernmost town in California, as one of the evil plants' destinations. So who knows?

But beyond noting the curious coincidence of the two towns sharing the same initials, Sierra Madre isn't really Santa Mira. Is it?

"I don't know . . ." John Delgatto says, somewhat guardedly. "Before the freeway came in, around late '75, we were still pretty isolated. Before then, you'd have to drive through the whole city of Pasadena before you could catch a freeway to go someplace else, so we were somewhat remote. And over the years, if you watch the movie, it's interesting to see that the town hasn't changed that much. A few little things here and there, but it's still pretty much the same town."

Gulp.

Photo from *Invasion of the Body Snatchers* courtesy of Republic Entertainment, Inc.

AN INTERVIEW WITH DANA WYNTER

Tom Weaver

"I HATE THE IDEA OF A DOUBLE," DANA WYNTER once told a *TV Guide* interviewer, adding that she always refused to allow herself to be doubled in her movies. She was referring, of course, to the standard use of stunt doubles and stand-ins during picture-making; but for fans of *Invasion of the Body Snatchers* the comment has a coincidental "double" meaning: it vividly recalls her costarring role as Becky Driscoll, the chic divorcée romantically pursued by Kevin McCarthy—then stalked and ultimately duplicated by the extraterrestrial pod people—in the 1956 science fiction classic.

The daughter of a noted surgeon, she was born Dagmar Wynter in Berlin, Germany, and grew up in England. When she was sixteen, her father went to Morocco to operate on a woman who wouldn't allow anyone else to attend her; he visited friends in southern Zimbabwe (then Rhodesia), fell in love with it, and brought his daughter and her stepmother to live with him there. Wynter later enrolled as a premed student at Rhodes University (the only girl in a class of 150 boys) and also dabbled in theatrics, playing the blind girl in a school production of *Through a Glass Darkly*, in which she says she was "terrible." After a year plus of studies, Wynter returned to England and shifted gears, dropping her medical studies and turning to an acting career. She was appearing in a play in Hammersmith when an American agent told her he wanted to represent her. She left for New York on November 5, 1953—"Guy Fawkes Day," a holiday commemorating a 1605 attempt to blow up the parliament building. "There were all sorts of fireworks going off," Wynter later told an interviewer, "and I couldn't help thinking it was a fitting send-off for my departure to the New World."

Wynter had more success in New York than in London, acting on TV (*Robert Montgomery Presents, Suspense, Studio One*) and the stage before "going Hollywood" a short time later. The willowy, dark-eyed actress appeared in over a dozen films, worked in the Golden Age of Television (*Playhouse 90*), and even costarred in her own short-lived TV series, the globe-trotting *The Man Who Never Was*. Married and divorced from hotshot Hollywood lawyer Greg Bautzer, Dana Wynter, once called Hollywood's "oasis of elegance," now lives in happy retirement in county Wicklow, Ireland.

Tom Weaver: When you first arrived in New York from England in 1953, things must have been touch-and-go for a while.

Dana Wynter: Yes, I was living on doughnuts, living on . . . absolutely nothing! The English only allowed you to take five hundred pounds out of the country—that was *it*. Then you were on your own, you had to make your own way. But I was very lucky, I was great friends with [composer] Richard Rodgers from England, and when I got my first TV show, *Robert Montgomery Presents* or *Suspense* or whatever it was, he had quite a few people watching it. I had the lead in the show—Eva Gabor fell out, and they pushed *me* in. It was one of those miraculous things that happens in America, one of those wonderful, crazy, no-reason things. (By the way, on that first show, I thought to myself, "How *kind* the Americans are, they employ deaf veterans." Well, I didn't realize all the floor managers had things on their ears so they could talk to the control room! I was *that* naive!) But Richard Rodgers had everybody watch, [TV producer] Martin Manulis and people like that. And after that, I was very lucky, all the rest of the live TV stuff happened. My life has really been blessed, it's all been quite magical.

Weaver: You also acted in a play in New York, a comedy called *Black-Eyed Susan* with Vincent Price.

Wynter: Vincent was the *most* enchanting man, a most civilized man, having taught art and being tremendously well-educated. *Such* a lovely person! I had never done comedy before, and so of course I was falling into everybody's laughs and I wasn't getting my *own*—it was rather awful. We got to Boston, where Elliot Norton was really *the* critic at the time—if you got a decent notice from him you were okay for New York, and if you didn't you might as well fold up. I got lucky, he said I was the best thing in the play. (Which wasn't saying much!) We opened in New York just before Christmas [1954], and—imagine—in the audience there were five people, all relatives of people in the play [laughs]! We closed in three days! It was quite an experience, I'll tell you—a baptism by fire!*

The best days—the *best* days were the *Playhouse 90* days. Oh, they were magic! I did three of those†, two with [director] Johnny Frankenheimer, and I'll tell you, that was a golden time in American theater-drama-live television. The excitement of that will never be duplicated. Think of the writers who came through, and the directors, and with John Houseman and Martin Manulis guiding the whole thing—it was just so civilized, you know?

Weaver: I found a quote from a 1958 interview where you talked about how much you liked live TV—and you even exclaimed, "I hate movies!"

Wynter: Yes. Quite right. I like the preparation, I *love* the rehearsal—it was absolutely intense, it was sort of total immersion, those rehearsals. The actors used to sit around and, if there was a problem with *any*body's lines or *any*body's speech or *any*thing, *everybody* tried to fix it and make it better. It was an *intense* experience! And then the excitement of playing. When we did *Wings of the Dove,* in the cast was Isabel Jeans, the lovely, lovely actress who played the aunt in *Gigi* [1958]. She kind of looked at me on the first day of rehearsal and she said [haughtily], "What do *you* play, dear?" And I was playing the lead, you know [laughs]!

---

*"[*Black-Eyed Susan*] is a farce," wrote a *New York Daily News* critic. "It also is a fiasco. Moreover, it is shoddy, sleazy, leering, vulgar, blatant, ill-mannered, coarse, witless, feckless, insulting, discouraging and unfunny." According to the headline of the *New York Times* review, "All Goes Well in *Black-Eyed Susan* until First Actor Steps on Stage."

†*Winter Dreams* (May 23, 1957), *The Violent Heart* (February 6, 1958), and *The Wings of the Dove* (January 8, 1959).

Well, after about three days, we became great friends, and one day she turned to me and said, "I've never *done* live television before, dear. How many people do you suppose *watch* this program?" This is *Playhouse 90!* I said, "Well, I don't know. On a *bad* night, I guess twenty million. On a *good* night, forty million." "Forty million people. . . . ? *Forty million people??!!*" Well, after that she was just pacing the corridors, gripping her script and muttering, "Forty million people . . . " We were on the air, in the middle of this scene in a conservatory in our lovely costumes and hats, and suddenly I saw "forty million people" go across her eyes [laughs]! I thought, "That's it! She's going to go up!" And we were only halfway through it. But I saw the old lady pull herself together . . . take a very deep breath . . . and go on. And she was just wonderful. But I'll never forget that silent moment of panic that just struck her in the middle of this production, because she knew that forty million people were looking at her. *That* was the excitement! When you heard the *Playhouse 90* theme come up and they were counting down, "ten, nine, eight, seven, six"—I can't *begin* to describe the adrenaline rush, the extraordinary kind of excitement. Because there was jeopardy—I mean, if anything went wrong, there were all those people looking in.

When I did *The Violent Heart*, a Daphne du Maurier show with Ben Gazzara, we were playing a scene and all of a sudden, out of the corner of my eye, I saw something go down and I heard a bit of a thud. Turned out to be the cameraman! We had four cameramen on this live show, and an electrician had been standing next to one with a klieg light. The electrician leaned on him or something, and the light shorted through his camera. The guy got a very sharp electric shock and fell off his camera. A cameraman from another set had just wandered onto ours, because whenever

Johnny Frankenheimer was working, everybody would come and watch because the crew absolutely worshiped him. This other cameraman climbed on the camera and he said over his microphone to the control booth, "Johnny, I don't know this show, but I'll *try* if you want to talk me through it." It was tremendously difficult, but Johnny called all the shots, all the lens sizes and the moves, and we got through the show and nobody knew that one of four cameras had almost been lost. The original guy climbed back on his camera for the last of the six acts. Now, *that* kind of thing never happened in film—I mean, it was all so *dull* by comparison.

Weaver: You started your Hollywood movie career under contract to Twentieth Century Fox.

Wynter: I was offered [contracts by] Metro and Fox, and I signed with Fox. [Studio boss] Darryl F. Zanuck later told me that he wasn't very lucky with his last few women contract players, and he hoped that he'd get lucky with me.

Weaver: But before you appeared in a single Fox movie, you costarred in *Invasion of the Body Snatchers.* Why did producer Walter Wanger think of you?

Wynter: Some time prior to that, I was in the William Morris Agency in New York. They weren't my agents, so I don't know why I was there; I was probably there with a friend or something like that. Walter Wanger happened to be there and he saw me and he asked somebody who I was. I didn't meet him at the time, I didn't know *any* of this.

Weaver: But he thought of you when he went to do *Body Snatchers.*

Wynter: Apparently Vera Miles had been penciled in by Allied Artists for *Invasion of the Body Snatchers,* and Walter Wanger said, "No, I want that new girl. The English one." That's when they found out that I was under contract to Fox, and Fox allowed me to push the [start of the] contract a few days backward so that I could do this picture. *Invasion of the Body Snatchers* was my first movie.

Weaver: No, you *were* in some English movies—

Wynter: No, no, don't, don't, I really wasn't *in* them, you know. I was sort of trying to make a living doing whatever I could while I was studying.

Weaver: So *Body Snatchers* was the first movie you had a sizable role in.

Wynter: Oh, yeah.

Weaver: Any "first-picture jitters" on *Body Snatchers,* or had you had enough experience on TV to walk right in and go to work?

Wynter: Not jitters, no, because everybody was awfully nice. Well, *most* people were. From live TV to *this,* it was a *dawdle,* you know what I mean? You could kind of gather yourself together. Also, I was quite young and inexperienced, and . . . well, "fools rush in," you know [laughs]! And the cameraman was very kind to me, too, Ellsworth Fredericks. Just terribly concerned and kind of "there" and friendly and helpful. People gathered 'round and the crew gathered 'round—I think it was probably my English accent, they probably thought I was an orphan!

Weaver: "*Most* people" were nice, you just said. Who *wasn't* nice?

Wynter: I must say I learned a lot from her, but Carolyn Jones was . . . strangely unfriendly and unhelpful. But I learned a lot from *that,* too, because I learned that if there's somebody in your cast who's kind of new and hasn't been around much, you gather 'round and you try and help them through. That was the only . . . "strange" event.

Weaver: You had to have a plaster cast made of your body for the pod scenes. What was that experience like?

Wynter: [laughs] Well, worse for Carolyn, because she had claustrophobia. For me, it wasn't bad, except they were "funny," the guys who made the thing. I was in this thing while it hardened, and of course it got rather warm! I was breathing through straws or something quite bizarre, and the rest of me was encased, it was like a sarcophagus. The guys who were making it tapped on the back of the thing and said, "Dana, listen, we won't be long, we're just off for lunch [laughs]!" In the end, we had to be covered except for just the nostrils and I think a little aperture for the mouth.

Weaver: One article said it got to be 120 degrees inside that thing.

Wynter: Yes, that plaster heated up, all right!

Weaver: I never quite understood why you and the others had to go through all that, why these dummies had to be made. Why couldn't the actors themselves just lay inside the pods in the scenes where they opened up?

Wynter: Probably because the special effects people hadn't decided *how* it was going to work, and if they had these [dummies], they could experiment. They weren't that advanced in special effects, I suppose. I only saw that picture once, and that was a very long, long, long, long time ago, and I really don't remember the scene with the pods opening.

Weaver: Did you read the short story that the movie was based on?

Wynter: Yes. This may sound stupid, but I really can't remember what I thought of it. I'll tell you something: Once something is *done,* I sort of put it behind me. I suppose one remembers the very important things in one's life and not the minutiae, you know. [My career] *wasn't* my passion, and that's why I left. Because I think you *have* to [have a passion for it] to devote your life to it. Kevin McCarthy, for instance, is a very fine actor and the theater is his passion. For *me,* I do things out of sort of intellectual curiosity very often. I once wrote for a year or more for *The Manchester Guardian,* the newspaper Alistair Cooke wrote for. It's one of the oldest English newspapers, and I had a series of my own, every fortnight. The fact that they took me on on that basis and that I had my series, that was lovely. But once I *did* it—it's like flying. Once you fly solo, that's the thrill; after that, it's on to something else. That's terrible, it's a very flibbertigibbet way of going about one's life, but it's great fun!

Weaver: Walter Wanger—how did you like knowing him?

Wynter: Walter was an extraordinary man. Tremendously civilized. I have nothing to say about him that everybody else doesn't say. He was highly educated and had beautiful manners and was well-read and had good taste. I don't know how he survived in that community.

Weaver: Was he on the set a lot?

Wynter: He was quite a bit, yeah.

Weaver: He called you "a brunette Grace Kelly with the zest of Ava Gardner. My best discovery since Hedy Lamarr."

Wynter: Oooh, how lovely [laughs]! A great compliment!

Weaver: In interviews, Don Siegel sometimes told a far-out-sounding story that he once broke into your house and put a pod under your bed.

Wynter: That *is* a bit far-out. Actually, he left it on my doorstep. He had a girlfriend who lived next door to me—I lived on Santa Monica Boulevard near the Mormon Temple in an enclave of five little cottages. Don Siegel was courting this girl, and he would pass my cottage all the time. And one night he just left it on the doorstep!

Weaver: And you found it—

Wynter: Yes, I did, leaving at five-thirty or six in the morning, and there it was!

Weaver: Did it have the desired effect?

Wynter: Yes, I nearly broke my neck, because when you open your front door to go to your car, you don't expect to find something large on your doorstep [laughs]!

Weaver: What was Siegel like as a director?

Wynter: Very interesting. He had so much *fizz*, he had that kind of New York buzz, fizz, energy. Enthusiasm and drive and sort of a wry sense of humor. It was all good. And then Sam Peckinpah was the dialogue coach.

Weaver: Peckinpah used to give interviews in which he claimed to have rewritten the script of *Body Snatchers.* Finally the real writer got fed up and threatened to sue, and Peckinpah never told that lie again.

Wynter: That's very interesting. I must tell you, he was a very nice man but I had no memory of him later. Even now, if he were alive, and I ran him over in the street, I wouldn't know him [laughs]!

Weaver: According to one of the trade papers, *Body Snatchers* was mostly shot on actual locales, and only four out of the twenty-four days was shot in the studio.

Wynter: That could be right. Bronson Canyon was where the final chase took place. Also in Bronson Canyon is the tunnel where Miles goes off and leaves Becky. They dug a trench and put planks over it and had the camera looking down at us. You know, people write *theses* about *Invasion of the Body Snatchers*; it's the most extraordinary thing about this film! One man was writing a thesis on this film for his degree, and he measured—he *measured!*—the distance from one corner to the other in the town where we shot. He said to me, "Dana, the line when you say, 'I'm here, Miles,' when Kevin McCarthy comes back to the cave. It's a tritonal line—you go from B-flat to E to G. Now *that* was brilliant. How did you decide upon that tritonal thing?" And I thought to myself, "These people are out of their minds [laughs]!"

Weaver: Have I given you the impression that I'm out of *my* mind yet?

Wynter: [laughs] *You* sound absolutely wonderful!

Weaver: Did you have a stunt double at any point in those strenuous scenes?

Wynter: No, and poor Kevin—p-o-o-r Kevin—had to carry me! I was quite chunky at the time [laughs], and all his good breeding came out. He didn't huff or puff or pull a face or anything, he was *terrific,* 'cause he had to run in and out of this muddy canyon carrying ol' Dana!

Weaver: It really looks like a very grueling chase. Was there enough time between shots for everybody to catch their breath, or was it a real hard day?

Wynter: The picture was shot in—what?—three weeks, and there were a lot of setups. So there *wasn't* much time in between, I seem to remember! They really got a move on, which was quite good.

Weaver: After you and Kevin McCarthy hide yourselves beneath the floorboards of the cave, the townspeople swarm in searching for you. At the very end of the shot, one guy steps between the boards and starts to fall forward. Did he fall on top of the two of you?

Wynter: I don't remember. I just remember an awful lot of bits of stones and things falling down on us [laughs]!

Weaver: Was the scene on the giant staircase a hassle?

Wynter: Yes. But it all went very well, the people were tremendously professional. That was one of the impressive things about that picture, that Wanger and Siegel were professionals and they got a crew together which was also very professional. And I think the actors were mostly theater people, so there was no waffling about and not knowing the lines. Also, there wasn't a lot of discussion about motivation and all this kind of stuff. Performances were thought through [by the actors themselves] and performed.

Weaver: Did you have an "approach," or what's the *key* to playing in a far-out movie like *Body Snatchers*? Or didn't your mind work that way?

Wynter: Well, you see, *on the surface* nothing was said about it being far-out. It was just supposed to be a plain, thrilling kind of picture. That was what Allied Artists thought they were making. By the way, we realized—Walter and Kevin and people who *can* think about things—that we were making an anti-"ism" picture. Anti-"ism"—fascism, communism, all that kind of thing. *We* took it for granted that's what we were making, but it wasn't spoken about openly on the set or anything like that. They were delicate times, and I think if Allied Artists had had the slightest idea that there was anything deeper to this film, that would have quickly been stopped!

Weaver: I don't know if Don Siegel ever owned up to it being an anticommunist movie. I think he always sort of ducked the subject.

Wynter: Well, maybe it was just one of these things that one thought. I mean, there's no point in talking about it, because the story was what it was, and it works. So there was no point in saying, "Well, now, look here, what we're really doing is *this*. . . ." I took it for granted that that's what it was, and I'm sure Kevin did, too. Now, Kevin has stories about the humor in the film that was knocked out by Allied—"We don't want any *laughs* in here!" Oh, they were *something*, those people, they *really* were something. I tell you, it took some getting used to, going into that town [Hollywood] and being part of it when you come from a completely different culture. Quite extraordinary! I remember being in Walter Mirisch's house—terribly nice people—and there were some extraordinary paintings.

It was the usual thing: Dinner (quickly!) and then right into the projection room and watch the latest movie from the studio. Out of the corner of my eye I saw what I thought was a very precious painting—a Matisse or a Renoir or something—plummeting. I cried out, "Watch it!" and everybody turned around. Well, they had had this painting fixed to the ports of the projection room—the projectionist had pressed a button to let the panels go down so that the glass aperture was revealed, the window the film was shown through. But the panels had precious paintings on them, and when I saw this painting falling, I didn't realize it was *nailed* to a panel that was going down! Everybody looked at me thinking, "What a fool *she* is," "What on earth is the matter with her?"

Weaver: You just mentioned that the humor was cut out of the movie by Allied Artists. Walter Wanger didn't have enough pull to keep that from happening?

Wynter: I don't know *what* his position was in the studio system at that time. I thought he seemed to have lost quite a lot. I mean, he was making *very* serious pictures at one time. He'd either lost his grip *or,* as Billy Wilder says, "You don't lose your talent in this business, you just become unfashionable." (That's pretty good, isn't it?) Anyway, I don't know what happened to Walter; I don't know whether the shooting of Jennings Lang* kind of made him into a bit of a laughingstock in that town. Maybe he was just too good for them, he was a bit too sophisticated, too highly educated. Maybe he

---

*In 1951, Wanger, the husband of actress Joan Bennett, convinced himself that Bennett and her agent, Jennings Lang, were having an affair, and he shot and wounded Lang in an office building parking lot. Wanger served a short prison sentence.

made them feel a little uncomfortable. That's understandable, isn't it?

Weaver: Your impressions of Kevin McCarthy?

Wynter: You feel there's not a shadow on Kevin: he doesn't speak badly of people, he's full of praise, he's full of enthusiasm, you feel that he's decent through and through and through and through. *Apart* from being so charming. And he doesn't *have* that "actor thing"—I really don't care for actors very much! I've had no actor friends, I can't bear "actor talk" [laughs]!

Weaver: And you felt that way about him in 1955, as you were making the movie?

Wynter: In 1955, I hadn't been exposed to many actors. I mean, I'd done a couple of plays and things, but I hadn't been exposed to that whole genus of "*ac*-tor." Actors always try to enlist you against *other* actors if you're in a play or something; they kind of gang up on each other and talk about each other. I can't bear it! But Kevin had such a *masculine* thing—there was nothing petty about him. Well, look at where he comes from—he and his sister are serious people. An absolute joy.

Weaver: In your early publicity, the first movie you made for Fox, *The View from Pompey's Head* [1955], got all the attention. If *Body Snatchers* was mentioned at all, it was referred to as a quickie, as something that had to be gotten out of the way before you could start your *real* movie career.

Wynter: That's because all that was done through the Fox publicity machine, and of course they weren't interested in doing anything for *Body Snatchers.* Also, remember that *Body Snatchers* was a B picture from the start—at the time, it was never considered to be anything other than a B picture, because that's what Allied Artists made. So Fox wasn't interested in that, the "push" was behind the new girl at the studio. By the way, one movie I made at Fox, *D-Day, the Sixth of June,* was just on here—every year they play it here in Ireland. That was my favorite, I *really* enjoyed that.

Weaver: Your favorite movie to make, or the best movie you're in?

Wynter: It was the one I really enjoyed, because it was with Robert Taylor and Richard Todd. We were great pals before the picture, and it just so happened we made it all together at Fox. That was kind of marvelous.

Honestly, this *Invasion of the Body Snatchers* thing—looking back on it, I'm not really mad about thinking about it. I was sort of new and looked kind of young and . . . boring. And my acting—I was boring *in* it. There was no edge. If you're lucky, you develop a bit of that as you get older. And you develop a bit of humor. In your first picture, you're so terrified that you're going to do the wrong thing that you just play everything straight. So it's nothing I'm *proud* of. Now, I was happy to be in it, especially because of Kevin and because of Don, and it was a fun thing to do. But I'd just as soon forget it.

Weaver: Did you feel, by making a B picture, a science fiction picture, that you were starting off in Hollywood on the wrong foot?

Wynter: Oh, no, it was very much the right foot for me. I was happy to be doing it because I liked Walter very much. Your first picture, you're delighted whatever it is. Mind you, I've always said that I was terribly embarrassed by that title. I begged Walter, I said, "Walter, you can't [call it *Invasion of the Body Snatchers*]! I mean, my *parents*! How can I admit to my parents that I'm doing a picture called *Invasion of the Body Snatchers,* for God's sake! They'll think that I'm demented [laughs]!" How do you explain *that* away? Even now, people who don't know it and haven't seen it, they kind of snicker, you know? Don Siegel wanted to call it *Sleep No More.*

Weaver: In 1955, before *Body Snatchers* had been released, you were already telling interviewers that the title was dreadful. You also said about it, "I suppose it will appeal to the science fiction kids."

Wynter: [gasps] Oh, dear . . . oh, Lord! It's terrible you can't *bury* your past, isn't it? It's always there to haunt you!

Weaver: I just thought it was interesting that you were so frank about your own first movie.

Wynter: You know, if you haven't learned the "studio speak," you say things like that. I don't like "studio speak," I don't like the hypocrisy. The publicity woman at Fox used to come on the set every single day, Sonia Wolfson. She was a terribly nice woman, but terribly . . . *driving.* She'd come on with the pencil poised on the paper and say, "Now, what did you do last night?" And it used to drive everybody crazy. I remember Robert Taylor really *telling* her—he made it up to such a degree, she fled scarlet-faced, and she never asked him *that* question again [laughs]! Publicity people would also *make up* things that weren't said, and that was really so terrible, because people believe what they read. If you're quoted as saying something that you didn't even say, you can never get away from it.

Weaver: Once you married Greg Bautzer, obviously you didn't worry about where your next meal was coming from, and yet you stuck with your acting career.

Wynter: Well, because I was under contract and Fox wouldn't let me go. I begged to be let out, because they wouldn't allow you to do *anything* [beyond the movie work], especially in television. When Martin Manulis and Houseman sent me the script for the Scott Fitzgerald *Winter Dreams* [episode of *Playhouse 90*], it was such a wonderful story, it was such a part of Americana, I went to Buddy Adler and I said, "Let me do this." He said, "No. None of our people can do television." I said, "But we can't *learn*, we can't *stretch* ourselves. Where do we learn if we just go from film to film to film? That's not a learning process." So I made him read it and they all discussed it, and then they said, "All right, she can do it." So at least I broke *that* open, I was able (while I was under contract) to do these three *Playhouse 90s*, because after a while they were recognized as being prestigious.

Weaver: But you couldn't get Fox to let you out entirely.

Wynter: That's right. And they kept giving me pictures like *The Lion* [1962] with Bill Holden, which was going to be shot in Kenya. I was assigned to that, and I told them, "I can't go, I've got a child who's two. If I take him to Kenya, I don't want him to have his head stuck on a pole!" (The Mau Mau thing was still going on then.) So I was suspended for the length of that. *No Down Payment* [1957] they also assigned me to, and I said, "I can't imagine why anybody is making this picture!" I said, "This is the most boring thing—life in a housing development, for God's sake?! Absolutely not." So I was under suspension for a good deal of the time. These contracts were in their [the studios'] grace and favor; the actor couldn't say, "Look, thanks a lot. I'm off." And if you're suspended, the length of the [shooting of the] picture is added to the end of your contract. The head of the William Morris Agency, who was a friend of my husband's and a very nice man, said he wanted to represent me and he tried to get me [away from Fox]. But Buddy Adler had some kind of a problem, he wanted to teach me some kind of a lesson, and he wouldn't let me go. I was there for seven years, and I could do nothing about it.

Weaver: What brought you to Ireland?

Wynter: They were making *Shake Hands with the Devil* [1959] here and the studio sent me. I had never been to Ireland before. I made a lot of friends here. And then I came back when John Huston asked for me for *The List of Adrian Messenger* [1963]—I played the mother of Huston's son. I had never ridden sidesaddle before, and I had to ride sidesaddle; had to play in hunting sequences sidesaddle; had to drive a Land Rover, and nobody ever bothered to ask whether I could do it or not [laughs]! So I did it! I bought the land here in 1966, built a house. But my son was at school, so I stayed in America until he went to university and was able to drive and stuff. That's when I started spending more and more time here. I love it, but the winters are pretty hard here. They're long and gray, and I was snowed in twice this year.

Weaver: So what's the best movie you were in?

Wynter: You know, there really *wasn't* a best. The best workout was, of course, the *Playhouse 90* work. Also [the TV series] *Twelve O'Clock High*—I had a wonderful time there. I did three of those, and they were love stories that were kind of tragic. *Unresolved* love stories, like *D-Day, the Sixth of June*. But I finally gave up. In the end, I found myself doing a *Magnum, P. I.* And even though it was a *Magnum*, and Tom Selleck is the loveliest man in the world, and the whole thing was fun,

I found myself at one stage with a gun in my hand, playing some wicked person. And I thought, "Hang on here. Here's a grown woman with a gun in her hand, and this is supposed to be entertainment? What am I doing here?"

So, to get back to your question, the *Playhouse 90*s were my favorites; as for the films, I don't know. *The View from Pompey's Head* was fun, *D-Day* was lovely, and *Sink the Bismarck!* [1960] I enjoyed. But there really aren't any movies that I did anything astonishing *in*, or *with*. I never read my own publicity, just as I don't see pictures that I've done. Once lived, once done—that's it. Onward!

DANA WYNTER FILMOGRAPHY

White Corridors (1951), *Lady Godiva Rides Again* (1951), *The Woman's Angle* (1952), *It Started in Paradise* (1952), *The Crimson Pirate* (1952), *Colonel March Investigates* (1952), *The View from Pompey's Head (Secret Interlude)* (1955), *Invasion of the Body Snatchers* (1956), *D-Day, the Sixth of June* (1956), *Something of Value* (1957), *In Love and War* (1958), *Fraulein* (1958), *Shake Hands with the Devil* (1959), *Sink the Bismarck!* (1960), *On the Double* (1961), *The List of Adrian Messenger* (1963), *If He Hollers, Let Him Go!* (1968), *Airport* (1970), *Santee* (1973), *Le Sauvage (Lovers Like Us)* (1975).

PHILIP KAUFMAN'S SECOND *INVASION*

Anthony Timpone

TOYING WITH A MOVIE CLASSIC IS ALWAYS RISKY business. The Hollywood landscape is littered with bad remakes, from Dino De Laurentiis's ridiculous *King Kong* to the Sharon Stone washout *Diabolique.* Not surprisingly, when director Philip Kaufman accepted the challenge to helm an update of 1956's *Invasion of the Body Snatchers,* he admits that he feared he might be stepping on hallowed ground.

But Kaufman's 1978 revamp is one of the rare ones that works, mainly due to the approach that he, screenwriter W. D. Richter, and producer Robert H. Solo brought to the familiar material. The trio set out to make "another version" of the Jack Finney novel, instead of a slavish copy, with the main difference being switching the pod takeover from small burg Santa Mira to major metropolis San Francisco. Kaufman took a "more organic" stab at the story and deftly orchestrated a "symphony of terror" that combined unsettling music, film noirish photography, and creepy sound effects to entrap the audience in a total paranoiac experience.

Born in Chicago in 1936 and educated at the University of Chicago and Harvard Law School, Kaufman taught for a while in Europe before returning to the States to begin work as an independent filmmaker in the sixties. His seventies films *The Great Northfield, Minnesota Raid* and *White Dawn* eventually caught the attention of producer Solo, who hired

Kaufman for *Invasion*. Since then, Kaufman has emerged as one of the American cinema's true mavericks, winning praise for such films as *The Wanderers* (1979) and Best Picture Oscar nominee *The Right Stuff* (1983), as well as his two erotic epics, *The Unbearable Lightness of Being* (1988) and *Henry and June* (1990). In addition, Kaufman shared a story credit with buddy George Lucas on the 1981 Steven Spielberg blockbuster *Raiders of the Lost Ark*. Though he may not be the most prolific person working in films today (his last effort was 1993's *Rising Sun*), he is certainly one of the most talented. "I try to make movies that interest me deeply," Kaufman says. *Invasion of the Body Snatchers* was no exception.

Anthony Timpone: What first attracted you to remaking *Invasion of the Body Snatchers*?

Philip Kaufman: To some degree, I really didn't look on it as a remake. I looked on it as just another variation of the original theme. If we were going to remake it, we would have done the same story in the same small town and with the same approach. So it was [a question of] how to take that theme and do some variation of it. To some degree I felt the original, which I loved, was more connected almost with the world of slightly film noir, but almost a radio show where everything was narrated and everything was laid out with a certain kind of tension. I felt we could come up with something that was maybe a little more contemporary and visual, and bring the film into a larger city from that small-town atmosphere. It made it more relevant to the time in which it was made, in the seventies.

Timpone: Besides the novel and '56 film, were you inspired by any other sci-fi or horror films?

Kaufman: Not really. I would say that I was really more interested in the theme of paranoia, more of the Kafkaesque thing, which I felt was told really well both in the [1956] film and the Jack Finney book. Of people lost in a world where all of a sudden everything becomes, and all their feelings are of, paranoia, and yet it's not paranoia at all, because it's true [laughs]. So we made it clear from the very beginning that it was a science fiction film, as opposed to the Don Siegel version, by beginning on another planet. It was really meant to be the feelings you could feel around San Francisco at that time, with really believable characters.

Timpone: Didn't you screen 1933's *Island of the Lost Souls* beforehand?

Kaufman: Well, for visual reasons, but not for content, really. It was for the camera work and for how to get a film noir look into color, which you still don't see very much of. Going back to that time, some twenty years or so now, color just never seemed to have that same shadowy look, and that's what [cinematographer] Mike Chapman and I were trying to get.

Timpone: What made you go for a film noir look?

Kaufman: Because it had a creepy quality to it, and I felt most horror movies were almost lit like comedies in a strange way, and they weren't given, in most cases, the kind of treatment that they really deserved visually. They tended to get a kind of campy quality, because the lighting wasn't as powerful and as focused as it should have been. The great thing about film noir was that it really focused your eye right on what the filmmaker wanted you to focus on, and the shadows really kind of became characters in the piece.

Timpone: Unlike the first film and book, the audience seems to be one step ahead of the characters in your film. Why was that approach taken, where you know right from the start something "alien" is occurring?

Kaufman: Well, that was really to establish the fact that this was a science fiction movie right from the beginning, where you know that something strange was happening here. And to some degree the book has more of that quality; you do feel a little more of that sense of wonder more than the [1956] film, in a way. Jack Finney dealt more with the science fiction aspects than Don Siegel did, and we just pushed it that way, so that we could see our characters reacting to something that was . . . in fact, it became scarier to know, as I said earlier, that their paranoia was not paranoia at all, but was in fact something really true. Whereas Don Siegel's film, which was great, partly because it was dealing with that time where one of the possible metaphors was the communist menace or something, people in an ordinary society were dealing with other people changing what seemed to be their political beliefs.

Timpone: As a director, it seems you were more comfortable with the psychological terror of the story than the action sequences, especially in the warehouse climax. Would you agree with that?

Kaufman: No. I'm a little surprised by that question, because I thought that the action and the effects were very well done for that time. I thought that the warehouse was a good climax, given the fact that the film was made for around $3.4 million. It was a big all-out pod central and got its just due. And there was as much action as we could put in; the running through the streets and all of that I felt was done in an exciting way. I like to do things like that.

Timpone: What kind of collaboration did you have with screenwriter W. D. Richter?

Kaufman: Well, we worked right from the beginning together and all the way through. He was off and on the set, and I talked to him quite a bit about what was going on, and if I had any new ideas I would call him and say, "Look we want to do this and that, what can you do, how can we help?" The film was very collaborative, it was a lot of fun to make, because to some degree I viewed it, we all viewed it, as a comedy in a strange way, even though it's about scary things. For us it was partly because of the quality of the actors we used. There was always something funny underneath the surface. When you had Jeff Goldblum playing Bellicec, as opposed to the Don Siegel version, where the characters were super-serious about everything, Goldblum's character was quirky and odd, and someone you could laugh at and laugh with. And all the things Donald Sutherland, who is also a very funny guy, brought to the piece. There was a playfulness that all of us had in the making of it. I'm sure it was a very memorable time for everyone. The film was made pretty quickly, efficiently, and with high spirits.

Timpone: Which elements did you add to the script?

Kaufman: I don't know specifically all the changes. The ending, certainly, which we didn't tell anybody.

Timpone: The ending was your idea?

Kaufman: Yeah, we didn't tell that to anybody. I mentioned it to Richter, how I thought it should end, and then we talked to Solo. We never told the studio, so the studio never knew how it was going to end until they saw the movie. And I told Donald Sutherland either the night before or that morning, and if he hadn't bought into it we might have had some problems. But it seemed like the only possible conclusion, particularly working off the idea that Don Siegel's original film had been given the bookends that made it seem like all the danger was gone away, and it kind of sanitized the paranoia. Don had told me that that was a studio thing, and they had some comedy in the original, but that was taken out. I had known Don for a number of years, and we were friends, and even Kevin McCarthy talked to me about all the things that were taken out. Richter actually had set the first draft in a small town, and then I just felt no, this was a thing where we wanted to in a way show how that same story would have played out twenty years later and in a big city. In other words, if the virus had spread to a big city, how would you take the same theme and play it out over again, even though some of the characters have the same names, more or less? The idea was to do a variation on the theme of Don Siegel's thing rather than a straight remake of it. So there were many things I came up with, many things Richter came up with.

Timpone: Solo says you chose San Francisco because you lived there. Were there any other reasons?

Kaufman: Well, I think San Francisco was the perfect place for the thing, for all of those characters. The idea was that in a way it would be more scary if it were a liberal society rather than a conservative military society or something, that it could happen to people who were like Leonard Nimoy's character, for example. His psychoanalytic jargon made you think everything was all right all the time, and in fact there's something deeply wrong going on, and that's another reason why we wanted to have the science fiction stuff more clearly put in there. So that the audience could have more perspective on the psychoanalytic jargon that the psychiatrist in his Birkenstock sandals was using, especially when Leonard Nimoy finally turns around and we discover to our terror, our horror, that he's on the other side.

Timpone: What do you remember about shooting the effects scenes in the film?

Kaufman: Well, we shot them; it wasn't stuff that you go in for now with computer-generated images, it was all done right there in backyards of San Francisco at night; that is to say, the pods were growing into their final stage, and it was all done in live action. I remember the opening stuff on another planet, which I had a lot of fun with, the gelatinous material. I looked all over the city and we couldn't figure out how to do that, and somewhere in an art store I found this gel, which we paid about three dollars for. By putting it in water and reversing the camera movements and so forth, we were able to create the effect of another planet, and the opening effects scene probably cost us fifty bucks or something like that [laughs]. That was a lot of fun to do. I like to do effects that have the old-time jerry-rigged quality to them, rather than the super multimillion-dollar effects. Unfortunately, that was covered over with credits at the beginning, to my regret. I don't remember how that happened, exactly. Somebody was trying to shorten the movie by three minutes rather than leaving that alone and putting credits elsewhere. Those effects of the spores or whatever they are drifting through space would obviously have been much more powerful without the credits.

Timpone: What was it like directing your pal, Don Siegel? I read that he was very nervous.

Kaufman: He was as nervous as any director who isn't an actor would be. He really hadn't done that before, and he just came up here and suddenly was asking all the questions a director hates to be asked [laughs]: "Why am I doing this?" But once he got into it he was great, and he really had fun doing it, working with the crew in a way that he didn't have to be responsible for every shot, every move; he was terrific. He was a tough, hardened guy and suddenly he had to be kind of vulnerable. But that was the homage to Don Siegel. The whole film in a way was meant to be a homage to his version, which I respected so much. I was honored by his presence, and in turn was giving him back the film as a homage.

You've probably heard that story with Kevin McCarthy, it has been printed in a couple of places, where Kevin and I were shooting in the San Francisco Tenderloin, the scene where he finally runs into the car and is killed. He's shouting the same things that he was shouting at the end of the first film: "They're here, they're here!" And he's being chased by the crowd and it's as if he's run twenty years from the first movie all across the landscape from a small town into a big city to try and warn us, and he's about to warn Donald Sutherland. He bumps into the car and Donald's in the middle of telling this joke, and we never really get the punch line of the joke. He's killed, and as we were shooting the film, we did a number of takes with Kevin bumping into the car. The Tenderloin, if you know San Francisco, is kind of a Bowery area, a down-and-out area. It was a sensitive area in which to shoot, so there were a lot of street people around there, a lot of cult players. There was this one guy who took off all his clothes, and he was lying there with his head on the curb watching us shoot, and you couldn't tell these people to move because it would be politically incorrect and cause a lot of trouble. This guy called us over and he said to Kevin, "Hey, wasn't you in the first one?" And Kevin said, "Yeah, I was," and the guy said, "That was the better of the two" [laughs]. It was like we were getting our first review. Here we are just shooting the second one, and the guy is already giving the review [laughs]! Kevin fell down laughing.

Do you remember that joke Donald Sutherland was telling, do you know how it finishes?

Timpone: No.

Kaufman: The joke goes, the British are in the desert surrounded by Rommel, and he brings all his men together and says, "Listen, there's good news and there's bad news." (At that point Brooke Adams said, "I heard this one.") "The bad news is we've got nothing to eat but camel shit. The good news is there's plenty of it" [laughs].

Timpone: What did Siegel think of the completed film?

Kaufman: He really liked it. In fact, he said wonderful things. I don't really remember exactly, but he was a really big booster of the whole project and his presence helped everyone. We all loved working with him.

Timpone: Besides the obvious (the relationship between Miles/Donald Sutherland and Elisabeth/Brooke Adams), could you explain why you saw the film as a "tragic love story?"

Kaufman: Well, in a way it's a group of people, all of whom are in love with each other. Donald sort of loves Jeff Goldblum, and Jeff Goldblum and Veronica Cartwright have their love story. I felt the problem we had in the movie was making the characters as human as possible, and that's where the humor came into it, like in the backyard where Brooke Adams rolls her eyes around. I discovered she could do this amazing thing where she can not only roll her eyes, but she can roll each one in the opposite direction. There's something so human about Donald Sutherland cooking Chinese food, and just the feelings that they all had for each other. So if you establish that humanity, then the loss of that humanity becomes that much more tragic. It wasn't just some cardboard characters that you sort of liked, or the people that were branded as your heroes suddenly became monsters; it was that when Jeff Goldblum became a pod, he was no longer that human being that you loved. However hurt and paranoid he was as a poet, you loved him. And Brooke Adams, she totally loses this great quality that she has in the movie. That's where the real tragedy lies. So in the film, we really tried to work on that tragic dimension.

Timpone: While shooting the film, you occasionally had to shut down production to discuss metaphysical pod problems. What were some of those discussions like?

Kaufman: I remember particularly one time when we were shooting, my friend George Lucas had come to visit me on the set just at the time when Donald Sutherland didn't see how he would play one of his scenes a certain way. So we went into a room, and George sat outside for about two hours and then finally left. Donald was just going through some metaphysical anguish about how to play the scene. But fortunately, all the other actors felt, as Leonard Nimoy said, "I know my role and my character, so that no matter what Donald wants to do, I'm fine because I know how I'll react to anything he does." After discussing it, the actors and myself all worked out how we would approach the scene, and for Donald, suddenly something clicked in for him. It's one of the problems that you have when you don't have enough rehearsal time; he arrived at a scene and suddenly Donald didn't feel it made enough sense. He's an incredibly bright, sensitive actor, so we just wanted to make sure that the pod, prepod and postpod characters were in place for everybody.

Timpone: What led you to hire a Marin County psychiatrist, Denny Zeitlin, to do your score?

Kaufman: First of all, I've known him from college days. He was a wonderful jazz musician, and I just felt he would have some insight into paranoia. In discussing this with him, he got very enthusiastic about it, and we went over different types of music that I thought would be interesting, including Bernard Herrmann and various other composers. Denny sat with us and sat with it and really worked hard and came up with a unique and great score to the film. He said he never wanted to do another score because it was such hard work and took so much time out of his practice, but the idea of having a psychiatrist, an expert in the loss of self and paranoia, doing the score, seemed to me exciting.

Timpone: Could you explain how you attempted to exploit urban paranoia in the film and why that theme appealed to you?

Kaufman: It has to do with neighborhoods, the lighting in neighborhoods, the lurking feeling that there's always something dangerous around the corner. Other science fiction movies deal with this kind of thing, that there is something scary in the world and you just can't explain it away. It is there, and there is the potential for something fearful, and to some degree that's why people go to horror or science fiction movies. It's because they have inklings, things that cannot be logically explained, that there is a terror lurking. I think anybody who walks through the city, particularly late at night, learns to walk in a kind of guarded way, and you're silly if you don't.

Timpone: Do you think the pop psychology elements date the film today?

Kaufman: No, I think that same psychology is around and in some ways is even more popular; it has spread even more. In a way, San Francisco was the avant-garde of that at the time, but now it has spread even more over the whole society more than it was then. So people who see the film now still seem to enjoy it.

Timpone: Were there any other themes that you hoped to explore in the film?

Kaufman: I was pretty happy with what it was, and the way we made it.

Timpone: In what way did Michael Chapman light the pod people to offer subtle visual clues to their nature?

Kaufman: Chapman is a great cinematographer, and I talked about all different ways of lighting it, and I don't remember the codes exactly that we worked out, but we had stages of pod-dom that were lit in a certain way. When someone really became a pod, it was a much more low-angle lighting on their faces. There were even some tints of color that we put to color them a little greenish around the gills. There were also those shadows, like when they're running away from the pods, the whole group, and you see all these huge shadows suddenly growing up on the wall. The shadows become another character in the piece. Using color almost in a way that color hadn't been used much before, because in color films, particularly Technicolor films, the idea was to get all the color you could get into a film, and here we were trying to take out as much color and only put in certain colors that we wanted there. Certainly Gordon Willis did that kind of stuff in the first *Godfather*, and Chapman was actually the [camera] operator on *Godfather*. But when you go back to the early seventies, that was something that hadn't been played around with as much. And we really didn't use a lot of long lenses to give it that smoky thing, we were using short lenses and trying to get crisp colors, and I don't think we even used a lens over seventy-five millimeters.

Timpone: Could you discuss the importance of sound in the film?

Kaufman: The sound was a big push for a long time. Dolby said it was the best soundtrack that they had, and they still use it for demonstrations of the use of Dolby. We really wanted to get that sense of the use of surround sound, the low rumbling. For example, when Don Siegel is riding through that tunnel and the motorcycles go by, being pursued, there were things that we did that really hadn't been done before, where the sound goes from rear screen where you see the motorcycles into speakers on the side and into the surrounds so that you really got the full effect, if you saw it in the right theater. You might not get that at home unless you have a surround system with a laser disc or something. That's the problem, unless the theater is really equipped for Dolby surround and the speakers are tweaked properly, which often doesn't happen. Now it has become more commonplace, but then we were pushing. By that I mean to say of all the people who did sound effects, the San Francisco people were very much in the avant-garde of sound effects at the time. For the mixer, Mark Berger, it was one of the first movies that he mixed. He's mixed hundreds since then. But we were trying to push the envelope a bit on the use of Dolby.

Timpone: In the seventies era of feel-good science fiction films like *Star Wars, Close Encounters of the Third Kind*, and *Superman*, do you think audiences weren't ready for a downbeat SF picture like yours?

Kaufman: Well, the film did very well, considering what it was. I think it would have done better had the release pattern been more of a modern release pattern, which hadn't been perfected then. In fact, I think it went into four hundred theaters and never went wider. Now it could have gone into two thousand theaters and then be much more widely seen. It had basically really good if not great reviews and pretty full houses everywhere it played, and was tremendously profitable given what it made. But it was released about Christmastime, and was up against a lot of big movies, like *Superman*, which came out the same time. Some of those movies were in much wider release, so there was a problem with what theaters we could get and so forth, and it was released in that transitional time, before modern release patterns were perfected.

Timpone: Was the film tested in front of an audience?

Kaufman: I think it was. I was busy making *The Wanderers*. Bob Solo took it around and tested it in a lot of places. I remember him calling me from Chicago, and the screenings were all good.

Timpone: And United Artists' reactions were the same?

Kaufman: Yeah, the studio was great. Once they saw it, they really liked it.

Timpone: Were you aware of some of the film's ratings problems in Dallas and the subsequent lawsuit?

Kaufman: No, I never heard that.

Timpone: The local Dallas ratings board ruled that children under sixteen could not see *Invasion of the Body Snatchers* without a parent or guardian, thus challenging the MPAA's own PG label for the film. UA [United Artists] sued the city.

Kaufman: No, I never heard that. I've had my own share of ratings problems, so that's interesting.

Timpone: *Invasion* was your only major attempt at science fiction, before or after. Why?

Kaufman: I don't know. I love to do sci-fi, and I was going to do the original *Star Trek*. That's where I met Leonard, and really cast him, because I was building a whole script for *Star Trek* around Leonard Nimoy, around the Spock character, and I just wanted to work with him. I thought he was a wonderful actor, and I love science fiction and would love to do it [again]. I've tried to do a couple of things but nothing's come to fruition, and if you have anything that you think would make a great movie, send it to me immediately [laughs].

Timpone: Looking back on *Invasion of the Body Snatchers,* is there anything you would do differently?

Kaufman: No. I never really look back at my stuff, and I thought that it was fine at the time, and I never view [any] film again really. I've seen it fifty or five hundred times or however many times while I'm making it, I go through it over and over and over. And then once it is released, I never look at it again, and that's that, it is what it is.

AN INTERVIEW WITH W. D. RICHTER

Matthew R. Bradley

QUITE LITERALLY A CHILD OF THE POSTWAR ERA, screenwriter W. D. "Rick" Richter was born in New Britain, Connecticut, on December 7, 1945, four years to the day after the bombing of Pearl Harbor and just months after the end of World War II, and educated at Dartmouth College and at U.S.C. Film School in Los Angeles. It is perhaps appropriate, then, that it fell to this lifelong genre enthusiast to reenvision, at times radically, such classics as *Invasion of the Body Snatchers* and *Dracula* for a new generation of filmgoers in high-profile remakes made during the late 1970s. The 1980s brought both an Academy Award nomination for the fact-based prison drama *Brubaker* and Richter's directorial debut with the cult favorite *The Adventures of Buckaroo Banzai Across the 8th Dimension*, starring such up-and-coming actors as Peter Weller, Ellen Barkin, and Jeff Goldblum. More recently, Richter has returned to the director's chair with the offbeat romantic comedy *Late for Dinner*, adapted Stephen King's bestseller *Needful Things* to the screen, and written the screenplay for *Home for the Holidays*, directed by actress Jodie Foster.

Matthew R. Bradley: *Invasion of the Body Snatchers* (1978) seems like quite a switch from your earlier comedic credits on *Slither* (1973), *Peeper* (a.k.a. *Fat Chance*, 1975), and *Nickelodeon* (1976). What prompted your entry into the fantasy film genre?

W. D. Richter: When I was a kid, I liked horror and science fiction films as much as I liked anything. I actually probably watched them a little more religiously. I'd go to the movies by myself to see *The Day of the Triffids* [1963] and *The Blob* [1958] and all that stuff. It's just a wonderful release of the human imagination. I think that's its ultimate appeal: it takes you somewhere out there and makes you picture a universe that's just far more fantastic than the little town you're living in, or whatever your particular arena is at that time. So always in the back of my head was a sense of the magic of thinking about other worlds. I was a fan of that type of film, and then somebody comes along and for whatever reason gives you a chance to play around with one of them that you've really enjoyed all these years. I think the question might be, why did [producer] Bob Solo come to me? I guess he just liked the way I wrote, and maybe saw something in the eccentricity of some of it, I really don't know, but it was a delight to get the call, and I didn't have to hesitate.

Bradley: Did you work primarily from Jack Finney's novel *The Body Snatchers,* which was serialized in *Collier's,* or from Daniel Mainwaring's earlier screenplay?

Richter: The Mainwaring script could never be found—it was an enormous frustration to all of us—so we had basically the novel and the movie to work from. I'd say equally from both. I certainly read the novel very carefully, and the biggest, most dramatic part of that development process is that the first incarnation of our version was also set in a small town—contemporary, but a small town. Now, Phil Kaufman had already accepted from Bob Solo the job of developing the material, and Bob called me without telling me Phil was on it. I'd known Phil casually through Ronda Gomez, who's a very successful agent now and recently married Howard Zieff, the director of *Slither*. After I said, "Yes, I'd like to do it," Bob said, "Oh, great, now we can all sit down with Phil and we can start working on this." I said, "Who's Phil?" "Phil Kaufman, didn't I tell you? He's going to direct it." I said, "Bob, thank God I like Phil. What if you had told me somebody that I was uncomfortable with?" He said, "Oh, I thought I mentioned it." We had a delightful process of development, but everybody's first instinct, without much analysis, was, "It's enough to make it contemporary." Phil lived in the San Francisco area, and we'd settled on shooting in the outlying communities. So we were looking at all sorts of small towns around San Francisco, trying to get the feel of what that meant, like orchid houses out there that they might be hidden in and stuff. That was the draft that I wrote, and that's the draft that Mike Medavoy gave the green light to. We were in preproduction, and I don't remember how far in, I think about seven or eight weeks from the start of principal photography. Phil and I were talking one day in the office, and he was, I think, losing confidence in the concept of making a small-town film. It came out of this conversation that maybe we'd miscalculated, and that it was more interesting to locate the paranoia in a large city—that it might be easier for them to hide, and that that would be a more energized version of it. If long ago we thought the communists were taking over the heart of America, our small towns, then if we had fears today it had more to do with how we were losing the center of our civilization, because our cities were starting to seem strange. They weren't necessarily representative of the best of us, but maybe the worst of us. So Phil and I said to each other, "We have made a mistake here. What if we set in a big city? Are we being crazy?" We talked for a little bit and decided that the narrative we'd come up with wouldn't be that radically different. People's occupations would change, but the essential plot moves might not be that different. He said, "How on Earth can we tell Medavoy this?" Well, we just got up out of the office, and I can picture the two of us as if I'm a fly on the wall, watching these two guys go down the hall. He said, "We have to be really good in this room." Mike was very sympathetic. He heard the new version of it, and he said, "You guys are right. I mean, I wish you'd thought about it a year ago, but what will it take? Can you do it, Phil?" He trusts filmmakers, that's the wonderful thing about Mike Medavoy. Phil said, "We will do it. Rick will be there every minute. We will locate it very quickly for logistical purposes in San Francisco." It didn't take long to come up with notions of mud baths and things like that, but to get the dialogue more urban, et cetera, I was going to have to be writing during the whole production, which I did. I stayed in San Francisco, and I finished well before they were through with principal photography, but I'm sure I was doing rewrites during the whole movie. I was there all the time. I saw all the dailies, I was on the set an awful lot, but a lot of times I was in the hotel writing. It was an exciting thing to be doing, because we all felt we were really making a film that we believed in, and had had the nerve to change our minds at the last minute and try to make it better, and had the total support of the studio [United Artists] to do that. I think that was a time when films were made perhaps a little more on content than on release dates. The target was to get a good film rather than to get it out in August, although we had to go right away, not because of a release date but because so many people had been put on who were working. Mike Medavoy said, "If I shut everything down, I'm going to have to pay all these people off," and we said, "You don't have to. We're trying to be mindful of costs." I think the movie cost $3 million or something, and we thought we owed everybody. Staying on the original schedule seemed to be our responsibility at that point. It was fun, kind of guerrilla filmmaking.

Bradley: Like yourself, Kaufman is both a screenwriter and a director. Did he work with you on actually writing the screenplay, or just conceptualizing?

Richter: Just conceptualizing. He functioned completely as a director developing a piece of material.

Bradley: In terms of resetting the story in a major city, Phil Hardy's *Overlook Film Encyclopedia* states that you and Kaufman "wittily update [it] by replacing the simple contrast between rational 'pod' people and emotional humans with the more complex idea that urban alienation makes it virtually impossible to distinguish between pods and people." Was that in fact your intention?

Richter: Absolutely. I think that what the film is about on some level is not how something can take over the person closest to us, but how we're all so complex, that we have many facets that we reveal. Never mind do we ever really know ourselves, but do we ever really know the person we're living with, having a conversation with, working with? It's just a chilling fact of life to me. It's not so much urban alienation but the human condition, that we are very complex. We are playacting a lot of times to do the right thing in a given situation, and construct a personality that's full of layers, and you may not really understand the person that you're putting in an awful lot of time with. I don't want to say that that was something I was aware of in every scene, because we were really trying to write something that was spirited and moved on the surface as much as beneath it, but those are the things I was thinking about at the time. You're talking to somebody and you don't know if they're really listening but they're sure having a conversation with you.

Bradley: I presume that was why you added the character of the heroine's lover, Geoffrey, who has no analog in previous versions of the story?

Richter: Right, exactly.

Bradley: Were you daunted by following in the footsteps of the original film's director and star, Don Siegel and Kevin McCarthy, who both made cameos in yours?

Richter: No, because we respected their work, and they made it much the same way. They didn't sit down to create this timeless masterpiece, they had a good time making that movie, and we were just trying to do the same thing. It wasn't like it was a perfect movie, and we thought we were doing something different enough that we weren't truly in their shadow. Also, certain people would see our version who had never seen theirs, unless you were a real serious film fanatic. People don't necessarily get to see the other, so we thought, "Well, we'll just do the best we can here, and who knows whether it'll be better or worse or just sort of equal in a different way?"

Bradley: Was the chance to use more sophisticated effects an impetus for the remake?

Richter: I don't think so. I think this was a time when we were still making movies about human beings, and of course you knew you'd have more resources, but it wasn't a world that flew in special effects people and other camera crews to do digital moves that would later be added. There weren't experts, so we all sat around and I watched production designers try to figure out how you make a pod, what's inside it. That wasn't sophisticated stuff, so it wasn't like, "Wow, do we have the tools now." It was more like, the story resonates, the themes can be evocative, and wouldn't that be nice if that's what was motivating films today? But no. Now, we know what we can do, so therefore we'll devise something that will demonstrate our technical skills. We were still coming from the center of a movie, from the heart of it.

Bradley: Jeff Goldblum, who later appeared in Kaufman's *The Right Stuff* (1983) and your own *Adventures of Buckaroo Banzai Across the 8th Dimension* (1984), was quite effective in his supporting role. Did you sense a star in the making?

Richter: Not a star, because Jeff is a true wonderful eccentric, but certainly a presence that was not going to go away, and if he was handed proper roles would be an indelible mark on the American filmscape. I mean, he's just special. You know it when Jeff starts looking at you or talking to you, off camera or on, you just grin, because he's a wondrous creation. I love that he was in that movie, because he did things with it that you hope can happen.

Bradley: Wasn't that Robert Duvall as the priest on the swing in the first scene? I know he'd been in Kaufman's *The Great Northfield Minnesota Raid* (1972).

Richter: Yes. He was swinging on the swing as a priest, just to do that for Phil.

Bradley: I kept thinking maybe he would turn up later on as a pod priest.

Richter: See, that's the problem with those. You get all excited when you do them, but then you tend to forget that it's saying something to the audience, and it's misleading. It's truly misleading, because that's just Robert Duvall on a swing. That was just game-playing, and you have to be careful about that.

Bradley: And then you spend the rest of the movie wondering who else will pop up.

Richter: These are the buttons you're pushing that you don't think about, and as you get more experienced you say, "Oh, nice idea, but that's just going to be an indulgence, and cause slight little weird problems that'll send tremors through the audience that we're not trying to do."

Bradley: Was the strange hybrid of a street singer and his dog, produced by a damaged pod, inspired by the dog in a human mask from *The Mephisto Waltz* (1971)?

Richter: Boy, I don't know, because I know that movie. I used to kid around and call it *Rosemary's Piano.* So obviously, you know, if it's in there . . . I just don't remember whether we said, "Oh, that would be cool," or if we just thought of it. You couldn't get at films as easily as you can now, they weren't bouncing all over the airwaves, so unless Phil remembers, I would have no idea.

Bradley: The frequent references to conspiracy by the characters in the remake seem to suggest that the post-

Watergate era provided just as fertile ground, if you'll excuse the pun, for this particular tale as the Cold War hysteria of the 1950s.

Richter: I'm sure it did, because it was part of our reflexive thinking at the time. We were just so convinced that everything was happening behind our backs that unconsciously, I suppose, you approach the creative process with that in the air, but I don't think there was any sense that that's why we were making this movie. We just thought it was a really good story, and it seemed to still have a reason for existing in the complicated world of the present tense at that time, but there wasn't any axe to grind. It wasn't like a new way to talk about conspiracy theories or anything.

Bradley: Though the invaders are driven off in Finney's novel, many have expressed dissatisfaction with the studio-imposed happy ending of Siegel's film, on which McCarthy's fate in the remake seems to be an ironic commentary. Was this a contributing factor in the decision to end yours on a downbeat note?

Richter: I suspect it was less political like that than it was just our feeling that that would be the most unsettling way to get to the audience, and I suppose express maybe that sense you brought up, that there were forces out there that were not going to go away, and you just might be overwhelmed by them. Maybe that's too cynical a thing to admit, but I think we were talking about it in the middle of that feeling that there were serious problems out there in the culture. The film is certainly not presenting a solution, but probably trying to reflect the danger of not being aware of what's going on around you.

Bradley: I've noticed that each successive incarnation of the story seems to grow darker in tone. In the novel, for example, all of the main characters survive, while in Siegel's film Becky and the Belicecs become pod people, and in your version even Bennell loses his humanity. Is everything just going to hell?

Richter: Well, if you have a vast historical overview, you say, "It was pretty difficult in the thirteenth century, and it wasn't a lot of fun in the fifteenth," but we tend to watch the progress of our own life spans. We can't help it, I mean, that's what we're living through. I'm a child of basically postwar America, and it was pretty great when you first got a sense of, "Oh, I live in America, and I make snowmen, and run around in the summer." It *has* gotten darker, or if not gotten darker the darkness is seeping out into the light, and we're aware that it's a much more dangerous, complicated, and threatening world than it felt like to most people in, say, 1952. I don't think the culture feels like it's on a journey right now toward a new renaissance, so I suppose we're getting more and more nervous with each passing year. No matter what the stock market's doing, people know down deep that it can't go on forever and it's being motivated by screwy needs people have to protect themselves for a dark, scary future by making as much money as they can, so that when a wolf comes to the door they'll be able to shoot it. So yeah, we're getting a creepy feeling that things are getting slightly worse if not better.

Bradley: And whereas in the fifties, despite the fifth columnists and Reds under the bed, the threat was mainly external, but in the seventies, with all the awareness of what our own government was doing, the threat was within.

Richter: Maybe if there's a point about the pod people, it's that they represent something that's right in front of us all the time, and we might not recognize it. You keep the metaphor that it came from somewhere else, but it seems to me that it's us. We'd better be very careful we don't turn into something that seems so alien from where we began that we're just destroying ourselves.

Bradley: How did you hit on the idea of the scream used by the pods to finger humans? It's certainly a key part of the effectiveness of the ending—it's devastating.

Richter: I don't remember. It's a very special sound, too. It has some of that African ululation, a tribal noise they make. We had endless hours of discussion about what the whole film should look and sound like. Mike Chapman is an extraordinary cinematographer, and we were trying to get such a weird edginess in. There are some passing shots in there that almost look like darker versions of Edward Hopper—an apartment building with somebody visible inside it, just sort of at a kitchen window or something, I recall. On the way back from locations, Michael was always shooting out of the windows of cars, trying to get textures of the city. We were listening to city noises, sirens and dump trucks, familiar sounds, so sound was always a very important part of this. Ben Burtt, who turned into one of George Lucas's major collaborators, did the sound in that film. I will always remember going to this little primitive room he had where he was creating the noises of the pods opening up. He had this delicate little microphone suspended off of an L-shaped bracket. It was, to my recollection, the size of a pencil eraser hanging four or five inches off the table top, and he was cracking zucchini and cucumbers and stuff. The sound design in that film was always essential to its working, so it's not a casual thing that you were unnerved by it.

Bradley: And I noticed that the cinematography creates so many unnerving, unsettling little moments where nothing significant is necessarily even taking place, but they combine to provide a cumulative sense of real unease and dread.

Richter: That's really nice to hear, and I love it when everybody's working together like that. There's a moment that comes to mind when they're all in Matthew's apartment, and Veronica Cartwright is into this speech about, "Why do we always expect aliens to come in metal ships?" There's a cutaway to Donald Sutherland as he's being deeply rattled by the depth of her confusion and fear, and he's standing on a dolly. The camera's stationary, and he is being moved just incrementally, but that's changing his relationship to the doorframe that he's in and the room behind him. That's a different effect than if you were creeping the camera, because only the frame would be moving. So Donald is actually moving inside the frame, and the background is not. The background and the camera are in the same universe, and Donald is sort of gliding through it, but at such a slow rate that you don't perceive it and say, "Why is that guy moving?", because the cut is so short. It's a very disconcerting image, because he's got a look on his face like his eyes are sort of screwed together and he's trying to figure it out. They've gotta know she's not talking bullshit here, and the shot has that internally. There's a slight sense of dizziness or light-headedness without it being shoved in your face. Probably a lot of people aren't even affected by it, and some are and don't know it's there, but those things are sprinkled throughout the movie, and that's really good storytelling, I think. It's also in another way an attempt, at least, to use the ordinary, like those red dump trucks. And even at the airport, there are these droning voices about, "the red zone is for loading and unloading," and then in that same cadence is some reference to pods in the same voices—"unload your pods," so you're hearing the ordinary and the extraordinary all mixed together in sort of numbing, almost muzak, public address stuff. Who knows what's penetrating the audience's sensibility? It's slyly funny and sinister all at once, and that's what we were trying to do.

Bradley: Strictly speaking, Abel Ferrara's *Body Snatchers* [1993] is neither a remake nor a sequel, but more a variation on a theme. What was your reaction to it?

Richter: I have not seen the film. However, I was sent the screenplay, and it had no acknowledgment of our movie, so I thought, "It's obviously based on the book." Bob Solo was one of the producers. Actually the reason I was sent the screenplay is because when the Writer's Guild gets a thing like that, they have a way of churning out of their database the fact that there were previous movies and other writers on them, and they're always protecting us. They say, "We noticed the producers are asking for a certain credit on it, so we're sending copies to the other writers," and in fact the scream was in there. I said, "Wait a minute—this is interesting, because this is a very subtle thing happening here." There were a handful of small things that I knew specifically did not come from the book, and we were into an extraordinarily dicey moment there. Warner Bros. made that movie and United Artists made ours, though I believe it was owned by MGM at the time, because the United Artists' library fell into MGM's lap when they took over the studio. I'm sitting here reading this script, thinking, "Not only are these things coming from my adaptation, but they are being, on a purely legal level—not that this is intentional—stolen by Warner Bros. from MGM, because MGM owns the rights to all the material that was created specifically for our film." So

I spoke to Bob Solo about this and said, "You must have shown them that script," and he said, "Well, I guess they did see it." Whether it was sloppiness on their part or whatever, they didn't remember where certain things came from. There was a slight settlement on that. I don't know if the studios ever directly addressed each other, but I was given some compensation just to acknowledge the fact that they used some of my stuff. It's that basic. I've had literally no desire to see it. I saw the final shooting script. That's what the Guild is forced to show you.

THE RORSCHACH PLOT OF *INVASION* II: THE LIFE AND DEATH OF COUNTERCULTURE

Tracy Knight

THE MOST CAPTIVATING AND UNFORGETTABLE fictions—the stories we embrace and absorb and never quite let go of us—are marked by their ability to perform several functions at once, to simultaneously affect their audiences on more than one level. To borrow from the field of linguistics, these tales have both *surface structures*—their basic plotlines—and *deep structures*—submerged, sometimes shrouded representations of and statements about human existence, the implicit worldview foundation upon which the plot rests. Consider your own experience: when a book or film mesmerizes you completely and lingers in consciousness long after you're exposed to it, more often than not it is because the story possesses a near magical combination: (1) a surface structure that is entertaining and compelling, and (2) a deep structure that is powerful, universal and delightfully elusive, demanding your repeated consideration and reflection.

It is the elusiveness of the deep structure that teases us, daring us to pry its exact meaning from the story's layers. In short, these stories have "Rorschach plots," fictional inkblots that playfully interact with us and our beliefs. Their ambiguity invites us to project our own interests and biases upon the story in order to wrest meaning from their tantalizing lack of explicitness.

The Body Snatchers, in all its incarnations, is a prime example of a glorious Rorschach plot. Although the deep structure of *Body Snatchers*—which decries the seductive dangers of conformity, of sacrificing the self to the mindless herd—is widely accepted and celebrated, more precise statements regarding the political leanings of its various versions have been consistently debated.

In his book *Cult Movies*, Danny Peary explored the debate regarding the political meaning of Don Siegel's 1956 *Invasion of the Body Snatchers*. Since the movie's release, parallel camps of thought have assembled, contending that the original movie is either a cautionary anticommunist tale or a polemic against the politics of the McCarthy era. Because of the main character's ultimate (and apparently well-placed) reliance upon the government to combat the otherworldly threat, Peary came down firmly for the anticommunist interpretation.

Kaufman's 1978 *Invasion of the Body Snatchers* (hereafter referred to as *Invasion* II) likewise encourages debate, albeit distinct in its focus. Because of the film's setting in time (the cusp between the counterculture era and the "me decade") and place (San Francisco, where flowers in the hair, if not the nervous system, were encouraged), as well as changes in the film's characters, the film appears to be making a statement regarding the life *or* death of the counterculture in America. But in what way, and from what perspective? Is it an admonition against the relentless lure of the "me decade," the temptation to relinquish the ideals of the hippie culture resulting in its absorption into corporate America? Or does the film demonstrate that sacrificing one's individuality *to* the counterculture proves every bit as dangerous and soul-numbing as forfeiting one's self to the establishment?

Kaufman's *Invasion* opens with the discovery of the alien spores and their inviting blossoms by Department of Public Health Lab Technician Elizabeth Driscoll (Brooke Adams), who takes them home and shows them to her husband. He soon seems to change in a quietly dramatic manner, to become less "human." She shares this observation with her boss, Health Inspector Matthew Bennell (Donald Sutherland). Although initially skeptical, Matthew soon sees evidence of this same phenomenon wherever he goes. People are changing throughout the city. Matthew and Elizabeth enlist the support of Matthew's friend, pop psychiatrist Dr. David Kibner (Leonard Nimoy), who has heard multiple reports from his patients of their spouses changing unnaturally, yet interprets these reports as indicators of the deterioration of relationships and eschewing of responsibility in modern American culture. Matthew and Elizabeth find more support and open-mindedness in his friends, free spirits and mud bath proprietors Jack and Nancy Bellicec (Jeff Goldblum and Veronica Cartwright). As the population of San Francisco becomes dominated by those who have been taken over by the pods, Matthew, Elizabeth, and their friends seek escape, working to keep one another awake to avoid being transformed into one of the robotic masses. One by one, the allies relent to the pods and join the other side. Finally, after Matthew and Elizabeth flee into the wilderness, Elizabeth falls asleep and is taken over, her new self beckoning Matthew to do the same. He runs away and destroys a warehouse full of pods. In the last scene, Matthew is seen having returned to work at the Department of Public Health, all outward signs leading the viewer to believe that Matthew is impersonating a pod person by not expressing any emotion. However, he then encounters a still-human Nancy Bellicec outside and—in a startling and chilling departure from the original film's climax—he shrieks and points to her, alerting the other pod people to her presence, making it clear that he has been transformed himself.

Clearly, like the book and the other films, *Invasion* II remains concerned with the bewitching dangers of conformity. But more specifically, is the film pointing to the value of the counterculture in resisting the fragrant temptations of the soulless establishment, or to the inherent dangers of the counterculture, or any mass movement, to becoming mindless drones of the larger group?

Changes in the societal roles between the characters in the first and second films suggest that the counterculture and its remnants are important to understanding the meaning of *Invasion* II. Physician Miles Bennell in the original film becomes Public Health Inspector Matthew Bennell in the remake. Donald Sutherland portrays the latter as a liberal do-gooder, a public servant empowered with the responsibility to look after the citizens' well-being.

Friend and patient Becky Driscoll in the original becomes career woman Elizabeth Driscoll, who becomes unafraid of pursuing her own life path once her marriage becomes irreconcilable. The original film's Dan, Dr. Bennell's friend, becomes pop psychiatrist Dr. David Kibner, who writes bestsellers that inspire readers even as the optimistic tomes render their readers more susceptible to the encroaching danger by blinding them to its existence. Miles's friends Jack and Theodora become aspiring poet Jack Bellicec and his wife Nancy, with whom he runs a public mud bath, which is certainly a symbol of hip self-indulgence. The characters with whom the film is most concerned are liberals who, each in their own way, are distinct from the society at large.

It can therefore be reasonably argued that *Invasion* II concerns itself with the *value* of counterculture and the danger of its demise should the enticements of Establishment America prove victorious. After all, it is the establishment that seems central to the success of the invasion, and on some level Matthew seems to understand this when he asks Elizabeth whether it's possible her transformed husband has become a Republican. Government and industry appear to have succumbed early to the invaders. And what of the church? An intriguing, fleeting early scene shows an uncredited Robert Duvall dressed as a priest, swinging with children on a playground swingset as he impassively observes Elizabeth picking the flower that begins her introduction to doom; the church stands idly by. For his part, psychiatrist David Kibner denies the invasion, preferring instead to couch the widespread social transformation in theoretical terms with which he is already comfortable. Government, industry, medicine, and religion appear to be complacent coconspirators, integral parts of the malignant transformation society is undergoing.

However, the more compelling view is that the counterculture that saw its birth in the 1960s contained the seeds (or pods) of its own demise, that the film chronicled the self-destruction of the energetic Left. Sutherland's Matthew Bennell, while a public servant, has a cynical worldview (apart from his desire to love Elizabeth); his first appearance in the film shows him inspecting a restaurant and apparently mistaking capers for rat turds. So narrowly bound is he to his own aims and goals that he remains oblivious to the approaching death of humanity, clipping small articles of personal interest out of the newspaper while completely ignoring the headline: "Webs Shroud Bay Area." And although he asserts a vaguely countercultural posture, he maintains a trust in America's institutions that is disturbingly naive, to the point that he continues to call the authorities for assistance—the police, the mayor, and other government officials—long after their uselessness has been made clear. It is not until he notices that when he tries to call for help that those receiving his calls already know his name (and by this time, he and his group are virtually surrounded by the pod people) that he recognizes the worthlessness of the establishment in rescuing him. In *Invasion* II's Matthew Bennell, we see the formula for destruction of the counterculture: increasing cynicism, a lack of awareness of the big picture, and a bewildering dependence on the government.

The use of characters and plot in *Invasion* II clearly point to the conformity being cautioned against being the conformity that, by the time the film was released, had become apparent. It wasn't that the establishment had co-opted the counterculture; it was that the counterculture had poisoned itself. Joyous, honest rebellion had become garden-variety cynicism; the value of individuality had been supplanted by the enticement of losing one's soul to a group; and the childish dependence upon social institutions to save us all prevented self-preservation. In important social ways, the counterculture became indistinguishable from the establishment and, in doing so, compromised whatever value it had introduced into the culture.

And what are the final defenses used to combat the invading danger of the pods? True to the descent of the counterculture, they are drugs (Matthew and Elizabeth ingest amphetamines to stay awake) and destruction (Matthew sets fire to a pod storage facility). Predictably, neither works.

The larger viewpoint proffered by *Invasion* II is that the seductive and sedating appeal of passive compliance exists for all of us, whether we be establishment or counterculture or somewhere in between. Cults of conformity seek out the same foundation no matter their natures. Elizabeth observed when she first found the alien flower—which she identified as a *grex*, a new species resulting from the cross-pollination of two other species—that these organisms "thrive on devastated ground." Human social groups—no matter their aims or initial impetus—commonly become "devastated ground" upon which sameness takes root as humanity dies.

Each incarnation of Jack Finney's *The Body Snatchers* reminds us—through the vehicle of a story that is chilling, suspenseful, and masterfully created—that conformity spells the death of identity, spoiling the very lifeblood of human existence. In *Invasion* II, Philip Kaufman demonstrates that even the social movements that appear most diverse and sincere ultimately serve as the "devastated ground" upon which virulent conformity grows and blossoms.

"Meet the new boss
Same as the old boss."
—The Who, "Won't Get Fooled Again"

ROBERT H. SOLO, POD PRODUCER

@ @ @

Anthony Timpone

AFTER AUTHOR JACK FINNEY, DIRECTOR DON SIEGEL, and actor Kevin McCarthy, the person most associated with the *Body Snatchers* films is producer Robert H. Solo, who shepherded both the acclaimed 1978 version and the ill-fated 1994 adaptation to the screen.

Born in 1932 in Waterbury, Connecticut, Solo has produced numerous films during the last three decades, including *The Devils, Scrooge, Colors, Winter People, Above the Law,* and *Blue Sky.* A fan of the original movie since his youth, Solo dug into his own wallet to purchase the rights to Finney's *The Body Snatchers* in 1975, a few years before the George Lucas/Steven Spielberg–driven sci-fi boom of the late seventies.

For this former talent agent, studio executive, and independent producer, *Body Snatchers* represents the best of times and worst of times. The best: his association with director Philip Kaufman's chilling remake that starred Donald Sutherland and reset Finney's small-town story in San Francisco. The worst: Abel Ferrara's moderately effective update, relocated to a southern army base, which became a victim of studio politics. Now semiretired and living in Nevada, the veteran producer is quite proud of his 1978 *Invasion of the Body Snatchers.* However, Solo's attempt to relaunch Finney's trendsetter as a filmic franchise for the nineties left him questioning whether the pods had already invaded Hollywood.

Anthony Timpone: When did you first see the '56 film?

Robert H. Solo: Probably the year it came out or the year after, and it was terrific, it just scared the daylights out of me. I've seen it once or twice after that, and it just always stuck in my head as one of those movies that registers very powerfully on you, and so it was part of my repertoire of movies that I remember. It was no surprise when later on I was thinking about things to do and what subjects to make, and I thought of *Invasion of the Body Snatchers.*

Timpone: Had you read the book before you saw the movie?

Solo: No. No, I had not read the book, I didn't even know it was a book at that time. And obviously I read the book more than once in '75 or '76, when I first got the idea to do a movie on it.

Timpone: Why did you decide to remake a film that many consider a classic?

Solo: Well, first of all, I thought that it had an opportunity to be remade in color, not black and white. And compared to what they had in '56, I thought we could do a lot better in the special effects area. Of course, by today's standards, even our special effects are from the stone age! Those were really the main reasons, other than the fact that I always felt that the ending of the '56 version was a cop-out and a joke, and always made me laugh, actually. You know, "Call the FBI [laughs]," like they're going to save the world. That was ridiculous. Having read the novel, I thought that one could do what was in the novel or something that was akin to what was in the novel, but certainly not what was in the 1956 movie.

Timpone: What made you take the risk of plunking down $10,000 of your own money to grab the rights?

Solo: I don't know. It was something I really wanted to do, and the only way to do it was to get an option on it. I had an exclusive two-year producer deal at Warner Bros. and had been trying to find projects for about a year when I thought about this. I suggested it to them, and they didn't want to do it. I still had time to go on my contract and I thought, "Well, I really want to do this, and I want to try and put it together, and Warners isn't gonna put money up for me. I'll just have to do it myself." I didn't have all that much, but I reached in my pocket and I got an option.

Timpone: Warner Bros. eventually began developing the film. Why did they then put it in turnaround and decide to pass?

Solo: To this day I have no idea. I have no idea why they just finally did develop it and then put it in turnaround. By then I had a script and I had full confidence, so I can't imagine.

Timpone: Besides the '56 *Invasion*, were you a fan of other science fiction or horror films?

Solo: Well, not as a general rule, no. I like science fiction. I used to read science fiction and fantasy magazines in the forties or fifties, maybe when I was in high school. So I always liked science fiction, and I always like the old H. G. Wells movies. I was drawn to science fiction, but not as an aficionado or freak. I didn't go to conventions.

Timpone: Were any other scripters hired to work on the project besides W. D. Richter?

Solo: No, he was the only one.

Timpone: Wasn't the original intention to set the film in a small town and follow the Siegel film more closely?

Solo: That was the intention. The original intention was to do a 1978 remake, and originally it started out in the same small town as it was in the book and film. But that changed in the course of development. Actually, it changed while I was out of the room. We were sitting talking about the script and what we were doing, Richter and Phil Kaufman, and I went to the men's room, and I came back and they said, "We're moving it to San Francisco." I gasped and my eyes bulged out, and I thought about it and it was just such a wild idea, so I said, "Terrific, great, let's do that." So that's how it happened. I don't know who broached it, probably Phil because he lives in San Francisco. And as I know Phil better now over the years—I didn't really know him well then—he likes to live at home, so I guess he just wanted to go home every night [laughs]. So he said, "Let's make this happen in San Francisco."

Timpone: What led to the hiring of Kaufman? He was somewhat untried at that time.

Solo: Well, he had made a couple of movies, and I had seen *The Great Northfield, Minnesota Raid*, and *White Dawn*, and they struck me as being very cinematically unusual. They weren't conventional movies the way they were shot. There was something really interesting and offbeat and off-key about the way those films were made. So that attracted me to him. I didn't know him, so I called his agent, and at the time he was working on *Star Trek* [the first feature film attempt], which I hadn't known. And then somebody at Paramount canceled *Star Trek* because they thought there was no future in science fiction movies, and so he became available to do *Body Snatchers*. We always used to laugh about *Star Trek*.

Timpone: What did you contribute to the screenplay in those early days?

Solo: I have no idea. I presume something. I mean, it's hard to keep my mouth shut. So I'm sure I made a contribution, but believe me, I couldn't tell you what it was.

Timpone: Let's talk about the casting of the film. What led to your ultimate choices: Donald Sutherland, Brooke Adams, Leonard Nimoy, Jeff Goldblum, and Veronica Cartwright?

Solo: I don't know. Jeff Goldblum and Veronica Cartwright came in as general casting. We had seen Brooke Adams in *Days of Heaven*. We needed to get some kind of a name in it for United Artists to go ahead with it, and someone said Donald Sutherland was back in the country. And he was an old client and friend of Mike Medavoy, United Artists' West Coast head of production. So between Mike and ourselves we approached Donald, and he agreed to do it, and everything keyed off of that. Of course, we didn't have much of a budget, and we had very little money for cast, and he got most of it. It was considerably lower than he had gotten in the past, but then he hadn't made an American picture in a long time. We didn't really have any money for anyone else, so all we could pay anybody else was $25,000. That's the most anybody got. That means Jeff Goldblum got $25,000, Brooke Adams got $25,000. I'm not sure Veronica got that, but the rest of the principals did. It was difficult to convince Leonard Nimoy to do the movie for $25,000; he had come off of *Star Trek* and was quite a name, but he did it for Phil, who got to know him while he was preparing *Star Trek*.

Timpone: So Sutherland was the first choice for the lead role?

Solo: When his name came up, we all said, "Gee, that's a great idea!" We wanted an actor who gave the appearance of being intelligent, somewhat aggressive, because he was going to be a health inspector who would go in and ask questions and be credible in that kind of occupation.

Timpone: How much was Sutherland paid?

Solo: Something between $200,000 and $300,000.

Timpone: It must have been a tough shoot: lots of locations, night scenes, not to mention the special effects.

Solo: Well, it was difficult because so much of it was at night. It was really exhausting for everybody, everybody except me, because I'd usually go home and go to bed at one o'clock or two in the morning. I'm an early person, so I'd be up at six-thirty or seven o'clock. But when it was night shooting, I couldn't handle it, having been up all day. It was very hard night after night after night, like out on the warehouse location where we shot the greenhouse where they were raising all the pods. It was right on the water, and it was very damp and cold. But compared to other locations I've been on, it was a picnic. It wasn't that difficult to shoot. It was difficult to shoot it with the time and money we had, because we had a lot we had to do.

Timpone: What was your shooting schedule?

Solo: About ten weeks. I don't remember what the budget was, it was around $3 million dollars, 3.2 or something. But the city of San Francisco was very cooperative. And all in all I don't think it was a nightmarish shoot at all, by any stretch of imagination. I can't tell you any horror stories.

Timpone: Do you have any location anecdotes, like when you were shooting in the red-light district?

Solo: When we were shooting in the Market Street area, South of Market, there were lots of drunks around all the time. It was sort of like the Bowery, that kind of area. I guess they're cleaning it up and have reclaimed it today. But then it was still a lot of drunks and people yelling out in the middle of the take and all that business, chasing after Donald Sutherland and Leonard.

Timpone: Was the Jack Bellicec character conceived from the start as comic relief, or was that something that Jeff Goldblum improvised?

Solo: No, that's the way it was conceived, a kind of a New Age character spouting drivel. And as was Leonard Nimoy on the other side of it, it was all because it was right in the seventies when all that stuff was going on. EST was very popular, and all these self-improvement movements were at their height. Everyone was into some sort of a group looking for self-awareness and insight and so on. So we incorporated all that into the script, and it was in the temper of the times.

Timpone: What other themes, besides EST and the New Age philosophy, did you wish to explore?

Solo: Just urban paranoia.

Timpone: Is it true that you started filming without a completed script, and the actors didn't know the ending until late in the game?

Solo: Well, we had completed the script but the actors didn't know the ending, and neither did Donald Sutherland. And of course that was crucial, because he had to do it! We had been shooting out of sequence about three or four weeks, so the time came when we were down around downtown San Francisco, where all the office buildings are. We had been shooting with Donald and we had to shoot the end of the movie the next day. It was the next *day.* We didn't tell Donald, he didn't know about it. So Phil grabbed me and said, "Listen, we've gotta go tell Donald the end of this movie" [laughs]. And we went to his trailer, nervous I may say, and Don said, "Well, I've been expecting you" [laughs]. And then we told him what the ending of the movie was, and he thought it was terrific, and we were very relieved.

Timpone: Cartwright said that Sutherland was a bit of an eccentric, and showed up at a three-hour rehearsal with pink curlers in his hair.

Solo: Well, Donald is Donald. He flew in his own crazy hairdresser from New York and wanted to be in curls for some reason in the movie. God knows why he wanted to have curls. I don't remember [Cartwright's] situation, but I'm sure it was true [laughs]. And I think we toned it down a little bit, but he wanted to have curls. Of course, Donald has always been a little eccentric.

Timpone: Did Nimoy see his role as a career breakthrough?

Solo: Oh, I don't think so. He did it because he thought it would be fun; he certainly didn't do it for the money.

It wasn't the lead in the movie, so it couldn't possibly be a career break. He did it for Phil and did it for fun.

Timpone: Did the four leads bond while you were shooting?

Solo: You mean personally?

Timpone: Yes, did they become a pretty tight-knit group?

Solo: Well, most of them, not all. Not all. I really don't want to go into where there was conflict, but there was.

Timpone: How did the uncredited Robert Duvall cameo come about?

Solo: He's a pal of Phil's, and he happened to be in San Francisco. So Phil grabbed him and said, "You're going to be in the movie, and I'm gonna make you a priest!" And I guess they had a priest costume on the wardrobe truck, and they put him on a swing. And that was it, just a spur-of-the-moment thing. Whereas Don Siegel was not a spur-of-the-moment thing.

Timpone: Was Duvall supposed to be the first pod person?

Solo: Yes, I think so. Yeah.

Timpone: Whose idea was it to cast Kevin McCarthy and Don Siegel?

Solo: It was all of our idea, because we all loved the [1956] movie, and so we thought it would be terrific to get them in. And Phil was a friend of Don Siegel, because they were both under contract to Universal. So we decided we'd make it a little bit of a homage to Don, and Phil called Don and asked him if he'd be in it. Don said he would love to, so that was easy. Kevin McCarthy loved the idea, but we started out with the equivalent of two dollars and ended up with two hundred dollars in order to get him. If you're going to get Kevin McCarthy you have to get Kevin McCarthy, you can't get anybody else. His agent kept asking for more and more, so we paid a lot of money, relatively speaking, for somebody to come out and work one day.

Timpone: How did Ben Burtt accomplish the legendary pod scream?

Solo: It's something playing backwards, a pig squealing or something like that.

Timpone: Whose decision was it to show more of the pods and their physiology, as compared to the first film?

Solo: Everybody's. We wanted to just make it more colorful and more graphic.

Timpone: Did the effects go off as planned, for the most part?

Solo: Yeah, for the most part. There were some problems with the pods and all that stuff in the beginning, but we worked it out, and of course today it would all be done in computers, and it would take a lot less time.

Timpone: Do you remember how the pod effects were accomplished?

Solo: Vaguely, only vaguely. I know that we dug a hole and we had some kind of a hydraulic thing that pushed the person up and it opened up.

Timpone: Was there a conscious decision to make the pod people more zombielike than in the '56 film? In the '78 film, they move more stiffly and deliberately.

Solo: A little bit. But you saw more of the pod people in the '78 version than you did in the '56 version. But on the one hand, some of them move slowly, and then at other times you have these dialogue scenes in the house with Leonard Nimoy, where he was just spouting his New Age philosophy to Jeff Goldblum, but he was a pod. And you didn't know that until the end of the scene when they go out and Nimoy says, "Tell somebody to go get them." You didn't know that he was a pod until the scene was over. So while we had some of them walking zombielike, it wasn't universal.

Timpone: Was George Romero's *Night of the Living Dead* used as a reference in any way?

Solo: I don't think so. It never came up at all.

Timpone: Was *The Exorcist* or any other film used as a model for an approach to adult horror while you were making the film?

Solo: I don't think so. I don't remember any of that ever coming up in any of our conversations. Phil wanted to screen some film noir for the lighting and stuff like that. Shadows, a lot of shadows and things like that. Just for visual reasons.

Timpone: Did you ever consult Jack Finney on the film?

Solo: No, he wasn't consulted. And he got a little pissed off at me, at us really. He and his agent were pissed off in the first place because we didn't pay him. We didn't *have* to pay him. We got the rights from the people who owned the rights to the book, and to the old movie. So when we wanted to do a remake, we got the rights from those people. And I think he and his agent were upset that he wasn't getting more money, which of course never happens. When someone buys the rights to a book, they own the book. If they want to sell it to somebody else, they sell it to somebody else, and he was not thrilled. By the time we were in San Francisco, Finney was quite annoyed, and then we belatedly invited him down to be in that book party scene with Leonard Nimoy, and he refused to come. So that was our association with him.

Timpone: Did you rekindle your association when it came time to do the nineties version?

Solo: No, it was just a lost cause by that point. What was the point?

Timpone: Were any other endings discussed for the '78 remake?

Solo: Well, there was the ending that was in the book, which was never shot, where they pour oil in the furrows in the field and set fire to it, and it burns up all the pods. They start burning and popping off the vines and then float up into the atmosphere, as if perhaps they're going to end up on some other planet somewhere. And the pod people that were already here had no future, because they weren't going to be succeeded by any future pod people without the pods. So that was the book. We had talked about that, or some variations on that.

Timpone: Do you think the film still holds up today?

Solo: I think so. I think the '56 film holds up, for the most part. And ours holds up, too. Of course, it was a reflection of the time, of 1978, what attitudes were, how people behaved, what kind of clothes they wore and the normal gobbledygook. But it's a very modern film and has done pretty well on video, and continues to do very well, so it's not on the dust heap of history.

Timpone: Do you think the film would have been more successful if it had ended more upbeat?

Solo: Of course; any film is going to be more successful if it ends upbeat, any film. Studios hate downbeat movies, and audiences don't want to walk out of the theaters grim, they want to walk out with at least a feeling of hope. Audiences like pictures to end on a positive note, whether it's brimming with enthusiasm or whatever, but not a negative note. Movies that end on a negative note usually flop. So that was the risk that we took, and of course we paid for it, because the movie was not a big hit. And we opened the same day as Clint Eastwood in *Every Which Way But Loose,* and it just killed us.

Timpone: The movie pulled in about $12 million in rentals.

Solo: Yeah, maybe ten or twelve. And it became a very profitable movie for its cost, because they sold it to network television. It was one of the last big sales to network TV; they sold it for something like $6.5 million to one of the networks for three or four showings. And then of course it has always had a pretty good life on video. So the movie was a profitable one, there was no question. It was sort of thrown away foreign because all those people that we had done business with at United Artists had left the company by then.

Timpone: What was your involvement in the proposed *Body Snatchers* TV series?

Solo: I had nothing to do with it; as a matter of fact, I don't think there will ever be a *Body Snatchers* TV show, because there's a problem with the rights. When I made the 1978 version I got the rights, and when I made the deal with United Artists I didn't have them all, but I had to give them rights to a television series, and the rights to a television series were frozen between them and me. In other words, they weren't really in the television business, so they couldn't make a series without me and I couldn't make a series without them. So then when I made the deal with Warner Bros., they took over my rights, so now Warner Bros. can't make the series without United Artists, United Artists can't make the series without Warner Bros. So the likelihood of that ever happening is slim. But seven or eight years ago, United Artists started developing a television series without even telling me, based on the movie. So I gather they got a script, tried to shop it, and couldn't sell it. Of course, they had no right to do it without me and there would have been a major lawsuit.

Timpone: Do you know what that series would have been like?

Solo: I have no idea, I never saw it.

Timpone: At what time did you decide to try the formula again and do another *Body Snatchers* movie?

Solo: Well, I thought that there was a way to do it that would be totally different—and of course it didn't turn out that way—but it would be totally different. My idea was that initially it was set in a small town in the Midwest, and nearby was an air base, and so basically they're taking over the air base, and from that the pods were going to take over the country through the military. So in a way it was going to be a kind of revolution, and it was going to be a military regime. That was the original idea.

Timpone: Was Raymond Cistheri hired by you to work on the *Body Snatchers* script?

Solo: Who?

Timpone: Raymond Cistheri is credited for the story with Larry Cohen.

Solo: Oh, yeah. I tell you, I don't want to go into the writing credits on this movie.

Timpone: Too complicated?

Solo: Yeah, too complicated.

Timpone: So then you probably wouldn't want to discuss Cohen?

Solo: I went to Larry to do it originally, and he did a script which was pretty good. Then the executives changed at Warner Bros., and they wanted another writer, and then there was another executive, so it was one of those nightmarish studio relationships.

Timpone: Was it your idea to go more youth-oriented?

Solo: Yeah.

Timpone: Were you a fan of Stuart Gordon's horror films before you hired him to script the film with Dennis Paoli?

Timpone: Yeah, Stuart did a very good script with Dennis. I thought that script was going to get shot. But it didn't because another new executive came in, and they gave him three or four scripts that they said needed looking over, and he looked at it and said, "Now I'm the executive of this project, and I loved your script." And then twenty-five drafts later . . .

Timpone: What made you replace Cohen and bring Gordon in?

Solo: It was the studio.

Timpone: Why do you think the film was cursed in its development and took so long to come together?

Solo: Well, we had an inept executive on it. He was completely inept, and every weekend he would see a movie and come back on Monday and say, "Look, we have to have a story meeting because I saw this movie over the weekend and we have to stick in this and we have to stick in that." It was just a nightmare.

Timpone: Is that part of the reason why the film is so unsure of itself, whether it's a sequel or a remake?

Solo: Well, ultimately I guess what happened was they got more secure the closer it got to the previous version.

Timpone: At any point, did United Artists make any kind of a fuss about the use of the pod scream or any other elements of the '78 version?

Solo: Actually, I don't know. After that movie I was out of there, I left L.A.

Timpone: It was such a bad experience that you just wanted to leave the business?

Solo: Yes, it was a terrible experience from start to finish, from the development stage through production and postproduction. For me, anyway.

Timpone: Was Abel Ferrara your replacement choice after Gordon left?

Solo: No, he was studio executive Lance Young's choice, and he sold him to the studio. He certainly wasn't my choice. I just thought he was the wrong jockey for the horse. While I like some of Abel's previous work, I just felt that he was inappropriate. He was great for gritty, realistic New York street movies, but had never done science fiction or had a flair for fantasy, and I just didn't think he was right for it. But ultimately, in a sense, he was given to me.

Timpone: Were any other directors considered who you preferred?

Solo: Yeah, there were other directors. Some directors didn't want to do it, they didn't want to make another remake or another version and so forth. But there was another very good director from Disney who wanted to do it, whose name I can't remember, and it came down to him or Abel, and the studio went for Abel.

Timpone: Was it Ferrara or Gordon's idea to toss the kid out of the helicopter at the end? That was pretty shocking.

Solo: I don't remember. I know that was a matter for some lengthy discussion with the studio. Should we or shouldn't we? This went on for quite a long time, and I was in favor of it, because I felt it was very shocking. And finally we shot it.

Timpone: Did you agree with Ferrara's decision to go back to the book and abandon some of the more visceral ideas that Gordon and Paoli had scripted—the pod people dissolving from the insecticide, for example?

Solo: That would have been more science fiction. And that's what Stuart does. That was a different approach, and I liked it because it was a very science fiction approach. After all, what are we selling? It isn't *War and Peace,* it isn't a love story. It's a science fiction movie, however you clothe it. Whatever the characters are like or the dialogue, it's a science fiction movie. You can't pretend it's not. Abel kept trying to make this not a science fiction movie. That was the problem; he didn't understand it. And when he was hired and went off with his pal, Nicky St. John, who's a very nice guy and not untalented, they came back with a draft where they took out all the pods! They took out everything that was science fiction! That was the plight—he never could get with what the material was, he could never get with it being science fiction. So he just kept trying to make it a New York street movie. When you've got a crew of eighty and you've got set designers and construction people, it's not the same as if you're making a movie with about twenty-five people in New York on 47th Street, and you want to shoot on 47th Street and traffic is too heavy so you say, "Let's run over to 46th Street." Which was the way he used to make movies. Well, you can't do that when you've got a crew of eighty-five and a regular schedule and sets are built and people have shooting schedules and so forth. You can't improvise like that. But that's the only kind of shooting he knows.

Timpone: So I take it this led to enormous friction between you and Ferrara?

Solo: Oh, terrible! Well, not personally. We had some words, but not personally. It was just that in effect finally I felt that I was in the hands of the wrong person, and the picture was going to be a disaster. I mean, I thought it was going to be a disaster, but it didn't turn out to be one. But it didn't turn out to be anything remotely like I hoped or expected it to be. He was, as I said, the wrong jockey for the horse.

Timpone: The film seems somewhat abbreviated at eighty-seven minutes. What wound up on the cutting room floor?

Solo: God knows. A lot of stuff. Dede Allen was under contract with Warner Bros. and was their in-house film editor, and she in effect oversaw the final cutting of the film. So by then I had really washed my hands of the picture. The postproduction was very prolonged and difficult.

Timpone: Is it true the film went over budget?

Solo: A lot.

Timpone: That must have caused trouble between you and the studio.

Solo: Well, my production manager, who was my line producer, quit about two days before we started shooting. The picture, because of Abel, was already a million dollars over and the camera hadn't turned! The production manager was an old-timer. I'd worked with him before and he knew his business, and he said, "I'm not going to be carried out of here feet first. I quit!"

Timpone: At any point, did you consider trying to replace Ferrara?

Solo: Candidly, yes. It was around that time. And Lance Young came down there and insisted that Abel stay on as director, and—well, what can I say?

Timpone: Why do you think *Body Snatchers* tested poorly when they finally got it out there in front of an audience?

Solo: I guess because it wasn't great! Most pictures test poorly because they're not terrific. So that's why it tested poorly. It ended up an OK movie. Not great and not terrible; it's an OK movie.

Timpone: At what point did you realize that Warner Bros. was going to dump the film?

Solo: After they saw it [laughs]! Just about after we had a preview. They thought so highly of the movie that they previewed it two miles away in Burbank. [Studio chiefs] Bob Daly and Terry Semel were basically horrified by the movie, and they sent the word out, "Guys, don't spend too much more money on this, just finish it and get it out of here." That's my guess.

Timpone: What do you think is the main problem with the film? Was it the fact that it abandoned those science fiction elements?

Solo: Well, it was a film that was neither here nor there, it really didn't have a point of view, it didn't have any engaging characters for the most part. Basically it had no prologue; you never really had time to get to know any of the people before it started. It all started happening too fast, and as a result most of the movie was one long chase.

Timpone: Didn't Ferrara keep the film alive by bringing it to Cannes?

Solo: Well, he tried, and they [Warner Bros.] were shocked that they chose it. And of course I was shocked, and nonetheless we all got a free ride to the Cannes festival, which was nice. And they all sat around, the Warners people, sort of surprised that the movie was even there. Abel was his usual self, he was late and unshaven. Abel was Abel.

Timpone: He is quite a character.

Solo: Yeah, Abel is a character unto himself. I don't dislike him as a person. I just wouldn't want anything to do with him professionally ever again.

Timpone: Four years later, you still sound pretty bitter about the whole thing.

Solo: Well, not bitter, just resigned to the fact that it was a project that started out with reasonably good credentials, and was gradually ground down by a studio executive who finally got fired. So that, coupled with the experience with Abel—I really took no moment of pleasure out of the experience. That's why I sound the way I do, not so much because the movie didn't turn out the way I wanted it to turn out, but because the experience was so unpleasant.

Timpone: In retrospect, would you do anything differently with the third film?

Solo: Well, I wouldn't hire Abel Ferrara in the first place; that's the first thing I wouldn't do. And then everything else would follow from that.

Timpone: If *Body Snatchers* had been the start of a franchise, which it was originally envisioned as, where else would you have taken the story besides Washington, D.C., which Gordon spoke about?

Solo: Yeah, exactly. They start coming into Washington, D.C. In the next one they get the president, they take over the government. Of course we all believe that everybody in Congress is a bunch of pods as it is, even now. So the idea is that they infiltrate the FBI, the CIA, and Congress and so on. And basically it's a kind of a coup. And what do you do with that, after that? I don't know the answer, but that's where it was going.

Timpone: Will you give the story another shot in a few years, or should it be laid to rest?

Solo: It's time to rest, it's time for a good long rest. Besides, other people rip it off all the time.

Timpone: Looking at the trio of films objectively, which do you think is the best version?

Solo: Well, I have to say mine.

Timpone: The '78?

Solo: Yeah, I just think so. I revere the old one and Don Siegel, but it wasn't nearly as sophisticated. And in addition to being scary, the movie that we did and Richter wrote was funny. It was sardonic, it was very hip for the time, it wasn't just your everyday science fiction movie. So I just think it was a much more sophisticated movie than either of the others, and that's why I like it the best. It's a smart movie.

Timpone: And the Hollywood system was a lot different in those days; you had much more control over the film.

Solo: Oh, yeah. Certainly with United Artists and Mike Medavoy, who was also a fan of Phil Kaufman's. He let us make the movie we wanted to make. As long as we brought it in on time, they really didn't interfere at all. There were only two or three executives; today there are twenty-seven thousand executives at every studio, and every one has an opinion.

Timpone: Why do you think audiences keep taking to Jack Finney's story?

Solo: Because we all think there's something under the bed. Ever since we were babies, little children, it was, "Mommy, don't close the door, leave the light on." There's something atavistic about it. We're terrified that somebody, something, is going to get us. The big bad wolf, the ghost, the bogeyman. That's just part of who we are as creatures at a very young age. So I think that's why audiences respond to it, it's something very basic to human nature.

Timpone: Before we go, is there anything else you would like to add about having worked on two *Body Snatchers* films?

Solo: Only to say that the experience I had with Phil Kaufman and Richter was terrific, and of all the movies I've made, working with Phil was the most pleasant experience of any of them, it was really a pleasure. One was pleasure, the other one was pain [laughs]!

THE MARK OF ABEL ON A CLASSIC: AN INTERVIEW WITH ABEL FERRARA

Gilbert Colon

BORN IN THE BRONX ON JULY 19, 1951, INDEPENDENT director Abel Ferrara has proven his considerable versatility at both television directing (episodes of *Miami Vice, Crime Story,* and *Subway Stories*) and feature filmmaking, starting with the low-budget thriller *The Driller Killer* (1979). It is only natural that he would eventually demonstrate his versatility with subject matter as well. Though widely known and regarded for his work in the crime genre with such infamous outings as *The King of New York* (1990) and *Bad Lieutenant* (1992), Ferrara burst onto the science fiction scene with his version of Jack Finney's classic, *The Body Snatchers.* Later, he went on to dabble in the horror genre with his black-and-white vampire opus, *The Addiction* (1995), before returning to the gritty urban morality plays that gained him notoriety with *The Blackout* (1997).

Ferrara immediately reveals a deep and obvious admiration for author Jack Finney, his book *The Body Snatchers*, director Don Siegel, and Siegel's film version *Invasion of the Body Snatchers.* Indeed, a respect for science fiction as a whole comes through. Ferrara is currently continuing his work in the science fiction genre with a forthcoming adaptation of William Gibson's short story *New Rose Hotel.*

Gilbert Colon: First, I wanted to know how faithful you were determined to be to Jack Finney's novel, *The Body Snatchers.*

Abel Ferrara: Well, it was Jack Finney's novel that got me into doing it because I knew the concept intrigued me, and I found the theme interesting. The Martians become you and take you, but only your physicality—and then they are what they are, which in theory is a big improvement on man, from their point of view. They're *you* without the screaming and yelling. But then again, is that an improvement or what? But you see, in the book Finney really worked on the angle that this is at the beginning of nuclear testing, and he was into the idea that man was now jeopardizing not only the planet but actually the universe with what he's doin'. And that's one of the reasons that he wrote it; to say, "Hey dudes, you can fuck up your own place, but leave the rest of the universe to us Zen Buddhists."

Colon: So mainly you were striving to remain faithful to Finney's themes.

Ferrara: Yeah. His book's a wild work of imagination. Basically the Martians came to Earth to bring everybody the good news. Now the earthlings naturally react with their paranoia and, well, violence, and they basically say at one point, all right guys, bye-bye.

Colon: So you're almost sympathetic to the body snatchers?

Ferrara: Oh, very much so. Now who's gonna make a movie like that? Don Siegel was a little bit in that groove. In other words, he tried to make it as far away from the obvious good guy-bad guy business as he could and still not get murdered by the financiers. But they retooled the movie on him. The studio reshot the beginning and the ending. Those things were done a year later, even though I think Siegel was there. Siegel's version started with that beautiful shot of the train coming into the station, not the bullshit in the hospital and the FBI going after him and all the stuff told in flashback. . . .

Colon: How different was Siegel's original vision?

Ferrara: Well, with the new opening, there's no tension anymore. Plus the music changed the whole thing.

Colon: By putting the story into a flashback frame, it becomes a happy ending.

Ferrara: Siegel's ending is when he sees them in the truck—great ending. They see a truck driving down the street—

Colon: And that's the real ending, or should've been the ending.

Ferrara: —and then we come back, and blow up everybody. Not bad, except all you need is one pod. Then again, who knows if the seedlings have gone all over the world.

Colon: But your version kind of tricks you into believing it's a happy ending. Gabrielle Anwar and Billy Wirth blow the pods up en route, and you think for maybe just a fraction of a minute they won.

Ferrara: Humanity saves the day.

Colon: Maybe everything's okay. And then they land their helicopter and it's not quite that way.

Ferrara: They could've gotten them all.

Colon: After all that, they don't even know.

Ferrara: Nobody knows. I always wanted to get that ending. And let me say something about that end—that Phil Nielson, who's a great stunt coordinator who also works with director Oliver Stone, he makes it. He hates for me to say it, but he did second unit work on these scenes—I say that at great personal risk to myself. I would have never taken on a film about the military without Nielson seeing me through from the very start. There's nothing worse than a film dealing with the military taken from the point of view of a pacifist draft dodger like myself. See, although I respect those of my generation who fought and died in Vietnam, I equally respect those who protested the war—some at greater personal loss than me. There was a common enemy, which is again like *The Body Snatchers*. Either way you look at it, it's group thinking.

Colon: Did you see the Siegel version and Finney's book as paranoid polemics against communist subversion, or warnings against McCarthyist red-baiting? People are divided on whether the pod creatures are communists coming, invading, infiltrating, or the whole thing is a parable about the gathering forces of witch-hunting. . . .

Ferrara: Now what are we talking about? The story or the movie? Are you talking about the movie as Siegel made it, or the movie that was fucking jerry-rigged together?

Colon: So you see them as different?

Ferrara: Yeah, in other words, you slapdash that beginning and ending on—somebody walking across the street and you hear nuh nuh, nuh nuh, nuh nuh, *nuh nuh,* you're gonna say, "Oh, I'm scared." But if you take the music out, it's just someone walking across the street. . . . You dig what I'm sayin'? The film Siegel made's left-wing, the fuckin' movie they tried to turn it into was right-wing, so what do they got? A fuckin' middle-of-the-road movie! A movie is left-wing *and* right-wing. A movie's a work of art, man, it's not political propaganda. Siegel's an artist. I mean to me, Picasso's an artist. But if any film director can be an artist in this business, then Siegel fits the bill. He's an artist—that's his politics, man.

Colon: Which brings me to your personal politics. They sound—

Ferrara: Antipolitics.

Colon: Wow, that sums up something. I was going to say, from reading other interviews you sound a bit like Vincent Gallo's communist character in *The Funeral.* And I wondered if you put any of that into *Body Snatchers?*

Ferrara: Most of communist politics is actually a fascistic mind-set—to control and achieve power rather than uplift. I'm a limousine liberal.

Colon: Did that bent affect your decision to set the story on a military base?

Ferrara: *I* didn't set it on a military base.

Colon: That was in the original draft?

Ferrara: I don't know which draft it was, but that was the Solo people. They didn't want me to change it and I didn't feel like arguing it, 'cause it's definitely—

Colon: As good a place as any?

Ferrara: No, it's not as good as any. But it's 180 degrees from the fuckin' point of the story. The point of the story is you are not who you appear to be. How do I know if you're not who you are if I don't know you? But if I know you from when we were kids I can say, jeez, you're not acting like you. In the book a great scene is him lookin' at the librarian who gave him his first copy of *Huckleberry Finn* and saying, "I know who you are." She says, "Do you?" It's a great line. The idea is truly beautiful. It's like, it's ambiguity. It's complexity. I wanted to do that film because the complexity of the source material transcends a particular zeitgeist of mid-fifties Americana. Like a lot of good science fiction, it's metaphor. But to try to simplify it, to say this is about, y'know, fuckin' communism or nuclear testing or whatever, it's too simplistic. You trivialize it. The book—it's beautiful. It's a metaphor like an image in a million mirrors—y'know what I mean? It's infinite.

Colon: Many of your films, like *Body Snatchers,* have very sympathetic portrayals of female characters—do you have feminist leanings?

Ferrara: We dig the bitches.

Colon: Were you approached by the studio, or did you seek the project out?

Ferrara: They came to us. Who would come up with this thing? It's an odd film for Warner Bros. to make, right? But you know, the way I looked at it was—not to compare ourselves to the Rolling Stones, we're not—it was like that band covering a Chuck Berry song, y'know? We're connecting to somebody else's shit.

Colon: Do you know how they chose you specifically?

Ferrara: No, I mean obviously it was Stuart Gordon and Larry Cohen. They were sniffing for that genre of director. I think they talked to a lot of guys like me, and I was the one who gave them the right bullshit. They definitely wanted bad guys and action, which I gave them. Warners Bros. basically wrote their own version. They had your typical mental midget script. I shouldn't say Warner Bros., and I'm not blamin' any of the screenwriters. I mean, on my version of the script we have five names, which I love, and somebody put a fake name on it, I think.

Colon: What was the fake name?

Ferrara: I don't know, but why put a bum name on it? Why not just not put one on?

Colon: I know it wasn't your longtime collaborator Nicholas St. John, obviously. Larry Cohen and Stuart Gordon—they're established names. And Dennis Paoli's scripted projects for Gordon, so it's not him. That leaves Raymond Cistheri, whose last screen credit was the film *Melinda* back in 1972.

Ferrara: Who knows. The bottom line is, I never met any of those guys and wouldn't know 'em if I fell over 'em. I think one of 'em came around at the end when we had one of the advance screenings and was sitting there with one of the fuckin' Warner Bros. executives and he's like, y'know, smarter than a fucking kitty cat and put his two cents in. He's there at the fucking screening at that point and he's fighting for some dumb thing he wrote.

Colon: By now it's too late.

Ferrara: It's *not* too late. If you got a problem with the film, talk to me in private. Don't talk about it in front of the executives. But he was one of these guys running up to the executives because he knew he might—y'know what I'm sayin'? Just an asshole. I wanted to say to him, That's my film, don't be fucking things up.

Colon: Was there a whole lot of resemblance to the first draft?

Ferrara: Are you kiddin' me? They were into the idea that the Martians were vegetables, y'know what I mean? But they were pods! I never understood where the vegetable routine came from.

Colon: I remember reading that they wanted to make even their insides vegetable matter.

Ferrara: Yeah, I mean this is ludicrous, a total misunderstanding. . . . But I guess they didn't give a shit. The original idea is that they totally duplicated whatever you were—they weren't vegetables on the inside, they were you. But these guys had somebody cutting them open with a letter opener and, y'know, stupid shit exploding out of them. I mean, *do you know how stupid that is?*

Colon: Did the studio like that?

Ferrara: I guess so. I mean, the studio, they were weird. There was the producer Robert H. Solo and there was a hotshot young [production] executive named Lance

Young and he was the executive regime's model. They were muscling him out, so it was a period of transition. Young was a closet writer-director anyway—he went on to write and direct his own movie, *Bliss* (1997).

Colon: Was there any interference on *Body Snatchers* by studio heads?

Ferrara: They were there. Dede Allen was one of their editors. At least the person they had tampering with the film was solid. I mean, Dede's a two-time Oscar-nominated editor. She cut *Bonnie and Clyde* (1967), *Dog Day Afternoon* (1975), and *Reds* (1981). But nobody, *nobody* ever wants someone screwing around with his film. But I knew when I got involved that I didn't have final cut. I knew that. I didn't have the juice at the time to demand it, and I still took the film, so I'm not gonna be fuckin' vicious about it. I knew what I was getting. It wasn't as bad as it could have been, and then at the same time somebody changes one fucking shot and it's hard. But I've had it worse having final cut, believe it or not. In other words, when people are in your face twenty-four hours a day, seven days a week—which the studio is when you're making that type of film—I don't care whether you have final cut or not, if somebody's sayin': "That shot's no good, that shot's no good, that shot's no good, that shot's no good, that shot's no good"—y'know what I mean? You could have final cut and after a while you're gonna be thinking, jeez, maybe that shot's no good.

Colon: You're going to doubt, right?

Ferrara: It's not just that, it's all kinds of things. Because when we do a film where we have total control, where I write the checks, it's different. But if somebody else has control—in a way I had more freedom not having final cut at Warners. It's ironic. They are very aware of their reputation as a studio. They were conscious of that. You see, they don't want it getting out that Warners fucks over directors. They have to be very careful, or word will spread and the directors they want they're not going to be able to get. If they want Oliver Stone they won't be able to get him if he thinks they're going to ruin his film. And another plus for the studio is if a film's a failure, you as the director carry the blame, not them. They don't want some director pointing a finger at them and saying, "The studio made me do that." Take for instance, even though they didn't want Gabrielle Anwar for *Body Snatchers,* they didn't stop me from casting her either. This way if the film's a bust, they can blame me.

Colon: Did you lose anything from *Body Snatchers* that you still regret?

Ferrara: That's hard to say. I dig the film. I'll stand behind the film as it is. There's one cut that I fuckin' can't stand, but—

Colon: Which one was that? Do you want to say?

Ferrara: I don't remember. But I'll tell you one thing, that film was in competition at Cannes, despite what Warners eventually did with it.

Colon: Apart from the body snatcher's piercing wail—

Ferrara: That was Solo. It came from the second film, which he also produced.

Colon: —was there any attempt to apply continuity or compatibility with the other two films?

Ferrara: We stole everything that wasn't nailed down.

Colon: Would you call *Body Snatchers* a remake, a sequel, or something else?

Ferrara: It was another interpretation of someone's novella, the third interpretation.

Colon: I know you like the first film, except for the tampering. . . . How about the Philip Kaufman remake—did you enjoy his interpretation?

Ferrara: It took me a long time to appreciate the second one.

Colon: How long?

Ferrara: It took me a *longer* time to appreciate the second, y'know what I'm saying? Then I saw where they were comin' from. I thought, maybe if I see it enough I'll dig it. The thing is, Siegel's is a tough film to top, y'know what I mean? And again, I just didn't quite get Kaufman's at first. I saw both of them a lot of times. The second—it took me a while to get into the groove of it. So I feel I just can't talk about that one like I can the first one. I thought I understood the first one better, that's all. I'm not sayin' one is better than the other.

Colon: Was the chance to work with state-of-the-art special effects on a science fiction film a lure for you?

Ferrara: We used Tom Burman, the same guy they used for the second film. I didn't want any of that morphing.

Colon: You could have, but you chose not to?

Ferrara: At $18 million, we didn't have the budget to compete with $70–80 million effects films, so we didn't try. We didn't have the budget of *Twister*, so we kept things simple—reverse motion, and just Burman's work. The guy, he's like the rest of us, know what I mean? He fucks up as much as he doesn't, but he can knock you out when he hits it. Besides, I don't go for postproduction effects. I'm a what-you-see-is-what-you-get kind of guy anyway. I don't want to wait two years later to see what's up on screen.

Colon: Did you tell Burman to do anything different than he did on the second film?

Ferrara: What we did different was work with Bojan Bazelli. So, y'know, we had a great cinematographer. I respect him. That movie was pure CinemaScope, not thirty-five millimeter blown up. How often do you see that?

Colon: Stuart Gordon's script was supposedly significantly more graphic in nature.

Ferrara: How can a draft be graphic? It's words on paper. His was ridiculous. Somebody gets cut and all of a sudden, fuckin' spinach pops out. How can that be scary? It's ludicrous.

Colon: I guess that's considered graphic.

Ferrara: Graphic? Spinach poppin' out of people. How the fuck graphic is that? Who are they?! Popeye?! Get the fuck out of here! I mean, the whole thing with these types of films is to make them play as if they can happen. I mean, whatever anybody says, the fuckin' movie I made, *that* could happen. It's a very scary movie, if I do say so myself. I don't mind saying that because I'm not the only one who made it, y'know what I'm sayin'? I didn't write it, I didn't shoot it, I didn't do the effects and I didn't act in it. What I'm tryin' to say, when I watch that film, it's not cinemafantastique, y'know what I mean? It's like, oh man, why not? I mean, if you have any imagination for otherworldly events, why is that not a possibility?

Colon: Maybe because it was restrained, it seemed very plausible for the kind of scenario it was. . . .

Ferrara: Sure is, man. I mean, the first one was like the fuckin' *Bicycle Thief*, y'dig what I'm sayin'? The black-and-white, the way they acted and all that stuff. If it wasn't for the ill-suited music—that wasn't Siegel's thing, man. That was never there. Forget it, man. I mean, it's too fuckin' bad there's not a version of it somebody could put together—

Colon: A director's cut?

Ferrara: Yeah, maybe I'll do it. That'd be a presumptuous thing to do. The director's cut of Don Siegel's movie, by Abel Ferrara. Why not? I should. We have all the reasons to. Take the front and back off, and dump all that inappropriate music.

Colon: *Body Snatchers*—they envisioned it as a franchise.

Ferrara: But we ended it [both laugh]! We put a stop to that!

Colon: Would you ever direct another one if you were asked, and what direction would you go?

Ferrara: I'd try to do the whole story.

Colon: *Body Snatchers* didn't screen well, like a lot of genre films don't.

Ferrara: Right.

Colon: But tell me, do you ever go by test screenings?

Ferrara: I'll try and get something from it, but not the way they would. Anytime you got a film in front of the audience, you should learn something.

Colon: Next up for you is *New Rose Hotel,* which you're in production for. Are you a fan of William Gibson?

Ferrara: I am now.

Colon: What did you feel about *Johnny Mnemonic?*

Ferrara: I didn't see it.

Colon: Are there any future plans to return to your other political science fiction project, *Birds of Prey?*

Ferrara: I don't want to talk about *Birds of Prey.* It's a film I've wanted to make for a long time. Twenty years and the idea's still viable and original.

Colon: Is that your script?

Ferrara: It's Nicky's [St. John].

Colon: Mainly you work in the crime genre. Is science fiction a favorite genre of yours?

Ferrara: I dug a lot of it when I was a kid. It's like nostalgia. I remember seeing *The Blob* with my father and him falling asleep in the theater, and me not waking him up till I saw it twice. I got my ass kicked for that one.

THE UNSEEN *BODY SNATCHERS*

Anthony Timpone

AS JUST ABOUT ANY FILMMAKER WORKING IN THE movies today can tell you, it's a miracle that any film gets made under the labyrinthine, bureaucratic Hollywood system. Endless corporate meetings, the fitful development process, mutating screenplays, etc., are enough to make one reconsider that job offer from McDonald's.

Body Snatchers, producer Robert H. Solo's second redux of the Jack Finney novel, was no exception. The screenplay went through at least twenty drafts and six scripters before Warner Bros. greenlit the film for production in the fall of 1991. One of the credited screenwriters, cult director Stuart Gordon (best known for the shock sleepers *Re-Animator, From Beyond, Dolls* and *The Pit and the Pendulum*), was also hired to direct the film. But frustrated by the development quagmire, Gordon jumped ship to pilot 1993's futuristic actioner *Fortress* instead.

The Chicago-born Gordon and his longtime writing partner Dennis Paoli took *Body Snatchers* through four drafts before Gordon handed the reins over to controversial director Abel Ferrara *(Bad Lieutenant),* who then brought in his writing buddy, Nicholas St. John, to take a few more whacks at the script. (The final film is credited to Gordon and Paoli and St. John, from a story by Larry Cohen and Raymond Cistheri.) After all the start-up delays, *Body Snatchers* suffered further indignities when dissatisfied distributor Warner Bros. shelved the sequel/remake for nearly two years, only giving the decently reviewed film a marginal theatrical release in the spring of 1994.

In the following interview, Gordon discusses *Body Snatchers*'s troubled birth and delivery, and reveals some surprising differences between his and Paoli's initial take on the project and what ultimately emerged.

Anthony Timpone: What guidelines did Robert Solo give you when he hired you to direct and cowrite *Body Snatchers*?

Stuart Gordon: He asked me to come in so we could pitch an idea. He'd sent me the script they had been working on, which Larry Cohen had written. What they were trying to do was to make it a sequel to the seventies movie. The main idea was to make it more youth-oriented and have the characters be younger. Larry's version is all about these teenagers, kids, people in their early twenties. The army base was not in it until the last act of the story. Originally it was my idea to make it about a family, but I felt that we didn't care enough about the kids [in Cohen's version]. It was more like a *Halloween* kind of thing going on, where the kids are getting bumped off one by one. I felt that it would be more upsetting with a family being taken over one at a time, the idea being that we wouldn't be sure who the protagonist was for a little while, and it would turn out to be the teenage daughter.

In the story setup, the characters are based on my family, right down to their names. My wife's name is Carolyn, and Marti, the daughter, is based on my daughter Suzanna. The reason we called her Marti was because when I brought Dennis Paoli in to write it with me, we were both envisioning Martha Plimpton in the role, so we named the character after her. As it turned out, the producers thought that she was too old by the time the movie finally would be cast, so we got Gabrielle Anwar, who I thought was great.

What we were trying to do was bring back the movie as a franchise, which Warner Bros. wanted. With *Body Snatchers,* Bob Solo had brought up the idea of making several movies, and mine could be part one. The ending of our movie had the trucks being sent out with the pods to all the various military bases, but they're also being sent to Washington, D.C. The last shot in our script was of the trucks driving down Pennsylvania Boulevard. And one of the things Bob Solo and I talked about was the next movie involving the president of the United States, the idea of the government being taken over by pods. That was where the next *Body Snatchers* movie was going, almost like Romero's *Living Dead* movies, that the whole world was going to be eventually taken over by pod people.

Timpone: How much of Cohen's original script wound up in the final film?

Gordon: Not much, really. The idea of the army base was the main idea that survived, which is really the last third of the story in Larry's version. Most of the story took place in this town. Our first draft actually took place in the town. In the second draft, Bob Solo and the studio suggested the idea that the whole thing should take place at the army base.

Originally, in our version, we had the town being taken over by fundamentalists. There was this whole church thing going on, the born-again thing. When they were taken over by body snatchers, they were born again in a way. But we sided to the idea that maybe the army base was something we hadn't seen before. While we were working on it, the studio realized that it had been so long since the seventies movie that the idea of this being a sequel to that one didn't make any sense. So instead, they decided that maybe it should be thought of as a whole new version of *Invasion of the Body Snatchers*.

Timpone: So at first it was pitched as a sequel, and then it was decided to make it more of a remake. The completed film is stuck somewhere in between.

Gordon: Yeah, it was. It was funny, because we borrowed things from both the first two movies. Some of the ideas, like the pod scream from the second film, we incorporated into ours. We also had things that got cut out of the film. I was originally supposed to direct the film, but then we were prepping the picture for so long, doing rewrites, in development hell and so forth, and I was offered *Fortress*. So I went off to do that instead. They got Abel Ferrara to come in, and he dropped a few of the things that we had developed.

When we were brought on, we were asked to try to make the thing scarier and more explicit than the earlier films. And one of the ideas that we came up with was the thought that the body snatchers, the pod people, look like human beings on the outside, but inside they're nothing like human beings. They are sort of mimicking the look of a human being, which was a departure from the original story. The original story idea is that they take over humans molecule by molecule in their duplication. We got into this idea that inside they're like a plant and that their organs work unlike human organs and that, like a plant, their ability to think is cellular, rather than them having a brain and a nervous system and so forth. And so if you were to chop the head off these pod people, for example, they could still function. So we did a lot of bits like that. There's one sequence in [our script] where the pod people are chasing after them and they go into a garage, and the heroes begin using tools in the garage to try to defend themselves. Things like garden shears and spades, chopping off their fingers, which doesn't seem to have any effect on them. Shooting them has no effect either, and finally Marti ends up grabbing a sprayer that's got some weed killer in it and sprays them with it. They start to dissolve with the weed killer, which led to the finale where they drop a defoliant, Agent Orange, on the plant people to kill them. That was a concept that we played with, and we even had Berni Wrightson do some illustrations to show how this would work, which looked pretty incredible, drawings of them dissolving and their insides being all over, looking like an eggplant or something.

Timpone: Why do you think that material was cut from subsequent drafts of the film?

Gordon: It happened when Abel came on. He wanted to stick more closely to the original concept and book, which was that they were completely duplicate human beings. They dispensed with it, although there were still elements of it at the end of the movie. They still drop and spray the defoliant on them, and they do dissolve, which is kind of unexplained.

Timpone: Were there any other graphic moments in your script that never made it into the film?

Gordon: Well, there was a cut sequence that I liked a lot that was actually from Larry Cohen's draft that we put into the beginning of our script. This guy is watching these bulldozers pushing thousands of what's left of the bodies into a big pit, and then covering the pit up in this massive burial scene. They see him and he's running, and these big earth movers are chasing after him, trying to push him into the hole as well. And [in the completed film] that soldier is the one who's in the gas station who grabs Marti; he's hysterical, freaking out. We had envisioned it being almost like a pretitle sequence. It could have been a very effective scene.

Timpone: Reportedly, United Artists, the distributor of the 1978 film, was upset that Warner Bros. had appropriated elements from their film for an unauthorized "sequel," the pod people scream being an example. Do you know anything about that?

Gordon: No. We were encouraged to use the scream. The garbage truck idea was in some of the drafts that we did, the idea of the aliens taking over the bodies and throwing them in the garbage truck, which is in the second film. So we were told by Bob Solo that anything he had developed in his version we could use in this one, that it was a sequel. Dennis Paoli used to kid around that we were making a sequel to a remake [laughs].

Timpone: At some point, Stephen King was approached to do a rewrite. Did you have discussions with him?

Gordon: Actually, I never had any discussions, but it was our idea. What happened was typical studio fashion. We had done about three or four drafts of the script. They said, "We'd like to bring in a new writer to rewrite it." So they asked us who we would suggest. We wanted to shoot high and we said Stephen King, so they sent him the script and got a wonderful letter back from him which I've saved, which said, "I really was interested in doing this, but I read the script and there's an old adage, 'If it ain't broke, don't fix it.' This script is great and you should just shoot it. You don't need me." But the studio didn't agree with him, apparently, so they brought in a couple more writers to do drafts.

Timpone: Next at bat was writer Nevin Schreiner. Did you collaborate with him directly?

Gordon: Yeah, I did.

Timpone: He replaced Dennis at that point?

Gordon: Yeah, he did. His stuff didn't change all that much.

Timpone: Was Schreiner someone that Solo brought in or was it Warner Bros.?

Gordon: No, actually what happened was weird. At this point, I was still the director of the film, so I was interviewing other writers. I interviewed several people, and thought that he had the best take on where to go from there.

Timpone: What impressed you about his take?

Gordon: He had a good feeling about the characters. What we wanted to do was try to make the characters as real as we could, and he had a good concept. I liked his dialogue and I liked the fact that he could flesh them out a little bit more. And he was not into doing a total overhaul. The thing that I was afraid of was, when you bring in new writers, they always want to make it their own. They end up throwing out everything that you've done, and it starts over again. I did not want to do that. I liked the way we had developed it, we'd done fresh work on it and he fine-tuned what we did without any major overhaul. When Abel Ferrara replaced me as director, he brought in Nicholas St. John. There were several changes that they did, the main one being the changing of the pod people's physiology. But he also changed the character of the pilot.

Timpone: The Billy Wirth character?

Gordon: Yeah. In our version—which I liked better, actually—he was a guy who pretended to be a pilot in order to pick up girls, and it turns out that he is actually in the helicopter ground crew. And in the climactic sequence, when he's got to make the escape and he gets into the helicopter, he doesn't know how to fly one! He's able to escape because he has been working around them and knows what the various things do, but he's never actually flown one before. So it was a much scarier thing. You've got this guy trying to take off in a helicopter who doesn't know how to fly. And you end up with the question of whether he's gonna be able to land it, if he's going to land it. But they decided at some point, I don't know whose decision it was, to make him more of a hero, a big hero from Kuwait, and references to him being an ace helicopter pilot.

Timpone: Coming from the independent scene, what was it like working for a major studio on *Body Snatchers?*

Gordon: Well, there were a lot of committee discussions, and that was the thing that got to be very frustrating, because different people have different thoughts. The thing about studios sometimes is that whatever movie happens to be hot that particular week, they want you to make your movie like that. I remember at one point having a discussion with an executive who had just seen *Terminator 2*. There's that whole sequence where Linda Hamilton is shooting from the back of a truck, and he thought we should have a scene like that in our movie. But looking back at the whole thing, the people were all very supportive of the project. There was a sense that everybody really wanted to make it happen and make it good. A lot of times on a studio film, you get involved with people with different agendas, and on *Body Snatchers* everyone was for it. But studios are slow-moving entities. That was the thing that just got to me. If this had been a low-budget movie, we would have had it shot and out in theaters in a year, and with the studio it just ended up taking at least two and a half years. The process is mind-boggling.

Timpone: Were you a fan of the '56 and '78 films?

Gordon: Yeah, yeah. As a matter of fact, the Don Siegel version is still the best. The energy in that movie is incredible. I like the second one, although I don't think it holds up as well. We watched both movies again while we were working on ours, and the one in the fifties seemed much fresher, much more involving. But [director] Phil Kaufman was very much a child of the seventies, so it stays there.

It's funny, when I was working on *Body Snatchers* I ran into Kevin McCarthy. When I told him I was working on the third *Body Snatchers*, he said, "I have to be in it," because he had been in both of the first two films. In our version, the doctor was kind of an older man, and we thought that he'd be great to play the doctor.

Timpone: Which character is that in Ferrara's film? Major Collins?

Gordon: Yeah, the character that Forest Whitaker plays.

Timpone: That would have been a totally different character then.

Gordon: Yeah, but I liked what Forest Whitaker did a lot; he was great in the movie. Abel did a terrific job with it, and the performances he got were sensational. And I actually would go so far and say it is Abel's best movie.

Timpone: What do you think were some of the strengths of the first two adaptations?

Gordon: Well there's something kind of primal and nightmarish about the first film, and the energy is incredible. It really builds to a very powerful conclusion, and it's one of those few movies that has such a bleak ending; it's so downbeat and terrifying. The version in the seventies did much more with the special effects; they had gone further to show how the body-snatching process was accomplished. That was one of the greatest strengths of the '78 film, the wispy things connecting the pod to the person, showing you how it happens. In the first version you didn't see any of that. All you saw of what the person became was when they find this half-formed pod person in the basement. And in the second version they show you the whole process, and how it's accomplished. At the time EST was very big, and that pop psychology thing was going on. The first movie was really about the Cold War and the fear of communists being among us, some of our friends being not really who they say they are and so forth. The second movie was much more in terms of people being taken over by cults like the Moonies. But the thing I got into that was in both movies was the issue of conformity. That you are made to be like everybody else. That's what the pod people are. One of the things that you wrestle with in this is, "What is so terrible about being taken and being made into a pod person? You're still you." But what's missing is those things about you that make you an individual. There's a collective mind that connects them all. What we got into is that, in a sense, the reason that the teenager works as the heroine in the third one is because she's rebellious. What's considered to be her bad trait saves her. Which was what we were going for—the fact that she is the rebel, that she's a nonconformist, she's not really part of her family, that she's not going along with the program, is what makes her able to survive.

Timpone: What were the main elements that you wanted to bring to your take from the previous sources, Finney's book and the films?

Gordon: Well, the whole thing is a big paranoid fantasy, and I love how each begins in a very subtle, insidious way. I love the way it starts out with people coming into the doctor saying, "Oh, my uncle isn't my uncle. My father doesn't seem like my father; there's something wrong." It kind of underlined the delusional paranoia, which is what the doctor thinks is going on at first. There's some sort of a mass hysteria growing in town. When the first movie came out, it tied in with the McCarthy hearings during the Cold War—is my neighbor a communist? People are turning in their family members and so forth. That is the core of what all the *Body Snatchers* are about. It's not a monster movie, in that these guys aren't turning into vampires, or sucking your blood or anything. They go about their business as usual. But they're not really who they are. They're not human. What I really like about it is that it is a very subtle fear.

Timpone: Did you go back to Finney's book when you began this?

Gordon: Oh yes, absolutely. We read the book and as a matter of fact, the title of the third movie is the title of the book, *Body Snatchers*. We originally called our script *Body Snatchers: The Harvest*.

Timpone: Of the three films, which do you think captures Finney's themes the best?

Gordon: I've got to say the first movie. The first film is really Finney's book. It's remarkably close. Although Finney's book actually has a happy ending. The pods start lifting off and floating away; they leave the Earth at the end of the book. When the hero realizes what's going on and figures out how to destroy them, the pods retreat, where in Siegel's movie he gave it a much darker ending. The second one went even further with the ending than Siegel originally intended.

Timpone: You had come up with different endings when you were drafting your script, right?

Gordon: We did, yeah. One of the things the studio did, which I think was done against Abel's wishes too, was that they added this whole voice-over thing in the movie. Which I didn't want—I hate those things, first of all. We wanted the audience not to know who the hero of the movie was initially. They think the hero is going to be the dad, the Terry Kinney part.

Timpone: With the voice-over, you know from the start that the heroine will somehow survive.

Gordon: Right, that's what bothered me the most about it, because it lets you know she's gonna make it. So the voice-over takes away a lot of the tension in the movie. That was one of the notes we got; they wanted it to be clear that this was Marti's movie. I like it better when you don't know. We used *Alien* as a model, where you think the hero of the movie is Tom Skerritt, and then he gets wiped out halfway through. At the end, it's Sigourney Weaver who emerges as the hero of the film. So we were going with similar thinking. But when they started testing the film, it wasn't testing well, so they ended up, out of desperation, using the voice-over.

Timpone: Did you consider having a downbeat ending?

Gordon: Well, we wanted to actually leave it open, and in a way the movie's ending is close to what we had, though we went even further. In some of our endings, when they landed it turned out that where they went ended up being taken over by pod people. So they were tossed out of the frying pan into the fire. But I think we got to an ambiguous ending, where we're not sure who these people are and where they flew to at the end.

Timpone: When Ferrara came on board with Nicholas St. John, he said he wanted to "fix" problems in the third act of your script. How would you respond to that?

Gordon: Well, I guess what he meant was that he did not want to go the way we were going, which was the whole idea of this sort of different internal working system for the pod people.

Timpone: At any point, did Solo ask you to write another sequel or promise you another film as a consolation prize, especially after Ferrara replaced you?

Gordon: No, we never really got into anything like that, but if the thing had succeeded, there would have been another movie. I have remained friends with Bob Solo; he's a terrific guy. And he had a real hard time getting the movie out, because it did not test well. Warner Bros. got scared of it and was going to dump it. They would not even risk [a theatrical release]. It was Abel who got it shown at the Cannes Film Festival, just on his own, which forced Warner Bros. to actually release the movie.

Timpone: How much of yours and Paoli's script was retained in the completed film after St. John took over?

Gordon: It's funny. Almost beat for beat it's there, with the exceptions of the things we talked about, in terms of changing the character of Billy Wirth. But all the events that are happening are basically scene for scene the same as our script. Again, in typical screenwriter fashion, the dialogue was all changed; a lot of it is almost like paraphrasing what we had done. In the beginning of Abel's movie, he has them singing a song about going to eat worms. In our version we had them playing a game called "Who am I," which is this kid's game where you have to give clues about somebody, and then you have to guess who it is. The scene [in the final film] is basically the same scene, with them driving in the car and playing a game and the character of Marti excluding herself from it all, listening to her Walkman while all this is going on. So I think the whole movie is like that. If you were to put the two scripts side by side, the structure would pretty much be the same.

Timpone: Is there anything that St. John and Ferrara added that you especially liked?

Gordon: The bit with the truth game and the fingers was not in our script, which I thought was a real nice bit, I liked that. But I think our idea of having the relationship with the pilot who's not a pilot was more interesting than him being this big jock war hero character. But they wanted him to be cooler. I thought he was more funny if he was more vulnerable. Some of the things that were added improved it and some of the things didn't.

Timpone: At least six writers worked on *Body Snatchers;* did it ever wind up going to Writer's Guild arbitration?

Gordon: Oh yeah, it did. In this kind of situation they ended up giving everybody a piece of it, including W. D. Richter, who wrote the version in the seventies, but who had nothing to do with ours. But the Writer's Guild's arbitration manual says that in order to be credited, your work has to reflect 60 percent of the script. Ours had more in common with Finney's book than with the seventies remake.

Timpone: Why do you think Warner Bros. dumped the film?

Gordon: When you look at Warner's history, they have not done very many horror films, and the ones they have done have been these big-studio kind of things. They're not really scary. The studio is dependent upon marketing, test scores, and so forth, and when they got the test score on *Body Snatchers,* at that point they said, "Let's forget this." And what they forgot is that horror films notoriously test low. A lot of times when you get a test audience in there, you're not getting people who would go out and buy a ticket to this thing. You're getting people who don't like horror films or science fiction, so the test scores reflect that. Plus *Body Snatchers* was very disturbing.

It's not your typical Hollywood finale where everything looks real great at the end. And that certainly was disturbing to people and made it test badly. At that point, Warners felt it would not be a big crowd-pleaser and wanted to move on. They were going to just release it direct to video. Then Abel, bless his heart, got it official entry at the Cannes Festival, where it got really good reviews and a French theatrical release. Warner Bros. felt silly and decided to release it, but by that point they just gave it a tokenistic release, almost as an art film. They gave it a platform release, put it out in a few theaters in the big cities. It did pretty well, but they never really gave it the push that it needed. Besides being Abel's best work, it's also Gabrielle Anwar's best movie. And if Warner Bros. had gotten behind the film, they could have made her into a major star.

Timpone: Do you think the film would have been more successful commercially if you had directed it and gone with your more graphic horror approach?

Gordon: I would honestly say no. Abel did a really good job with it; the movie was scary. Having that stuff maybe would have added more gross-out potential, but I don't think it would have been the difference between making or breaking the film. It really had to do with the studio not marketing it. That's really what killed the movie.

Timpone: Overall, would you say you're proud of your association with the film?

Gordon: Yeah, I'm very proud and I'm even prouder of being part of the *Body Snatcher* legacy. Going back to the book and the fifties movie, it's a true classic. To have the opportunity to be part of that is a great thing, and so I'm very happy that I was involved and very happy with the movie that resulted.

Timpone: Do you think these themes will be just as resonant in the twenty-first century as they are today?

Gordon: Oh yeah, absolutely, and I think that it's still possible that, knowing Bob Solo, there will be another *Body Snatchers* movie. Maybe it will be the one where the pod people take over Washington.

WILL THE REAL FINALE PLEASE TAKE A BOW?

Tom Piccirilli

"MANY HAD LOST, BUT SOME OF US WHO HAD NOT been caught and trapped without a chance had fought implacably, and a fragment of a wartime speech moved through my mind: *we shall fight them in the field, and in the streets, we shall fight in the hills; we shall never surrender*. True then for one people, it was true for the whole human race, and now I thought that nothing in the whole vast universe could ever defeat us."

So states the heroic Dr. Miles Bennell at the conclusion of Jack Finney's novel *The Body Snatchers* (Award Books, 1965), after the pods themselves desert the earth in a mass exodus to float once again against the nighttime sky, leaving a "fierce and inhospitable planet." It is quite possibly one of the most overconfident, self-assured, and expectant declarations ever made in so horrifying a novel of anxiety and personal dread. After Bennell finally finds his way to the acres of pod-strewn fields, where they lie "evil and motionless" at his feet, he and his love Becky manage to spill drums of gasoline and set the fields afire.

At first there is no reaction from the overtaken friends and citizens of Mill Valley, who quickly surround the hunted pair and simply stare without any curiosity, anger, or emotion at all. Within moments, though, Miles and Becky watch as the pods lift off for unknown worlds, the concept being that any fight that went on for a lengthy duration would be more than enough to drive away these incredibly adaptive extraterrestrial survivors from our planet. Such a sudden twist of fortuitous developments doesn't quite hold together for those of us encompassed by the finely wrought atmosphere of pure maddening fear created beforehand.

The disturbing theme of the novel was open to diverse interpretations, including issues of paranoia toward communism or the sweeping McCarthyism of the fifties, and yet despite the broiling political pit the world was facing in that era, of all versions of *The Body Snatchers* this is clearly the most optimistic conclusion where the fate of the human race is concerned. Even the "revised and updated" edition of the novel in 1978—written to coincide with the release of Philip Kaufman's movie version—the tale remains one of heartening promise and hopefulness in the midst of a mind-numbing whirlwind of alarm.

Don Siegel's 1956 classic adaptation, though, manages to deepen the horror we're left to endure afterward, if only by one additional frightening element. Kevin McCarthy, as Miles Bennell, squeezes every possible drop of shock and apprehension from his outstanding performance, his crisis and distress escalating moment to moment. The viewer is treated to the wraparound prologue/epilogue where we find the distraught and seemingly psychotic Miles relating his nightmarish tale to doctors in the emergency room. Although the doctors comment that he is "mad as a March hare," Miles is soon vindicated. His story is verified when a Greyhound bus and a truck coming out of Santa Mira (replacing Mill Valley) collide, and there's mention that the truck driver has to be dug out from under "great big seed pods." Soon law enforcement and government agencies promise to take control of the invading aliens by blocking highways.

The single most startling moment of the film might very well be where Becky is "snatched" in a scene of raw terror, veering from the original happy ending of the novel. After escaping into a mine, and barely evading the swarming pod folk, Miles lifts and carries his fatigued love through the tunnel, leaving her for a minute to check if the coast is clear. In a scene that has gone down in the history of horror filmdom as one of the most gripping ever, he kisses Becky and slowly draws back in revulsion from her cold, unresponsive lips, realizing that she's fallen asleep and been overtaken. Despite the fact that the situation is somewhat loosely threaded (Becky apparently falls asleep and is somehow "possessed" by the pod swarm mind, rather than actually being grown from a pod) there is a fundamentally evocative and genuinely disturbing realization that causes real shudders in the viewer.

By 1978, however, Philip Kaufman had decided to follow variations of themes from its predecessor, creating not so much a remake of the original film as an elaboration of issue and milieu. Set in San Francisco now, Donald Sutherland, starring as "Matthew" Bennell, is a public health inspector ably assisted by Brooke Adams as Elizabeth. When the city becomes covered in what appear to be spiderwebs, Adams is the first to notice strange behavior in people, beginning with her boyfriend, who becomes distant and secretive.

A real touch of wit comes from one of the earliest sequences when Kevin McCarthy makes a cameo as a fleeing madman chased by a mob who is almost run over by Bennell. This forms a resonant connection to the first film that is picked up later at certain other opportune points, like the play on the Siegel version when Becky screams at the sight of a dog in danger, thus showing emotion and exposing herself as an unsnatched human. Here, Brooke Adams again screams at the sight of a dog, and what a creature it is—a mutant, vagrant-faced canine created by a faulty pod. Rather than take himself completely seriously as either a horror aficionado or a social satirist, Kaufman ably tinkered with the film to poke fun at New Age claptrap that was all the rage in San Francisco at the time. No longer are we given to underpinnings of communism or government entanglement, but instead are held up to witness our own foibles and absurdity and held accountable for mind-numbing conformity.

Here too is the introduction of "the screech," that horrifying inhuman sound that pod people make to alert their fellow pods that a human still walks among them. This singular special sound effect—with face contorted into a leering mask, finger outstretched and pointed in accusation, with that hideous noise prevailing—makes for the most powerful ending of any film version. As Matthew and Elizabeth reach the well-guarded fields, again our heroine falls prey to exhaustion, and her body literally turns to dust in Matthew's arms as he sobs uncontrollably and watches in complete horror as she collapses and disintegrates.

It's also notable that this is the only version where our hero eventually loses his identity, becomes changed over, and follows his love to emotionless pod-dom. (If the lovers are reunited may this, in fact, be a sort of contented conclusion?) This allows for the awful and memorable last moment of the film where Matthew is approached by Veronica Cartright—a friend previously thought to have been "snatched" but who's somehow managed to escape—and leaves us with the haunting image of Matthew in full screech, pointing her out with that ghastly noise arising, calling forth his pod brethren.

Transposing political viewpoints from the original film, where the police and military promise to eradicate the alien infestation, Abel Ferrara's *Body Snatchers* takes place on a military base itself, the microcosms shifting full circle. No longer is the United States government our ultimate benefactor and savior of freedom and generations to come—now the infestation ironically *begins* with those who are to be our protectors.

For this 1993 effort we have the dutiful Environment Protection Agency official and his family encountering the pods in a southern military base. The fact that the setting is so isolated—shades of the secluded Mill Valley—is both a help and a hindrance to the ambiance generated. We're not given to the worldwide panic or nationwide (or at least citywide) frenzy, yet the detached environment shows us the step by step assimilation, imperturbable and coldly logical, the pods like the soldiers themselves performing their duty for God and country.

However, the concept of alienated teen is used to great benefit. After being put through paranoia hell—put so succinctly by Meg Tilly as the overtaken, creepy mother figure with terrifying clear enunciation: "Where you gonna go, where you gonna hide, when there's nobody . . . left . . . like you?"—Gabrielle Anwar as the feisty daughter, and her soldier-protector boyfriend, steal a helicopter and blow up the base and trucks leaving for all around the country.

The chopper lands at an airport in Atlanta, which may or may not be crawling with more of our favorite pod people.

While the ultimate fate of humanity is left "up in the air" (pun fully intended), one more modern Hollywood element that Abel Ferrara put into his film is the introduction of high firepowered vengeance. We may be having our world overrun by alien plant life, but that doesn't mean we have to sit back and take it lightly. No small gas fires set in distant fields here; we haven't been inflating that defense budget for nothing. Ferrara relishes in showing missile after missile blasting pods, convoys of trucks, and all interloping aliens to kingdom come. This gratuitous violence at this point—a cathartic moment for everyone who wanted to see the malefactors get at least a part of their comeuppance—undermined the pure horrific nature of being powerless. Still, Ferrara's vision is updated enough for us to feel the shifting tide of the nineties era, from terrorized, cringing helplessness to a take-charge, take arms, Hollywood action mindset.

Though the novel *The Body Snatchers*—in all three of its forms, including its original serialization in *Collier's* magazine—and the following three movie adaptations are all certainly products of their eras and American cultural influences, the thread weaving through all variations of this story is one that is especially ironic and biting concerning the subject matter at hand: what it means to be human.

Photo from *Invasion of the Body Snatchers* courtesy of Republic Entertainment, Inc.

AN INTERVIEW WITH KEVIN MCCARTHY

John McCarty

KEVIN MCCARTHY HAS BEEN A FIXTURE OF AMERICA's theatrical landscape for over half a century.

The eldest of three brothers, Kevin was born February 15, 1914, in Seattle, Washington; the boys' sister was the eminent American writer Mary McCarthy (1912–1989). "Until the age of four and a half, I was evidently a fairly daring, mischievous and naughty little rascal, having fun cutting up, however

I could," he says of his early childhood. But all that ended when the infamous flu epidemic of worldwide proportions struck Seattle in the autumn of 1918.

"During the course of it, in the waning days of October, unaware probably that the damned thing had already laid its deadly hand on us all, our young parents were in the final hours of their long-planned decision to give up their idea of living in Seattle, after four or five difficult years, and move back to our dad's hometown. All Hallows' Eve of 1918 found the McCarthy family, the six of us, installed in Pullman cars of the Great Northern Railway as the train departed Seattle en route to Minneapolis, Roy's birthplace and family seat. But we must have been carrying the deadly infection even as the porters got us into our berths—for a few feverish and scary images from that journey are still a part of me; and I vividly recall the consternation among all the people on the platforms in the big iron railway station in Minneapolis as we were all brought off the train on stretchers. We were put into beds in our grandparents' house; but unknown to us little ones, our parents were gone, within a day or so of our arrival—just before the armistice of November 11, 1918, which brought an end to the Great War. In my head, even today, I can hear the sounds of *that* day: wild bells clanging, all across the town they rang, the clamorous noise of auto horns mingled with screaming voices and shreiking factory whistles. In some way in my childmind, on that frightening day, the pandemonium seemed to be acknowledging the strange disappearance of our parents. That perception is woven through all the bedlam images of that terrifying morning. Our mother, only twenty-eight, had already had the four of us, and possibly a miscarriage as well. Our father, ten years older at thirty-eight, had suffered from severe heart trouble for years. As we children were growing up, we used to "hear" how Roy and Tess were very romantic and loving people [he a charmer, she a saint], deeply attached to one another despite difficult circumstances. Mary and I used to be mystified by the memory that we were never directly told of their deaths but did recall that, at some indefinite distance from the event, we got the news they wouldn't be "coming back" to us because "they've gone to heaven" (one day apart, on November 6 and 7, 1918); on account of "the epidemic"; whatever that meant! I suppose it was around that time that our parents got added to our 'Now I lay me down to sleep' routine as we knelt beside our beds. "God Bless Mommy and Daddy and let the Perpetual Light shine on them. . . ."

"We survived—my brothers and sister and myself. But nobody knew what to do with us and the macabre mistake was made to place us in the hands of a middle-aged couple, Meyers and Margaret Shriver, childless relatives of our grandma. Suffice to say here, they should not have been given children to raise; much of this is recounted in my sister's book *Memories of a Catholic Girlhood* [Harcourt Brace, 1989]. When it was discovered how we were being treated, and we got released from the four years of confinement under their harsh custody, my sister was sent out to Seattle to be brought up by our maternal grandparents, and my younger brothers and I were placed in a Catholic boarding school."

Kevin candidly admits to being pretty much of a ne'er-do-well for a long time after those grade school and high school and even early college years. "I had the sense of not belonging and was chronically self-conscious, to boot. Yeah, I 'had the blues' as an ongoing condition," he says. "Oddly enough, I usually play fairly *outgoing*, dynamic characters on stage and screen. That must be due to the fact that I can dig into all that repressed (Irish?) feeling in me, that came about from my parents' vanishing from my life—without explanation, when I was just a squirt. There's a formative experience for you! When I think about it, I realize that many of the characters I've played are often passionate to the point of being almost overwrought. At the same time, of course, for the actor *those emotions must be contained*, that's for sure! If the guy seems to be going berserk, losing his head, let's say, the actor for damn sure can't be losing his or going off the deep end—because of the job that needs to be done; going 'bonkers' won't do—particularly if '*survival*' is at stake." That's certainly true of the character he plays in *Invasion of the Body Snatchers* [the 1956 science fiction classic that is his best-known film and which is the subject of this book-length tribute]. Since one of the subjects of the film is *the absence of emotion*, and *his role* is that of a *reasonably sensitive person* with a normal capacity for *a wide range of feelings*, [director] Don Siegel may have seen Mr. McCarthy as on-the-nose casting for the role of the protagonist, Dr. Miles Bennell.

By his own admission an undisciplined student during his early years, he struggled to make the grade at Georgetown University's School of Foreign Service, but failed and wound up at a YMCA at 9th and La Salle streets in Minneapolis. After our hero's misadventures in D.C., his uncle/guardian, Uncle Lou McCarthy, had had to boot his shiftless nephew Kevin out of his temporary digs in Lou's house. The next fifteen months (at the Y) were a negative adventure that plumbed the depths of Mr. McCarthy's low self-esteem. He was living on five-cent White Tower hamburgers and five-cent O'Henry bars. Either some kind of survival instinct or a guardian angel roused him to save himself. He seemed to perceive through the darkness of depression that the laggard person he had been, had to reform. There was no work; the Great Depression was gripping the country; he had no special gifts, physical or mental; he was too timid to be a thief or a con man. He had to equip himself somehow. He tried proving to himself that he was not totally inept. He enrolled in a couple of correspondence courses at the University of Minnesota (nine dollars each)—Psychology I and English II. In three months' time, he realized he wasn't the abject student he had always allowed himself to be—he got an A in Psych, a B in English II. Two months later, he cadged tuition money (twenty-six dollars) to become a full-time student at the U. of M. and got a working-his-way-thru-college-job at Pioneer Hall, the men's residence there. After two semesters, the guy had reformed his dilatory ways; the attention-deficit lad learned to focus or concentrate without benefit of Ritalin. Kevin made the Dean's List. A certain Larry Gates is standing by in the wings of this pageant, awaiting his cue in 1936, while Don Siegel may be feeling odd (or pod), premonitions in his psyche as he is working as film librarian and assistant cutter at Warner Bros. Studios in Burbank, California—preludes to his "directorial" prowess.

Kevin made his Broadway debut in 1938 in a couple of bit parts in Robert E. Sherwood's Pulitzer Prize-winning play, *Abe Lincoln in Illinois.* Since then, he has appeared on the New York stage in works as varied as Shakespeare's *Love's Labor's Lost;* Chekhov's

Three Sisters with Geraldine Page and *The Seagull* with Montgomery Clift; *Alone Together; Poor Murderer; Joan of Lorraine* with Ingrid Bergman; *Brecht on Brecht;* O'Neill's *Anna Christie; The Deep Blue Sea* with Margaret Sullivan; *Marching Song* with Brooke Hayward; *The Day the Money Stopped* with Richard Basehart; *Cactus Flower; Two for the Seesaw* with Anne Bancroft; Kurt Vonnegut Jr.'s *Happy Birthday, Wanda June* with Marsha Mason and Bill Hickey; Sean O'Casey's *Red Roses for Me* with E. G. Marshall; and *Advise and Consent* with Richard Kiley and Ed Begley. During the 1949–1950 theatrical season in London, he portrayed Biff, the tormented son of the tragic title character in Arthur Miller's classic *Death of a Salesman,* directed by Elia Kazan.

He is a founding member of New York's venerated Actor's Studio, in which he is still active. The studio has spawned such acting luminaries as Marlon Brando, Geraldine Page, Maureen Stapleton, Montgomery Clift, Eva Marie Saint, Karl Malden, Anne Jackson, Eli Wallach, James Dean, Paul Newman, Joanne Woodward, Richard Boone, Faye Dunaway, Robert DeNiro, Holly Hunter, Matthew Broderick, Julia Roberts, and many of the big, as well as not so big, names gracing the stage and screen today, including McCarthy himself.

His favorite recent stage experiences include A. R. Gurney's two-character play *Love Letters* (in which he first costarred with Sada Thompson, then later with his wife, Kate); David Mamet's *A Life in the Theatre;* and Sam Gallu's one-man show *Give 'Em Hell, Harry,* wherein Mr. McCarthy appears as America's thirty-third president, Harry S. Truman.

His work in films has been equally varied. It includes the 1951 film version of *Death of a Salesman,* for which he received an Academy Award nomination; John Huston's *The Misfits* (1961), which starred Clark Gable, Marilyn Monroe, and his old pal, Montgomery Clift; the thriller *The Prize* (1963) with Paul Newman, based on a novel by Irving Wallace; Gore Vidal's prescient political drama *The Best Man* (1964); Arthur Hailey's *Hotel* (1967); Robert Altman's *Buffalo Bill and the Indians* (1976); the underrated romantic comedy about backstage life as an actor in summer theater, *Those Lips, Those Eyes* (1980); *A Big Hand for the Little Lady* (1966); the horror film *The*

Howling (1981); the Steven Spielberg–produced *Twilight Zone—The Movie* (1983); *Innerspace* (1987); the Eddie Murphy comedy *The Distinguished Gentleman* (1992); Joe Dante's *Matinee* (1993); *Greedy* with Kirk Douglas and Phil Hartman; and, of course, *Invasion of the Body Snatchers* (1956), the film for which he is best remembered.

Kevin's television credits are no less extensive. He has guest starred or appeared as a regular on virtually all of the most popular TV series of the 1950s through the 1990s. Among them are Rod Serling's *The Twilight Zone; Mission: Impossible; The Man from U.N.C.L.E.; Honey West; Hawaii Five-O; The Wild, Wild West;* Harold Robbins's *The Survivors; Banacek; Flamingo Road; Murder, She Wrote; Matlock; Dynasty; The Colbys; China Beach; Head of the Class; Tales from the Crypt; Dream On;* and *Boston Common.* Forthcoming is *The Addams Family Reunion*, wherein our man teams up with the esteemed Estelle Harris. They will give the world their idea of Grandpa and Grandma Addams.

Given such a substantial body of work, which has played for so many years to so many different generations, perhaps the description "fixture" is neither strong nor suitable enough for Kevin McCarthy. Perhaps "legend" or "one of the acting profession's enduring and genuine *greats*" is more apt, especially when you hear him tell an anecdote or spin a story, as I have had the pleasure of doing during the course of this extensive interview conducted for this book.

He has the ability to bring you into the scene with him and make you feel the situation as he and/or the character he's playing does. It is an experience (for example, his recounting of Montgomery Clift's horrific, near-fatal automobile crash) which more than once left the hairs on this writer's neck standing on end due to the vivid, you-are-there, emotional power of his recollections and the quickness with which he slips himself, seemingly so effortlessly, into recounting them.

At a question-and-answer session before a live audience of fans in New Jersey, I saw him reduce his listeners to stunned silence while recounting an anecdote about a revival of Arthur Miller's play *All My Sons* in which Mr. McCarthy appeared, and how during a brush-up rehearsal Miller (directing) voiced his disagreement with Kevin's interpretation of the drama's climactic scene. "I played a guy who discovers that his industrialist father cut costs on a war materiels order, sacrificing the lives of a number of American soldiers for profit," he remembered to the audience. "Arthur felt I was too emotional in the scene where I confront my old man about this," he went on, illustrating for us how he had played the scene *before* Miller's comments and then how he went about it for the next performance *after* listening to Arthur's suggestions. One could have heard a pin drop in the room as he slipped into the scene and the character with such amazing swiftness and potency, then out again with equal speed and ease. Even before he could go on and finish the anecdote, the audience burst into applause.

Amusingly, I'm not sure Kevin himself knew why, so second-nature does this ability seem to be to the veteran actor—who, by the way, is also a very warm and wonderfully nice man to spend some time with.

John McCarty: Is it true that Larry Gates, one of the costars in *Invasion of the Body Snatchers,* was responsible for you becoming an actor?

Kevin McCarthy: Sure is! He's the one who got me on the stage. That goes back to 1936, when I was at the University of Minnesota. I was in dire shape, working my way through college at the men's dorm as a sort of desk clerk. Larry, too, was working *his* way through college, in the kitchen and dining room. He, a Speech major, was involved in the college drama society called the Masquers and one day he said, "Hey, Kev, you gotta do me a favor: come over to the Music Building after class tomorrow; I want you to meet an assistant prof in the drama department, who has a problem; he's directing Shakespeare's *Henry IV, Part One;* and there are *lots of men's parts*—but *more girls* than guys are coming to tryouts and they need the opposite." I told him I'd be useless; I was taking Shakespeare 101 and it was mostly Greek to me. "Doesn't matter! All you have to do is pick up the script and read a speech or two for the guy—the director." "Larry, you don't get it. I *can't figure out* the sentences—*or* what's going on in that Shakespeare stuff. That's my toughest course; I won't make any sense!" He said, "Making sense ain't necessary, Mac; ya talk loud, just talk *loud!* I dare you." Well, naturally, on his dare, I went over there. I *never* had a thought about acting, or becoming an actor; had probably seen no more than a couple of plays in the entire twenty-one years of my life. Well, at this prof's office I tried reading a speech or two—in my head it felt like noisy gobbledygook. Result? I was given a minor part: Sir Walter Blunt, (type casting?) . . . forty lines. Frankly, because of "the guy shortage," he would have given me a part if I'd have whispered, or palpitated in some way. But get this! A few days into rehearsals, one of the students playing a key part couldn't show up. By that time I had begun to make sense out of the dialogue and to figure out (sorta) what was going on. So, that day I grabbed the chance to "cover" for the absent actor whose mouth at that moment was open for his dentist. It was the part of Owen Glendower, a great Welsh chieftain who with Lord Mortimer of Scotland and Lord Harry "Hotspur" Percy, was conspiring to overthrow the English sovereign King Henry IV (1404 A.D.). I've probably always got a grin of pleasure on my face as I recall that scene wherein the Welshman Glendower is bragging, in a great roaring voice, about his "magical powers" to the hotheaded Lord Percy, "*I* can call Spirits from the vasty deep!" To which Hotspur tartly replied, "And *so can I—and so can any man,* but *will they come when you call them!*" (big laugh from the audience). The director exclaimed, "McCarthy! Why the devil didn't you read like that when you were auditioning? I would have given you a much more substantial part!" What an unforgettable moment for me: *realizing* that I *could do it! I could act!!* Oh my God! It was as if some huge and heavy millstone had suddenly slipped from the upper deck of my psyche and plunged away into the deep dark sea of my unconscious.

McCarty: Words fail me!

McCarthy: John! For the *first time* in my life, I think, since the death of my parents and all that came afterwards, I felt valid! *I* could actually *do something successfully.* Whereas, until then I'd *never* been able to do *anything* successfully! I'd found a direction at last, and Larry was responsible for pointing me toward it. (Yep, Larry Gates—seventeen years later, in the unknowable future, our *Body Snatchers* pod psychiatrist! How about that!) After getting into the next ten or twelve university productions and getting to know the raptures and difficulties of the acting business, I was impatient to follow my heart. I quit the U. of M. and skipped east with no thought or regret about not getting my sheepskin, my Bachelor of Arts degree; *I* was "Broadway bound!"

McCarty: You were one of the *founding members* of the Actor's Studio. How did that come about?

McCarthy: The Studio didn't "come about" until many years in the future. I made it to the island of Manhattan in early '38 and spent the next several years scrounging around and seeking to make my fortune (humph!) in the histrionical sector, landing a few parts here and there. In 1942 Elia Kazan . . . etc., etc. down through that "failed work of art" [Cast as the "Redhead" in this "play in four panels" by Ramon Naya] was Kenneth Tobey, a stellar figure in another key science fiction film of the 1950s, Howard Hawks's *The Thing from Another World* [Christian Nyby, 1951]. Five and a half years later, in the autumn of 1947 an impulse similar to the "DollarTop" one by Kazan, Lewis and Cheryl Crawford brought about the inception of the Actor's Studio.

McCarty: Wasn't Lee Strasberg one of the founders, too?

McCarthy: No, Strasberg was a latecomer, but he became a paramount figure as time went on. I can remember Karl Malden, another founding member of the Actor's Studio, saying he'd heard Kazan declare that Lee Strasberg was the one person who must never be involved in the Actor's Studio. But Kazan, who has become used to being typified as an "opportunist," began to call on the dreaded Strasberg (a formidable capacity for self-advancement was his) to fill in for him at his group's sessions. "Gadge" did try various other "mentor" figures as his "reserves" whenever he was tied up making a film or staging a theater piece, but it was a hit-or-miss situation and too often it ended up with the one guy that was always around, and that was Lee Strasberg, who quickly established himself as the "in charge" person; and made his moves to the point where he became an almost guru-type celebrity and artistic director of the Actor's Studio, displacing Kazan.

McCarty: What, in fact, was the Actor's Studio?

McCarthy: It wasn't a school. It isn't a school. Not that we don't learn (and unlearn) there. The idea was to create something on the order of a craft "guild" where fellow members could get together and work together and comment on each other's work. That was the spirit of the thing. Kazan, Lewis, and the producer Cheryl Crawford, the female member of that triumvirate, had all been with the Group Theater in the 1930s. Their agenda then was to nurture a more naturalistic style of performance in the American theater. They missed their Group Theater days, I suppose, so they said, "Let's get some of the actors we know that we think have certain qualifications or qualities that we favor and start doing something." In addition to those I've already mentioned, they got Marlon Brando, Maureen Stapleton, Eva Marie Saint, David Wayne, Tom Ewell, E. G. Marshall (who withdrew early on), and many others, actors who had demonstrated, either by appearing in plays Kazan and Lewis had directed, or whose work had been seen and admired for its naturalistic elements: that is, who had qualities Kazan, Lewis, and Crawford valued.

McCarty: You care to try describing that?

McCarthy: Simply put, I'd say you had the feeling from watching them on stage that they knew about life, that they were "street smart" even if not "of the streets," and were more "natural" in their work than, let's say, their British brethren whose "mannered" style was "natural" to them in those bygone days (but not today, of course). The studio was composed of two sections. One, for known or more established actors, and a second section for unknowns, mostly young talents on the threshold of their careers. They had to audition successfully to be granted membership therein. Kazan handled those young "unknowns" just learning their craft, while "Bobby" Lewis was mentor to the more accomplished and versatile members. I had worked with Lewis, and with Kazan, here and there before the inception of the studio and thus got invited to be part of Lewis's collection of tested thespians. Sessions twice a week, Tuesday and Friday, from eleven in the morning to one in the afternoon.

McCarty: Did casting decisions come out of those sessions?

McCarthy: Not often; yet that's how I happened to be chosen to play the great role of Biff in *Death of a Salesman,* in the London run of the play.

McCarty: Rise and shine! Tell us the "glory" story.

McCarthy: Hah! Look inside me and you might see how *that* word may get amended or replaced by a four-letter word: drop the 'l'.

McCarty: *Gory?* Bigod, there's a *pod* lurking in the sod!

McCarthy: Hold on! (*That's* a bad three-letter word which is an anachronism at this time that we are learning our trade—so that *when a pod does come along we can tackle it*. Stand by!)

McCarty: Okay, the floor is yours; but giant steps, *please!*

McCarthy: I was doing a scene from *You Touched Me,* a Tennessee Williams/Donald Windham play, at the Actor's Studio one day, with an actress named Maggie Phillips and Cheryl Crawford, one of our trio of "Chieftains" (as you may have heard) happened to be there, sitting among those watching us. Evidently, she liked what she saw and (I later heard) had telephoned Kazan at the Barrymore Theatre where he was reading actors on the stage for a new play that he would be directing. She told him she'd discovered just the guy to play Biff, the elder son in a new work by Arthur Miller; namely, me! After the session, she took me aside and said, "Run down to the Ethel Barrymore Theater this minute—Gadge wants to see you." Hell, I was down there, pronto. And Kazan said, "Kid [he always called me 'kid'], I want you to take a good look at this play, *Death of a Salesman*, over the weekend and come back and read the *older son* for me on Monday; Cheryl said you did a hell of a job this morning." Monday found me back on the stage of the dark and empty Barrymore Theatre, the only illumination the single garish worklight. Del Hughes, the stage manager, read with me while I did most of the Biff scenes. It's a vivid experience waiting tremulously for a decision to be forthcoming in that ghostly kind of atmosphere. At length Gadge came up onto the stage from his seat in the darkened house, grinned at me, gave a friendly swat, and said, "Well, kid, you've got the part; you'll make a helluva Biff!" Imagine! Just the three of us there in that hallowed hall and I, feeling an indescribable emotion, seemed to have climbed the peak of my dreams. Of course, it was a great moment that I have to follow with a lesser one: Del Hughes coughed an "If . . . uh . . . Gadge—?" and I, still in the clouds, heard, "Yeah, there *is* one possible drawback—Artie would *like* to see 'Johnny' Kennedy playing Biff but he's out on the coast locked up in a seven-year contract at Warner Bros. and no one is very confident about getting Jack Warner to spring him."

McCarty: Was Kennedy a member of the Actor's Studio?

McCarthy: Nope. Never saw him there.

McCarty: Was John his real name?

McCarthy: John Arthur Kennedy was his legal moniker. In film he is known as "Arthur"; but around Broadway was better known as "Johnny"—to avoid confusion with Arthur Miller (Arty) who had Kennedy as a principal in five of his plays. At this time in our story, Kennedy had been in Miller's play *All My Sons* on Broadway, and previous to that had been in Miller's first Broadway show, *The Man Who Had All the Luck*; so Miller had had two dramatic adventures with the guy and liked him, thought highly of him. The public often got Johnny K. and Kevin McC. mixed up, even though Kennedy and I didn't look *that much* alike. It did seem we shared similar vocal qualities and personality textures; our voice-prints were practically interchangeable. *And the beat goes on*: "How's it goin', Mr. Kennedy?" still comes my way fairly often, even though Johnny is no longer with us; I suspect *he* got the "McCarthy" salutation on occasion. How d'you think he responded to, "*You* scared the hell out of us in *The Body Snatchers* again last night, Kevin!" [laughs and sighs]. Anyway, Jack Warner sprung the Kennedy fella out of his Warner Bros. contract, so he got to play the role of Biff on Broadway. Vividly do I recall the pain of seeing a performance of "the Loman story" [*Salesman*] in Philadelphia before the New York opening, and roiling with frustration and bad karma, damn near moaning to myself, no doubt, "Oh God! Why can't that be me up there under the lights—I can do Biff to a fare-thee-well!

McCarty: Which *you* did in the London production.

McCarthy: Don't know about that but it was a fabulous six months for my wife and our little son, Flip, and myself. When the play was such a huge success in New York, Kermit Bloomgarden, who produced it, gave me jingle at our digs down in Peter Cooper Village and announced, "You might like to know, Kevin, the play is so hot we're going to send out a couple of companies, one, the 'National' tour, starring Thomas Mitchell, will take to the road, hitting all the big cities in the U.S. *and* I'm sending a troupe to London, starring Paul Muni as Willie—so whadya say, kid; you were terrific and first up for Biff after you read for Gadge way back when; so now you can take your choice, guy—no reading or any other bullshit. Talk to me!" Bloomgarden had signed Harold Clurman to direct the road company, and Elia Kazan, the London company. I had worked with Clurman and thought he was a terrifically intriguing guy, a guru (almost unknown word, then). It was dynamite the way Harold could stir your feelings to a feverish pitch, stimulate your soul, and get your imagination bubbling. With *his* prompting, you'd find yourself bringing vivid, emotive life to the character you were trying to interpret; it could be funny; it could be tragical, but he was not in the same league with Kazan when it came to putting the play on its feet. Gadge had the gift of making movement and stage action *come alive* in a way that was extraordinarily dynamic! So I voted for a transatlantic voyage, "Hell, I'll go to London with Muni and Gadge Kazan—count me in!"

McCarty: Ship ahoy!

McCarthy: Aye aye, Sir John! Anyway, that's how I went to London, and played for six months, at the Phoenix Theatre. Interestingly, for such an old pro, the great

Paul Muni wasn't ready for opening night and we were opening cold! He was finding so many things in the character of Willy Loman and still sorting out his choices as curtain time neared. Kazan, concerned, could see it and, of course, with all those scenes Loman had with Biff, so could I. About four in the afternoon before the opening performance, Gadge took my arm in a strong clasp, drew me into a darkened angle of the set, and in urgent but low tones spoke as follows: "It's up to you, kid, to take this thing and make it *go*. You've got to just drive this play from front to back with your performance—which *tonight*, kid, is about getting Paul through this play!" I felt pretty stupid to be doing Sir Speedy instead of concentrating on Biff's tasks. We got away with it, but the opening night wine did have a somewhat bitter aftertaste. Within ten days or so, Muni was all tuned up and was his great, brilliant self for 192 performances.

McCarty: You, not Arthur Kennedy, got to play the part of Biff in the 1951 film version of *Death of a Salesman*. How come?

McCarthy: Probably a matter of money, because Kennedy had already appeared in films and the producer, Stanley Kramer, was making *Salesman* as a low-budget film. I believe the picture cost Columbia Studios less than $500,000. My only film experience up to that time was while I was in the service—a moment in a U.S. Air Force film, *Winged Victory* [George Cukor, 1944] based on Moss Hart's patriotic war play of the same name—while Arthur Kennedy already had a screen career going; no doubt he was getting five times more for a picture than Kramer/Columbia Pictures would have to pay me who had no established fee. I was dirt cheap; does that make my work priceless?

McCarty: You got to appear opposite another acting legend, Fredric March.

McCarthy: A well-known figure to moviegoers, a star, was wanted by Columbia Pictures for the film version of *Death of a Salesman*—rather than Lee J. Cobb, who had created the part of Willy on Broadway (brilliantly). I had heard that March was sought for the play in New York before Cobb was chosen but he had insisted that his wife, Florence Eldridge, star opposite him as Linda, Loman's wife in the play, and Arthur Miller preferred Mildred Dunnock, so March said, "Count me out." Apparently March considered Florence to be sort of a good-luck charm for him on stage and wouldn't go on the boards without her. But films were a different matter, and he worked outside their partnership, so when asked to portray Willy Loman in the *Salesman* movie he was able to reply, "Count me in!" A relatively unknown director, Lazlo Benedek, was chosen to take the reins of the film. For the most part the cast was made up of actors who had previously appeared in one production of the Miller drama or another. Millie Dunnock, Cameron Mitchell, Don Keefer, and Howard Smith were recruited from the Broadway troop. Most of us knew the play. March didn't.

McCarty: But what an actor! With credits like his on stage *and* screen; a major star—how can he fail?

McCarthy: That's the mystery—evidently Freddy never investigated Willy Loman in depth and with the guidance of a Kazan or his ilk. Talent flowed through March like a natural force that must put the possessor of it in danger. You feel its flourish and go with it: perhaps that happened in this case. But Loman is a complex case and has depths and aspects that should inform the performance, and his pain and failures must be factors to be encountered and made manifest.

McCarty: Pretty heavy duty.

McCarthy: Yep, and if, like Freddie March, you play the part off the top of your head and enjoy the free play of your talent without putting your mind or brain to work, it will seem frivolous, however gifted you may be. Possibly he was led astray, too, by Benedek's benign personality. Arthur Miller couldn't bear his performance. I think he felt March's Willy came across as more of a goofball than a guy who was suffering the excruciating pain of a salesman who is not well-liked on the road while family life at home is a torturous one of *un*quiet desperation.

McCarty: What's your opinion of the movie?

McCarthy: It's hard to discuss all that went on—I have poignant feelings about that experience. I discovered I was a neophyte jumping into a sticky La Brea tar pit.

McCarty: In twenty-five words or less.

McCarthy: Look! Stanley Kramer gave the job adapting the play to the screen to a guy named Stanley Roberts, who absolutely *loathed* the play and everything it said. Roberts wanted to eliminate all of what he labeled the "Millerisms," including such famous lines as "Attention must be paid!" or "You're killing that man!"

McCarty: By God, we've got drama on drama! What happened?

McCarthy: My wife, Augusta, and I and our four-year-old son, Flip, were out in Los Angeles (found a house in Westwood) before anybody else in the cast because I was gung ho to be totally ready and set to go on my first picture. On a Saturday morning in August (six-day work week, 1951) screenplay copies of the Robert's *Death of a Salesman* script were emerging, still damp, from the machines of the Mimeograph Department at Columbia Studios in Hollywood. Grabbing one of the first off the griddle, I headed full throttle to the seaside in Santa Monica, spread out my towel on the beach, and started reading it. I fell apart. It was an absolute mess of a disaster, my character, Biff, the conscience and engine of the play, had all but vanished in this so-called screenplay! Kazan (the *Salesman* theater director!) was in Hollywood too, directing the film version of Tennessee Williams's *A Streetcar Named Desire* [1951] with Marlon and Vivien Leigh. So, I jumped into my car—shaking uncontrollably at the steering wheel—but I tracked Gadge down in Malibu that afternoon on Marty Ritt's tennis court—tried to give him an idea of the script disaster. He said, "Kid, it's not your problem. This is Arty's problem. Get Arty on the phone (and I—so un-Hollywood and provincial—I'm thinking, as Gadge is advising me, "Gosh, a long-distance phone call!"—not an everyday occurrence in our house). But I talked myself into it and reached Arthur at his home on Willow Street in Brooklyn and gave him the sad news: "Arthur, the screenplay is just awful—a calamity! Its relationship to your play is damned distant—Biff and his problems have all but vanished, etc." Miller didn't seem concerned. Brooklyn was a placid place to be, I guess: "Don't worry, Kevin, I've got an understanding with [Kramer] that gives me script approval. Take it easy, kiddo." Pause.

What now? Rehearsals were ten days off. I spoke to my agent, Ingo Preminger [Otto Preminger's agreeable brother], told him about the script problems; he thought a visit to the director, Laslo Benedek, was in order. Found him in his office at Columbia Studio, where *Salesman* would be shooting, and discovered that to Laslo the screenplay was okay! Imagine me in that spot—oooff! But after some timid questions from me about all the missing material at the very center of the conflict between Biff and his father, Laslo began to entertain traces of doubt about what he was proceeding with . . . called in the screenplay "wordsmith," Stanley Roberts who, after five minutes one could see, clearly had no use for a tenderfoot like me. But Benedek's benign personality came into play and he proposed that Roberts and I sort things out between us over a cocktail up the road at the Player's Club on Sunset Boulevard.

McCarty: Wasn't that the show biz restaurant owned by [writer-director] Preston Sturges?

McCarthy: Uh-huh . . . gone now; but it was just below another film-star habitat, the Chateau Marmont. Anyway, it was tenterhook time for me with Stanley. After all, he was a veteran screenwriter, but about my age, I figured. An innate sort of disdain was operating his persona. We were out on the terrace with our drinks, Sunset Strip traffic zipping by and I, a nobody trying to get his first break in films, am trying to launch a diplomatic question to this guy with the condescending, long-suffering smile, but instead blurted out, "You don't like this play, do you?" A look of distaste worked into the disdain, "I *hate* this goddamn play." Bump. "And you don't like Biff?" Roberts's reply: "Biff, that son of a bitch. All he does is steal basketballs and fountain pens, hasn't any use for his dad whatsoever, and treats his dad miserably. How can I sell him as 'the hero' to an audience? Your brother Happy is the only decent one in the house!" The old one-two! Right in the puss—! Staggered, I was—but a gasp of dismay escaped my lips: "Why did you agree to write the script if you don't feel too keen about Arthur's play?" The *finisher*: "O.K. kid, here's why. [Stanley] Kramer promised me, if I would do this for him, get this out of the way, *I* could then write the screenplay for *The Caine Mutiny*; that's the story. Well, got to be off, take it easy, fella!" A minute later he was out of there, with a benign parting smirk. Time stood still. The traffic was whizzing by on Sunset and my head was spinning. I sat there in a very blue daze, wondering if somewhere there was a place for me. *That* strange interlude got followed by the news that Arty was mistaken—he *didn't have* script approval *in writing!* But Kramer was not about to alienate him, and have Arthur Miller—whose *play* won the Pulitzer Prize!—making comments against the *film* to the public. So Stanley Roberts was shipped back east to work with Miller. Before the disdainful fellow reached Brooklyn, Miller had already tackled and rewritten or revised Robert's inane adaptation but stuck to the structure and form of that man's *screenplay*, and managed to reinsert essential elements and much of the power from his *Salesman* play that the wily west-coast artist had eliminated. The two men did not get along. Well, a day or so later Roberts returned to Hollywood with his darned and revitalized work and popping into Benedek's office found a meeting going on: most of the key members of the cast (not March) had shown up by then and were getting briefed on production plans, rehearsals, etc. I see the scene still: Roberts identifying himself to the actors with a comical smirk, saying, "Yes, I am the villain who wrote your screenplay and here I am back from the horse's mouth with a *new* batch of 'Millerisms'!" Arthur told me on a long-distance call: "He got me so damn angry, I had to throw the bastard out of my house!"

McCarty: That's a Hollywood story for you.

McCarthy: Tough times were had by all. But it's a great play, a fairly strong film; and I don't regret a moment of my experience with Arthur Miller and his work.

McCarty: Was Kramer's *Salesman* a financial success?

McCarthy: Nope.

McCarty: You did get an Academy Award nomination out of it, though.

McCarthy: We all did: Freddy, Millie Dunnock, and yeah, me too. But it was the year of the *Streetcar* so the *Sales* force got shut out.

McCarty: Brando got shut out, too.

McCarthy: Yep. Something in common for Trivial Pursuit! What two of three Actor's Studio alumni didn't get their doorstops, that night of March 20, 1952? And which alumnus did?

McCarty: I've seen a snapshot, taken that night after the awards of Monty Clift and your friend Fred B. Green and you emerging from the Pantages Theater onto Hollywood Blvd. and *you are not looking gloomy*.

McCarthy: Hooray! At a post-Oscar party, Hedy Lamarr, "One of the most beautiful actresses to grace the screen" [Leonard Maltin] . . . staggered me, as she took my hand, leaned to me, kissed me on the cheek, and in an exotic silken voice, said, "Kaevin, your 'Beeff' was beautiful: *You* had *my* 'inside award' tonight!" Wow! Don'cha think there oughta be a "marker" at the—at Charles Feldman's house on Coldwater Canyon, there in Beverly Hills, with Hedy's utterance inscribed on it? You can have our "STARS" on H'wood Blvd. if they'll just give me that. I wonder what award Hedy might have had for Marlon had he shown up there. . . . Hmmn! You realize Brando was the only actor up for an Oscar from *Streetcar* who didn't win? Incredible!

McCarty: Well, the *veteran* Humphrey Bogart was a sentimental favorite and his work as the boozy riverboat skipper in *The African Queen* was too good to overlook despite the fact that Brando, the *twenty-seven-year-old new kid* on the block, was an unparalleled talent. His "Stanley Kowalski" was a superb achievement, made Marlon a star. How well did you know Brando?

McCarthy: Ah! Let me tell you about our first encounter—*but hang in there!* On a dazzlingly beautiful autumn morning in September after thirty-eight months in the service, Staff/Sergeant McCarthy received his discharge papers from the U.S. Army up at Camp Edwards on Cape Cod, Mass. Within an hour he/I was off that base and out on nearby Rte. 6, New York City–bound, with barracks bag in one hand and hitchhiking thumb of the other aloft and waggling at the oncoming cars, while lustily lilting "Happy Days Are Here Again!!", or "La la la-ing," to the passing traffic, some artfully melodic phrases from Beethoven's Violin Concerto. Just big, young me, enthralled with the freedom and the glamorous light shining its blessing down on me. One of the great days! Prosaically speaking, I got home on two "hitches" to my little flat on East 56th Street in Manhattan; hugged and kissed my wife, Augusta; and went out to find work. No longer a G.I., but an actor on the prowl. Sam Zolotow's legendary theater column, "News from the Rialto" in the *New York Times,* told me where to start looking, so before long I was waltzing down Broadway to the old Empire Theater, just off Times Square, on 39th Street. And, climbing the stairs to the office level, I found a door marked "*Truckline Cafe,* Inc.—Production Offices." Half a minute later, I'm inside the place, to find hearty and friendly shouts bouncing at me: "Hey! Soldier boy!" and, "So how does it feel to be out? Migod! . . . it's *more than three years!*" Etc. An exhilarating wave of pleasure hit me where it didn't hurt. I was back on theatrical turf and hungry to be a part of it once again. The office was alive with the excitement that comes with getting a new play on the boards and they were doing just that with the newest work of one of our finest playwrights, Maxwell Anderson's *Truckline Cafe*—and as a kind of welcome home gesture I was handed a copy of their play to take home and "have a look." Euphoria! There was one hell of an interesting part in *Truckline Cafe* for an actor of my age and type! So on my return a couple of days later I volunteered to read for it. Harold Clurman (directing) and "Gadge" Kazan (producing), very friendly about it, admitted I was "a natural" to play the young soldier, *but*—"Can't offer you that role, Mac—it's gone: young fella named Marlon Brando will be playing the part." That hurt! Who the hell was this Marlon-whatever? I'd never heard of him.

"No, no! Mac, don't worry, we know him—and he's a student . . . of Stella's," says Clurman. Stella Adler, a most remarkable person and teacher, was the great and good friend of our *Truckline Cafe* director, Harold Clurman (of Group Theater fame)—so whoever this Brando geezer was, he had the inside track—"Well," I thought to myself, "*I'll* show them how that part should be played. I'll understudy it—learn it by heart fast and if and when the kid falters, I'll sail in and 'raise the flag'!" They agreed to *let* me understudy and also play one of the truck drivers, who show up at the seaside eatery. My guy sat at the counter for his order—had only a few lines; was just part of the 'atmosphere'—so I had plenty of time to learn the part they'd given to this unknown Brando. The role was that of a young World War II soldier, back in the States after duty on one of the Pacific Islands; sent home when Japan surrendered and now hitchhiking up and down Pacific Coast Highway for some reason—to find his unfaithful wife and "make her pay." He finds her waitressing in our *Truckline Cafe*, and that's where he makes her pay. Anyway, put yourself in my shoes, we are deep into rehearsals and I am avidly watching our juvenile and itching to get out on stage and show my stuff—hell, he had barely walked through his scenes in the two weeks we'd been working. Then, a day came (with Clurman and Kazan out in the darkened house) when the Brando "kid" came out onto that bare stage of the Belasco Theater—and—suddenly—a wild, anguished shreik of horror erupted from him, "*I killed her! I killed her—and killed her—and killed her!!*" His fellow actors, watching from the wings, dumbfounded, can hear the kid's passionate outcries go echoing through the empty house, then fall away to an eerie stillness. After a moment, a low moan of grief seemed to bleed from the killer's lips . . . another instant later . . . a searing scream of rage against himself jams the air . . . then . . . stark scary silence again. The watchers in the wings are turning to each other, shaking their heads in wide-eyed disbelief—yet still the scene played on as the young soldier flings himself down at one of the cafe tables, buries his head in his clutching hands, his whole being wracked by a chaos of sobs and despair. . . . Well, that dazzling, terrifying, heart-stopping scene—the climactic one in the play—has not, as you can tell, gone dim in my brain. *God! I was standing there with a case of the shakes!*—the emotional impact of the man's performance was beyond anything I'd ever experienced! "What kind of petty damn fool am I? Holy Mother, whatever made me think I was in the same league with this Marlon 'whoever'?!" He was so—so—yup! he was *so*—sure as hell was and still is; thank God. It was a devastating four or five minutes. "Wow! didja see that!! Every histrionic thing hit the fan out there today, huh?—whadda we got here?"

McCarty: There's a pertinent question! C'mon, soldier, do your duty, things are *hangin' fire here!*

McCarthy: Well, what we got, *offstage*, was something like a stand-up comic (a phrase you never heard back then); a very damn likable, *whimsical* kind of a guy—180 degrees different from the devastated soldier he created that day in rehearsal. Well, as the *Truckliners* began to come together as a family, in no time the Brando boy would have us chortling with laughter from the nutty things he'd be taking a crack at: "weirdo clowning" and bizarre impersonations, etc. Clurman and Kazan got a great kick out of his hijinks, too—the "kid," vibrant youth personified, was ten years younger than I was—but hell, I looked young, too (even in my young days!) and was in shape, so to speak, but, damn it, around Marlon I felt like an old fossil sitting on the sidelines with a case of the chagrins! Lithe and strong, the kid would use the occasional ten-minute rehearsal break doing sit-ups or push-ups on the backstage floor. Still another way he'd exercise his physique would be to grab a backstage rope and, hand over hand, pull himself up on it, over our heads and then, after swinging through the air in wide arcs, the goof would let one arm hang free and, while holding on with the other as he swung to and fro, he'd be using that free hand to scratch himself like a chimpanzee—and put on the face to go with it! Quite a believable anthro*pod*, eh?

McCarty: Oof!

McCarthy: As Caesar said somewhere, "Where there is an unknowable there is a promise." And I can promise you, that more like that comes to mind when trying to relate facets of this man that was a boon companion for much too brief a time.

McCarty: *Time out!* We're in November of '45. *We've got ten years to do before the pods come looking for you!* Dana Wynter is only fifteen years old, and the thirty-two-year-old Don Siegel hasn't made a feature film—he's only now a film editor and learning montage techniques at Warner Bros. Studio. Maybe we could skip ahead?!

McCarthy: Whatever you say, stout fella! Oddly enough, early on, I had the fun of introducing my new pal Marlon to my old friend Monty, who seemed a little leery of Brando. I think he picked up on the powerful pysche and consummate self-confidence (uranium-fed!) just under the surface of Marlon's calm, soft-spoken exterior.

McCarty: It would have been hard to find two more dynamic personalities.

McCarthy: Agreed. I have never been able to give *myself* any "specific gravity" in what the hell *I* was—*to those two high-amperage mortals*. What did they see or find in me? I draw a blank trying to dope out what I must have been like in 1945 or '46!

McCarty: Maybe *you* were *becoming* . . . the average man. . . . As just noted, this is ten years before a very average chap, Miles Bennell, had to rise to some god-given potential that he had *never dreamt was in his genes*.

McCarthy: Yes! Yes! But ease off, we'll get there! Perhaps, back then, I was a devilishly obsequious social director standing between two titans, eh? Monty was already a brightly shining star of film and Brando at the outset of a fantastic career, relatively unknown except to professional theater people who, yes, were beginning to become aware of his astonishing talent and his free and easy, occasionally eccentric ways. And *daring*—both those fellas had more than their share of that in their genes.

McCarty: How so?

McCarthy: Well, first, here's material from the Brando file. One vivid memory of Marlon comes swimming right up; early in '46, we were in Baltimore, with *Truckline*—trying it out before the Broadway premiere . . .'twas a beautiful, wintry Saturday morning, fresh snow gleaming in the sunlight all over the city, a few hours before the 2:30 P.M. matinee . . . and I said to Marlon, "C'mon, lets do something. . . . There's a beautiful park out here, I recall, with a neat little art museum in it. Let's have a look. We can grab a streetcar and be there in no time." Well, Marlon agreed to grabbing one and we headed out to the park. It had been snowing the night before and there was a glistening white blanket over everything. When we entered the park you could see this little jewel box of an art museum which was also glistening, with its sparkling glass and all. It was early; 11:00 A.M. is early for theater actors, but the gallery was open, so in we went—to warm up a bit, probably. It was an attractive place, but seemed to be deserted—nobody else inside except maybe an attendant or two wandering around somewhere. Almost immediately, as we moved into this very quiet, sacrosanct atmosphere, we damn near bumped into a group of startlingly life-size sculptures—the nearest figure: an original work of Edgar Degas (1878), a bewitching young dancer in her tutu . . . and, standing just beyond her, an oh-so-lifelike female nude, reeking of beauty and sexuality! The snow-splashed light was beaming through the windows of our little "jewel box," quickening the sinuous and seductive powers of that white marble form. And as we moved closer to this beautiful thing to better appreciate her finer points, my Brando buddy suddenly climbed onto the low, elevated platform, where this daughter of Eve was standing, and as a yearning sound came issuing from his throat he put his arms around the lustrous, alabaster lady, murmuring sweet everythings to her—"and aren't you cold, my dear?"—the next moment holding her closely, and (would you believe this!!) opens his mouth slightly and is kissing her passionately on the lips!—and possibly elsewhere! I dunno—I was *panicking*: "Good *God. Marlon!!!* What are you . . . !?!" and I'm whispering fiercely, damn near audibly, I bet, "Hey! Hey, Marlon!! *Marlon!* Watch it! *God Almighty!* somebody'll *see* you!!" (Ah me! Telling this makes me feel slightly despondent.) Here was this "timid soul," the McCarthy guy, totally beside himself, *quaking* with worry that we'd get thrown out, or arrested! And not get back to the theater in time for the matinee. Cripes! But all Marlon was thinking, apparently: "Oh, God, I must be near this creature. I must be with her, infuse her or be infused by her. . . .

McCarty: When was the last time you saw Mr. Brando?

McCarthy: We used to bump into each other occasionally in New York, at Elaine's possibly; hell, who knows where; but now that we are living out here in Sherman Oaks—actually just down the hill from the man's bailiwick on Mulholland Drive—the sightings are rare. I must admit with a trifle of chagrin on my chinny chin chin, that something is keeping us apart—what *can* it be?! The last time we were face-to-face was, maybe, nine or ten years ago when Kate and I were having dinner at a little cafe here on Ventura Boulevard; I was facing the entry and as he walked in the door we spotted each other, instantly; he came directly over to our table and with a charming grin on his puss said, rather emphatically, "You never change, Kevin" [laughs]. You can take that any way you wish. . . . I've always liked seeing him—feel real affection and respect for him—which comes easy: the guy is without a peer, and as I am without a pier to stand on, I'll just have to keep treading water and say, as another good pal, Kurt Vonnegut, would, a rueful "So it goes."

McCarty: What's your favorite memory of Montgomery Clift?

McCarthy: Monty as is known from photos, film, etc. was a creature of spectacular good looks; a dazzling smile was his; he gleamed with male beauty mindful of a young Greek god. On top of these almost perfect attributes, he was a downright gracious, generous fellow; forthcoming when you met him, though you might be put off by the glittering good looks. But once the charm of his lively personality rippled in your direction you'd be quick to vote for him. Can't come up with a *favorite* memory because we spent *so* much time with him, had so many experiences with him.

McCarty: Monty and you and Augusta had been pals for years before he made his first film, *The Search,* for Fred Zinnemann in 1948?

McCarthy: Since the DollarTop. That reminds me, listen to this! Augusta and I went to a screening of it, with him and his mother and several others. It seemed very low-key, but it *was Monty's debut* in *film.* It was exhilarating to be a party to Monty's nascent career. The event took place early afternoon, in your basic grungy Times Square office building and in a very commonplace small screening room; a far thing from the kind of ambiance that soon would be surrounding our friend! Fred Zinnemann's work in *The Search* earned him an academy nomination and gave the public its first look at Monty on screen; and it was very beguiling and impressive. Our pal manifested all kinds of talent and it was astonishing how convincing he was in his portrayal of the central role of the young soldier. However, as our group emerged from the screening room, my young friend's mother, "Sunny" Clift, was exclaiming, maybe even groaning to Monty, "Oh, dear! You sounded just like Kevin in that picture!" Not intended as a compliment to either of us, I'm afraid.

McCarty: This is very mysterious to me. I'm on your side, Mac.

McCarthy: What Monty'd been trying to do was convey the sense that *his character*, the young G.I., was just an *ordinary* guy from let's say, the Middle West. His mother liked *elegant*. Normally, Monty *had* the air of someone who belonged to the upper crust in—in Manhattan—came from a well-to-do, privileged world. Hell, when we were first acquainted, he was being kidded about imitating the elegant *Alfred Lunt*—Monty, at eighteen, had spent close to two seasons playing the juvenile lead in Robert E. Sherwood's wartime drama *There Shall Be No Night*, which starred that *renowned* actor, and his wife, the great actress, Lynne Fontaine. The "Lunt" voice and his delivery were unique; and Monty had many months in which to cultivate it—but in no way should it be the sound coming from the lips of the young G.I. guy in *The Search!*

McCarty: Couldn't he take speech lessons?

McCarthy: Hear me! Listen as Monty did; aha! In those first years of mine in New York, as I was just edging my way into cosmopolitan life, the flavor and accents of the Corn Belt could be detected in my speech—got me my first job on Broadway in *Abe Lincoln in Illinois*. Unknown to me, Clift heard the midwest twang and went for it—sponged it from me; also another I.D. factor of mine, my unvarnished behavior looked and *was* sure as hell down-to-earth—latched onto *it*. Clift coveted those ingredients for his G.I. and stashed them into his thespic psyche—yep, that lad he played was secretly modeled on the McCarthy persona! A few years later, I was up for a part in a picture at Twentieth Century Fox that was being directed by Henry Hathaway, one of those hard-nosed, tough directors who had been in the movie business since the silent days. After reading a couple of scenes for him, Hathaway said, "Christ! You sound exactly like Monty Clift!" So, for the hell of it, I told him the story about Monty's mother's accusing him of doing me in *The Search*. Hathaway snorted and shot back, "Tough shit, pal. He got there first. He's copyrighted you. You'll have to find another way to go. Do yourself a favor, lose that guy—people are thinking you two are shacking up." And he was gone—outa there—before I, *whoever* I was, *or would have to become*, could regain my equilibrium.

McCarty: My God! Where do we go from there?

McCarthy: Onward; upward and onward with the arts.

McCarty: Yessir-ree-bob! Well, let's see. Tell me, was James Dean part of that first Actor's Studio group?

McCarthy: No. He came on a little later. Never met Dean who, then, was just beginning to make his way, I think. But, catch this! He'd gotten Clift's unlisted phone number somehow, and used to call Monty at any old hour, just to listen to Monty talk, so he could pick up Monty's speech characteristics and his way of talking. Monty was teed off. "Dean's trying to imitate me!" he'd gripe. Which is a bit ironic. . . . If Dean imitates Monty—who imitated Kevin so well—does that make little ole me, in some crackpot way, an intrinsic ancestor of the inimitable late James Dean [laughs]?

McCarty: And where do we go from here?

McCarthy: [Great times were spent in Paris and in Italy from early February till the Ides of March, 1950] I guess he and I had conned ourselves that we had a rendezvous with destiny. More than six months earlier, we came up with a plan to construct a screenplay from a theater piece *You Touched Me!* by Tennessee Williams and Donald Windham, in which Monty had appeared at the Booth Theater on B'way back in '43 or '44. A perfect part for Clift and an ideal thing for us to work on. We'd show 'em! Monty's agent, Lew Wasserman, then head of MCA, worked out a very favorable deal for us for the rights to *You Touched Me* from the authors' agents. Thereupon, all charged up dates were set; resolve reaffirmed! To accomplish our dreamplay adaptation, Clift and McCarthy pledged to splice a minimum of six months of their time together, with no diversions, immediately after he wound up filming his role (opposite Liz Taylor) in *A Place in the Sun*. Well, it happened that during the six months or so that he was needed in California and forced to behold the beauteous Miss Taylor day after day after day in *A Place in the Sun*, I was on stage eight thousand miles and eight time zones away—in Britain on a six-month contract to play Biff in the London production of Arthur Miller's *Death of a Salesman*. Yep, I was doing theater: having to behold the great Paul Muni and play those intense scenes with him as Willie Loman for 175 performances. Happenstance had it that his film and my theater venture concluded their endeavors almost simultaneously. Monty flew away from sunny California and Kevin and family got out of rainy London and over to France, pronto, on January 31, 1950. And who showed up in Paris the next day?!

McCarty: The timing worked out.

McCarthy: Our watermelon-sized egos allowed us to convince ourselves that we were something else: we had insight, talent, taste, imagination, humor well beyond the authors of 95 percent of the scripts that were being offered to Monty. We'd show 'em!

McCarty: Back to the business of Monty. You mentioned that he was quite a daredevil?

McCarthy: Dare I go on? We were in Rome in 1950 after I had finished with *Death of a Salesman* in London and he had finished the movie *A Place in the Sun* [George Stevens, 1951]. We were going to use our free time to write a screenplay together based on a play of Tennessee Williams and Donald Windham's called *You Touched Me!* that Monty had appeared in on stage in 1945. We didn't accomplish much work, but we had a great time. Monty was a big star by then because of *Red River* [Howard Hawks, 1948], so we met everybody; the directors Vittorio De Sica and Luchino Visconti, a.k.a. the Duke of Milan; the writer Alberto Moravia, etc., you name it. Monty was *always* daring and ready for adventure of some kind, and he would do things like hang from the balcony of the hotel over the Arno River by his fingertips. The same kind of deed, witnessed by Gusta and I, six months earlier, occurred outside a New Yorker hotel-room window one fine night; testing his coordination and musculature, young Clift hung from the window ledge of a pal's guest room—

dangling by his fingertips thirty stories (thirty!) above Penn Station's evening traffic on 34th Street!

McCarty: Let's you and I keep our feet on the ground.

McCarthy: Can't happen: we've got an equinoctial williwah to attend. Here's a final derring-do incident from the M.C. pages of my memory book: after our European holiday, the wife, our son Flip, and Monty took a ship back to the U.S. from Le Havre—and after two or three days out, we ran into a terrible storm—wild seas and tearing winds, a bloody tempest (mid-March, 1950: the vernal equinox). The ship was just tossing, rolling, heaving. Monty calls into our stateroom—Augusta prostrate from seasickness—"Let's go up on deck." I'm negative, "Good Christ, *no*, No, NO! We could be swept away." But he pulled me along, and when we got up there—top, *open* deck, Clift surveys the howling storm scene, says, "Great! Let's take a picture," gives me [trying to keep vertical] his camera and says, "I'll go down to my stateroom, get the porthole open, and climb out with my umbrella and attaché case. You can get the shot from here—but *wait to take it* 'til I appear to be stepping off the Queen [Mary] having had it with the old girl and the stormy weather . . . *then—Snap it!*" He did his part—I mine . . . got the picture of his incredible act; which can be seen in La Guardia's biography. [perhaps here, too—KM copyright].

McCarty: Was he addicted to alcohol?

McCarthy: Not early on—almost the reverse. Illness (chronic amoebic dysentery) called for pain pills—when booze got into the mix he became a different creature—especially later on, in the years after the accident; it was painful to watch his deterioration; got to the point you couldn't bear to be around the lost soul. But this anecdote is one from a more benign time. He liked to drive and you trusted him behind the wheel, but he could get playful. My wife, Augusta Dabney, and I were appearing in a play, *Jason,* at the Buck's County Playhouse. Monty came out to take it in and afterwards we returned to the city together, Monty driving us in his powerful Buick Century. One can't forget that for several stretches at a time the speedometer arrow stayed at the automobile's top speed, 120 miles per hour, on those moonlit back roads; but he was steady and concentrated while Gusta and I were basket cases, assuming an incongruous nonchalance.

McCarty: Of course, drinking and driving were what almost did him in when he had that terrible accident that almost killed him. You were the first one on the scene, weren't you?

McCarthy: Yes, and the shocking part was that he wasn't drunk. Nobody believes that, of course, but it's true. Monty always wanted to emulate you if he thought you were doing something of value. I was on the wagon to encourage him to do likewise. That night he didn't even have a glass of wine, was sober as could be. We were at Liz Taylor and Michael Wilding's house just above Benedict Canyon. Rock Hudson and maybe six or eight others there, too. Liz's husband, Michael, was not feeling well, had a terrible back and was laid up. Anyway, I was first away from the lovely dinner; had to get up early in the A.M. to go up to Berkeley to visit my father-in-law before catching a plane back east. Monty packed it in, too, so as to follow me in his car, inasmuch as I could point out a turnoff for his house from Benedict Canyon Drive which he was unaware of. We stood around in the Wilding driveway a while, under a beautiful starry sky, he chatting about his disappointment over the picture he was currently making, *Raintree County* [Edward Dmytryk, 1957]. I'll say it again, he was as sober as I'd ever seen him. Then I took off in my car and he followed in his as we made our way down to Benedict. There were a batch of hairpin turns. The first one came maybe two or three hundred yards down the hill from the Wildings'. Glancing in my rearview mirror, I became aware of Monty's car coming up behind me, just too goddamn fast. I thought: "If he tries to pull one of these stunts of giving my bumper a little playful smack with his front-side steel, he could send me right through the one house on that hairy road—located dead center of this 'g.d.' hairpin curve." I hit the brakes and made the turn very sharp and fast to avoid his bump, and I thought: "I'm going to have to put distance between us, so this nut can't pull the same stunt on me again." I gave my Chevy more juice; got ahead of him by fifty yards, maybe more; saw in the mirror that he got around the turn also, though I was really fearful he was going too fast to do so. I kept going pretty smartly to stay well clear of him as we went around the next turn. Finally, at the last sharp curve before the straight run down to Benedict, something went wrong. In my rearview, I could see the lights of his car dancing and swinging wildly around, and then he wasn't behind me anymore. So, I braked to a stop—hopped out of my little Chevy. His engine was making quite a racket and I figured he was stuck in a sandy ditch, so I ran the fifty yards up to his car, its headlights were still on. His car was a wreck. There was still dust in the air from the crash, but the motor and the lights were still on. Figuring the gas tank might catch fire and explode, I reached in the broken window on the driver's side and turned the engine off. But I couldn't find Monty. Panic inhabited every part of me. I thought he'd been thrown from the car. I ran back down to my car, drove up to the site—pointed the headlights toward the wreck so I could see better, and finally found him. His whole body lay crumpled and unmoving under the dashboard. Oh my God, he's gone . . . my dear friend! Nooo!! Not simply that! Millions loved this man! A world was crashing and I'm here alone and helpless—locked away from the victim. I could hear myself moaning desperate animal sounds—death was all around He was dead. . . . I could get one arm and shoulder in—reached and touched him. He was still warm, of course, but otherwise—no sign of life at all, but blood everywhere and the wrecked car smashed shut. What can I do! . . . precious time was passing . . . doors *jammed* shut—couldn't get in to him, then realized better not try to move him, not safe to do so. Had to leave a dead or dying man alone in the middle of the road in the middle of the night . . . sped back uphill to Wildings, jumped from the Chevy, banged on the front door—trembling violently, trying not to scream. Michael opened the door, took a look at me, limped forward, "Quick, call the hospital! Need an ambulance!—Doctors! Monty's—been I—don't know!—maybe!! Terrible accident!" At that moment, Liz Taylor appears at the door. I can't stop shaking like a leaf. . . . I'm begging her not to come down, "No! No! Liz, you better stay here. You won't want to see him." She exclaimed, "The hell with that. I'm coming *down!*" Which she did. Then she and I are back down at wrecked car scene, no way of getting the jammed car doors open. Others arrived from the house—wrenching at a rear door, Rock Hudson and another figure got it partially ajar. Liz got to Monty by scrunching through it and climbing over onto the front seat. I wedged my way in—leaning forward from the backseat—saw that Monty, though barely animated, showed signs of consciousness,—was a horrendous sight—face and scalp drenched with blood, head beginning to swell—looking ripped to pieces. Very gently, very carefully, Liz somehow drew him to her so his battered head was on her knee, and she kept talking to him gently, no alarm in her voice, a heroic pioneer woman from time past was what I saw as we awaited the ambulance. Monty, in a strangulated voice, conveyed to Liz that his front teeth had been knocked out and were stuck in his throat, choking him . . . would she try to get them out? She opened his mouth, calmly, in a most natural way, put her fingers down into his throat, and pulled out the broken teeth. Shortly thereafter, a doctor arrived, an ambulance pulled up. The doctor was Rex Kennamer, a guy Monty went to, Liz didn't know him. So, as half-dead and delirious as Monty was—out of that battered, bloody, broken face in his unfailingly courteous manner he choked out a hoarse introduction, "Liz, I . . . want you . . . to . . . uh . . . meet . . . Rex . . . Kennamer—Rex . . . this is . . . Liz . . . Taylor." I have all kinds of memories of Monty, but that is the most indelible.

McCarty: I can imagine. That accident happened in May of 1956. *Invasion of the Body Snatchers* came out earlier that year in February. How did you get involved in one of the key science fiction films of the 1950s which caused my generation and many others to have so much lack of sleep?

McCarthy: I had done a couple of pictures by then, including one with Mickey Rooney called *Drive a Crooked Road* [Richard Quine, 1954], where I played a bad guy, one of the hoods who forces Rooney, a small-time race car driver, to drive the getaway car after a big heist.

McCarty: That was an excellent little thriller, written by Blake Edwards, I think.

McCarthy: Right. People often ask what the difference is between acting on stage and for the screen; I use Mickey Rooney as an example. On stage, the difference is one of freedom of action, or movement; there is a much broader range for you vocally, as well; in a full-scale performance, on stage, your body language, which can be a subtle and revealing feature, is in film, often enough, useless to you when so much of your work is being viewed in close or medium-close shots. On stage, almost anything goes; jump around if it's fitting—be as "large" as you like without worrying that the director is telling you to "confine your movements," etc. I recall with pleasure hearing, from a marvelous veteran actress, "Honey, I've been in the theater for thirty-five years and you take a big piece of the cake—the way you feel at home in front of an audience!" I'm saying, "Dunno—I'm more me here, is the way it feels."

McCarty: White men can jump!

McCarthy: Whoa! Early on I found it difficult to adjust to "being in confinement"—in movies. But you learn, thank God, that you are adding technique that enriches your capabilities—making more of you rather than depriving you. Just had to learn it and let it become second nature because the camera lens *is* a magnifying glass. To delineate a part so that it's not overdone, yet still get it up there, can be a rather delicate thing, sometimes. For example, there was a very critical scene in *Drive a Crooked Road,* where three hotshot, smug thugs are involved in a bank heist with Mickey Rooney (our dupe), a whiz of a teenage racing driver, at the wheel of a souped-up sedan. Sitting in our getaway car, the fierce tension among the hoods as we await the escape moment with the swag is something to behold—*or not*—depending on whom you are looking at. We three thugs are doing Versions of Tension; lots of "indicating"—giving grim glances back and forth, etc. . . . not Rooney—I, thug #1, looked at him. Nothing going on. Immobile as a statue—a still life . . . uninvolved. What the hell?! Well, I caught on, when I saw the film: rigid as a sphinx, Mickey seemed frozen at the wheel as he regarded the entry to the bank, but no (unobtrusively) a single finger of his, tapping in measured, slow time on the steering wheel during those breathless moments, illuminated the whole critical situation. That did it: the suspense vibrated! Being with "the Mick" was a learning experience!

McCarty: All right—let's pick up the ball and the pace; Podstown is just beyond the horizon.

McCarthy: Funny, *I've* already got my cleats on and am calling the signals. Come along! I'd done a couple of films when I got called about a part in *The Annapolis Story* [1955]; had a session at the William Morris Agency with the director, Don Siegel (a name unknown to me) a slight, interesting-looking, sardonic fellow, wore a moustache who said he wanted me for the role of John Derek's younger brother. We would play cadets at the Naval Academy. Diana Lynn was going to play the girl who came between us. Derek was a very toothsome, very youthful rising star at Universal, where he played in lots of boxing melodramas and spear and sandal epics. The dampness of adolescence still sweated from his gorgeous torso, whereas I was nudging forty. So I didn't quite see how I could play John Derek's *younger* brother, a junior cadet, or whatever it was, at Annapolis, given the age and sweat difference between us. I took a chance and informed Mr. Siegel of the incongruity that was bugging me. God knows I'd played younger guys on stage and screen: Biff in *Death of a Salesman* was supposed to be around eighteen years old in the flashbacks, and word never came my way that I seemed unconvincing playing *that age*—even in the film version—despite the thirty-five years I had chalked up by *that* time. But Derek was a case where "disbelief could not be suspended." So, I suggested to Mr. Siegel, "What if I play the older brother instead?" He smiled his bittersweet smile, said he'd check with Derek and, bigod, a day or so later told me Derek was agreeable to the switch. Now I would play the older brother, which meant I would get the girl.

McCarty: So there was a method in your madness.

McCarthy: No! Come on, that wasn't my objective! (I *didn't foresee*, then, that I was to be caught for many a day and year in the warped strictures of Hollywood casting. On the stage in New York as "juvenile" or "leading man" I played good guys, heroes, whatever, but in films seemed destined to be proposed only for parts in the "not-so-good" guy category, or "antihero" types—or what was called a "New York *heavy*"—who *never* gets the girl!) Matter of fact, shortly after *Death of a Salesman* came out, I was up for *the romantic lead* in a Twentieth Century Fox picture. At this date I can't come up with the title, but I sure do recall how I was all revved up to hit the jackpot with—*at last!*—a perfect part for me—who was fancying himself, at that lovely moment, as the next great romantic leading man: *along the lines of the quintessential Ronald Colman*, but . . . ohhh, *God!* According to my agent, Ingo Preminger, the bloody producer-guy at Fox was *dubious about my ability to pull it off* because, after all, I hadn't gotten the girl in *Death of a Salesman!* After giving it some thought, Ingo rings the guy back and says, "What the hell are you talking about!! There *isn't any girl* in *Salesman!*" And the genius replies, "Just the same, he didn't get her!" Click! That cooked my goose; I did not get the part—or even get a look at the girl. Got a well-cooked goose, however!

McCarty: Siegel often joked about the fact that due to budget limitations, not a frame of *The Annapolis Story* was shot at Annapolis.

McCarthy: U.S. Navy stock footage was used, but otherwise the film was shot entirely in and around Los Angeles. We did the helicopter and air battle scenes, oceanside on a pier, sticking out into the Pacific at Ventura, California. That's where I had my first experience with special effects. It was quite thrilling for this neophyte. Those little things called "squibs" were exploding around my neck and under my shirt during the air battle I was involved in. I was slightly wounded but I maintained my heroic poise and avoided being shot down. Ironically, I have a somewhat different memory of another scene involving the midshipman I played in the picture. Not just a dashing combat pilot, my character was also the quarterback of the Navy football team that year. There was evidently some stock film footage of an Army-Navy game that could be cut in and used in the movie. Now, *my job* in those fictional scenes that would be interspersed with the genuine stuff—my assignment was to *duplicate the actions of the real U.S. Navy quarterback* as seen in the stock footage; Don Siegel had set up some close shots on me—in Navy football gear, of course, running several plays. However, after taking a good look at the stock film of the game via a portable *movieola* on the set, it became apparent that *my guy was right-handed—passed right-handed! and I am a lefty*! Well, that was hardly a stroke of luck. I had to become that guy! Whew! We were shooting our live-action scenes at the UCLA practice field with eleven hefty UCLA playing defense (in Army uniforms). And, in Navy garb, seven Bruins from the UCLA football team on the scrimmage line, plus three more "Navied" Bruins in the back field—aided and abetted by our "Navied Hero—" the future Dr. Miles Bennell who is to run the Navy juggernaut today, and call the plays.

McCarty: Think I'll go to Blockbuster and try to rent that flick and *check out your moves.* Perhaps one catch a glimpse of what Don Siegel saw in you to make you a pod chaser—you sure you didn't have a double and don't want to reveal it?

McCarthy: Nope, that was me, all the way, taking the snap and running back to escape the Army rush—then (ostensibly) tossing a long game-winning pass, no one recorded where that left-hander's right-handed pass *really* got to. However (to lay it on the line!) all our timid soul, KM, was experiencing was excruciating doubt. . . . Instead of giving himself a pep talk, his inner voice was babbling, "How can I look like the hero when I'm petrified with fear?" I hardly knew where my *right arm* was attached to my body. "Don! What if one of those mammoth defensive tackles comes smashing in and sacks me!" Siegel is unconcerned. "They've all been instructed to go easy on you, dear boy! *If* one of them does come tearing in at you, being a Bruin, at heart, he might give you a *bear* hug but surely he'll stay shy of your kisser!" The fearful hero quakes, "God! Is this going to be believable?" "God ain't around," says Mr. Siegel. "If you can just hang on to the oval, kiddo, and draw your arm back to an even halfway reasonable position and have a confident look on your puss as you begin your throw, I don't give a hoot in hell where the pigskin goes—I will have called, 'Cut' and we'll go to the game footage. So—hup! Hup!" I saw the "flick" and it looked okay. I await another opportunity to be ambidextrous!

McCarty: Had you become friends with Siegel by this point and planned on working together again in the future?

McCarthy: We weren't *un*friendly. Actually he was damned decent. Took me to dinner, introduced me to some interesting folk—including his mother! At any rate I was back home in Westchester County, New York (before zip codes) with my wife and three children again, picking up an occasional TV or radio or commercial spot; try to be choosy, of course, but constantly in need of income like most of us attempting to eke out a living in "Theater." I was on our Dobbs Ferry, New York Central Railroad platform, there beside the Hudson River, four or five days a week, commuting into the city to make the rounds, seeing "Theater," taking voice lessons (wanted to get into a musical) and working on whatever, maybe Shakespeare, at the Actor's Studio, etc. Then, big deal!—a long-distance! (1955 A.D.) phone call from California: Don Siegel! On the horn about a story that had been recently serialized in *Colliers*, the popular weekly magazine. It was a novel called *The Body Snatchers* by an author named Jack Finney. Was to be transformed into a film with Siegel at the helm, as they say. . . . Surprised and glad to hear from him, you bet, but, after hanging up, I had only a foggy notion of his story. "Weird" and "definitely *offbeat*" were terms he used (the term "sci-fi," not concocted by 1955 A.D.) I guess Siegel *sent* me the pertinent issues of the mag or I dug 'em up myself! But *what* a strange, far-fetched and unlikely story it *was*! I get a kick now as I picture myself at that time; looking no doubt like a middle-class icon, conventional, sincere, straight as a die—I prided myself that my "Actor's Studio persona" was undetected outside that "Strasberg precinct house." Not for me the trademarked "torn sweatshirt" of my friend Marlon—"jacket-and-tie" was *my* protective "dress code." I would have been sitting in our moderately conservative middle-middle-class house in Westchester County reading this Jack Finney fantasy—muttering, I'm sure, to my wife, Augusta, "Oh, boy! Is this ever nutty!" So, see me now as I was then and you will say that I was perfect casting for the part of Dr. Miles Bennell in the *Body Snatcher* tale. But the darn story had me baffled—but intrigued, too. Then, even as I was feeling the nutty thing just couldn't be made—an offer *was* made! Cause for celebration! I was wanted! And, man, what a helluva job for the actor who got to play that part and it had *my* name on it!

McCarty: I understand that it was producer Walter Wanger who acquired the rights to Finney's story and brought it to Siegel's attention.

McCarthy: He did a good thing.

McCarty: Walter Wanger had a reputation for being a maverick, independent kind of producer, who had worked with all the greats, including John Ford, Fritz Lang, Alfred Hitchcock, and Don Siegel.

McCarthy: Yeah, and he and Don had already made a film together called *Riot in Cell Block 11* [1954]. It was the first picture Wanger made after getting out of prison. He'd been doing time because of the *indiscretions of an American actress and a Univeral Pictures executive* (work in progress?). Before the "hoosegow" confinement, Walter was married to the much-admired, beautiful actress Joan Bennett. Unwisely, Jennings Lang, an executive at Universal, had been doing some secret admiring of the lady—but not secret enough—when Walter heard that Jennings had been cuckolding him with Joan, he confronted the "lecherous lady's man" in the parking lot of Universal Studios, pulled out a gun, and shot him. As Wanger was a much shorter man than Joan Bennett's not-so-secret, *tall* lover; the bullet hit Lang, rumor hath it, in "the family jewels."

McCarty: Kevin, that "warm Siberia" of yours out there (Moss Hart quote) is a landscape thick with PG anecdotes.

McCarthy: Siegel said Wanger wanted to make *Riot in Cell Block 11* to expose the evils of the penal system (and indirectly, the penis system, wouldn't you say?) having had firsthand experience with them.

McCarty: *Conformity* and *regimentation* are also factors of prison life, and a protest against them carries over into *Invasion of the Body Snatchers*. Maybe that's why the project appealed to Wanger. What was your impression of him?

McCarthy: He seemed an urbane, pleasant man, a touch on the bland side. I had the feeling that Siegel's appreciation of him was tinged with faintness.

McCarty: Really? In an interview with [director] Peter Bogdanovich, Siegel, who seemed to have a natural antipathy toward producers in general, gave Wanger pretty high marks.

McCarthy: Yes, I've read that interview, which was *re*published in Bogdanovich's book *Who the Devil Made It* [Knopf, 1997]. Maybe *I'm* off the mark, but I sure as hell got the impression that, on occasion, Don felt that Wanger was being urbane or *diplomatic* rather than *effective* in his dealings with the front office. I think he might have called Wanger a pod, if the two of them hadn't been partners.

McCarty: Walter's earlier crime of passion doesn't seem very podlike behavior.

McCarthy: No, it doesn't, does it? A *damn* good point, John. You've got me in your crosshairs! I feel myself to be on very soggy ground: with me, a quiver of uncertainty is the equivalent of a stab of guilt! You have just zapped me.

McCarty: Did you like Don Siegel?

McCarthy: If this were a tailor-made effort we are working on, I'd have to admit Don was a first-rate piece of goods—*Body Snatchers* was Act II of our opera. A well-known line in the theatrical game is: "How's your second act?" I'm glad to be here to reply, "It was a dandy!" and Siegel was the "maestro." He was a lot of man to know, though I've never felt I knew him more than 55 percent well. But when you were around him you felt life was worth living—all the while laughing at his "take" on things. He did have his sardonic streak. His smile was often close to a smirk; jiving remarks to and about his associates came easily from him—but beneath that crusty, saturnine exterior, beat a heart of gold. A very witty man, too; and lots of great gray matter inside that skull. Now I can say it: the answer is yes, I liked the poor S.O.B.

McCarty: You suggested a different title for the picture also, didn't you?

McCarthy: Don *hated* the title *Invasion of the Body Snatchers*, especially the "invasion of" part. Thought it made the film sound like a cheap horror picture.

McCarty: Of the kind American International Pictures would soon be cranking out, like *Invasion of the Saucer Men* [Edward L. Cahn, 1957]. Why didn't the studio just go with the title of Jack Finney's original story?

McCarthy: To avoid confusion with an old Boris Karloff/Bela Lugosi picture called *The Body Snatcher* [Robert Wise, 1945], which was still in circulation. I think the studio added the "invasion of" to capitalize on the success of *It Came from Outer Space* [Jack Arnold, 1953]. About the title: I asked Don during the course of the filming what he had in mind as a better title or a "classier" one. But he was always so damn busy dealing with the endless details of getting the story on the screen. So *he urged me* to come up with something—"C'mon, kiddo! Think! Cudgel your goddamn brains while you're sitting on your butt waiting for your next shot!"—which was pretty hilarious. I don't recall ever having a chance to sit down at the rate he was putting Dana Wynter and me through our paces. However, before I'd come west to do Mr. Wanger's film, I had been doing some Shakespeare—at the Actor's Studio, there on West 44th Street of the Big Apple—working on some scenes from Hamlet and trying to incorporate the "melancholy Dane" into my being—and so the Bard of Avon's remarks were, and still are, very much a part of me. It's astonishing how, as you run through his soliloquies, how all manner of great phrases and concepts imbedded in them are familiar to us now, as titles or quotations. Anyway, sir, put me back in Hollywood now, in your mind's eye, on location up in Beachwood Canyon (circa 1955), and, if you will, see me as "Doc" Miles standing by to do a two-shot with beautiful Becky Driscoll; but running Hamlet's words in my head, as we wait to get before the camera . . . eureka! the bolt from the blue came zipping through my noodle—I am struck by three very appropriate words in the famous "to be or not to be" soliloquy: "To die, to sleep, no more—and by . . . a sleep to . . . say . . . we—Hold on! To . . . sleep no more . . . SLEEP NO MORE!" *How about that!* Maybe that . . . could . . . be . . . our new title!!??? Don! Listen! It's damn pertinent, too, isn't it?" Don, delighted, kept exclaiming, "*Sleep No More! Yes*! That's *it*! That's *it*!" Of course, a decision to ditch the "invasion" moniker would be up to the studio brass, and Don was sourly pessimistic about his chances there. "Those *pods* will never let us use it." Correct! They didn't. Again a case of Vonnegut's, "So it goes!" Ah, me!

McCarty: Why did he immediately think of you for the starring role in *Invasion of the Body Snatchers*?

McCarthy: Who knows if I was his first choice! I don't think it was any big thing. It was a job and he was casting, some of the scenes would be very demanding physically and he needed someone who was up to it. In *The Annapolis Story,* he had seen I could handle a variety of tough or strenuous jobs. Where my vigor and stamina comes from I don't know, but I've always had more than my share of energy.

McCarty: And you weren't too expensive.

McCarthy: I believe I may have picked up seventy-five hundred "Georges" (or possibly, I made ten "Clevelands" *overall* for *Invasion of the Body Snatchers,* but that's a guess). We made the picture in a little over three weeks, so, let's see, that would be twenty-five "Ben Franklins" per week, or five "McKinleys" per week; a remarkably modest fee. Peanuts. What the hell, I was a *small soldier* serving Titans whose pockets were choked with "Chases" and "Woodrow Wilsons." Today, the treasury no longer issues anything larger than "Ben Franklins."

McCarty: Did you do a screen test?

McCarthy: No, no. Don just said he'd like me to play Miles in the film and I liked working with him, so I said yes.

McCarty: You've been quoted as not having particularly liked the script by Daniel Mainwaring.

McCarthy: Forget quotes! Anybody can drop them in the brew. I probably said his screenplay struck me as being a *less subtle* and *sophisticated* piece of work than Jack Finney's serialized novel, which had come out in a paperback edition by that time. Of course, it could be said that it is *Dan's adaptation* that made filming of Jack Finney's story feasible and is the source of the film's power. However, in streamlining the story from Finney's novel, not much depth of character is revealed in any of the participants—hardly a flicker of individuality emerges.

McCarty: So what can be done?

McCarthy: Don't you think the public has become pretty well aware of the various ways actors go about trying to enhance the humanity of parts that on paper are just *stock* characters? Actors try to put their minds and feelings to work to develop the *backstory* of their characters; in other words, they seek to imagine the life and incidents of their characters before the film story begins—material that probably won't show up in the plotted action but hints of specific humanity help to flesh out a flatly written role.

McCarty: In what way less sophisticated?

McCarthy: Look at these men and women we portray: Miles Bennell, successful small-town doctor; Dana Wynter's character, Becky Driscoll, a somewhat sophisticated lady, not just a small-town girl. And King Donovan's Jack Belicec was a writer. All educated, adult people, but most of their talk was simply "straight," lacking the curves and nuances that you often hear in the conversation of ordinary, mature men and women. We missed that—didn't find much texture in Mainwaring's script. Of course, in a certain way, there's hellish little time to get very well acquainted with the characters in our story, with events moving at the frantic pace which they do. But they were a touch too humorless. Wouldn't sophisticated adults have injected some kind of mordant remarks into a few of those interludes, as frightening as they were?

McCarty: Did Mainwaring make any changes in the script prior to or during shooting to bring more of that flavor out?

McCarthy: We went with what we got on the first day. I never met Mainwaring. It's known that Don thought highly of him. The actors had some chat with our director about letting a little humor—even guillotine humor—enter into the playing of a scene where it wouldn't seem incongruous. Don was all for it. So, if during the rehearsal of a scene it occurred to one of us, or to Don, that the moment almost called for a humorous line of some kind, you would find one of us going for it! For example, when Becky says to me, "Is that an example of your bedside manner, Doctor?", a saucy ad lib popped out of my mouth in reply: "No, that comes later!" (seems *tame* now—*not then!*) Yup, well, Don's attitude resulted in a lot more salt and/or spice getting into the original rough-cut film but, sorry to say, in the end they harpooned most of our tidbits of humor.

McCarty: Who is "they?"

McCarthy: The "Broidy Bunch." The "pod posse" from the production office lassoed our tiddledywinks and exterminated them! That was "early" Allied Artists, headed by a guy named Steve Broidy. This was the middle period in the studio's history, before Walter Mirisch came in to class it up by making pictures with A-list directors like William Wyler, John Huston, and Billy Wilder. The studio was once called Monogram, a poverty row kind of studio, comparatively speaking.

McCarty: What did Broidy and company do?

McCarthy: The provocation for the attack on the original rough cut of our *Body Snatcher* movie came about like this: I wasn't in town then, so I got the story secondhand from Ted Haworth, the production designer on *Invasion of the Body Snatchers,* who was there when it happened. When the film was in work print stage, Don and Wanger decided to take it to a theater in Long Beach one Saturday night to test audience reaction before going to a final cut.

McCarty: Sort of an unofficial sneak preview.

McCarthy: Completely unofficial. In fact, Don, Wanger, and Ted *sneaked* the cans of the *Body Snatchers* print off the lot and brought along a new Webcor wire recorder and turned it on in the theater to record the audience reactions to the film. I gather it was wild—went from shrieks and screams to laughter and back to shrieks and screams throughout the screening. The three "sneakers" were elated; convinced they had something very special. So, on Monday A.M. they brought the recorder [wire all *re*wound] to the Broidy office, and turned it on to regale the studio boss with the fantastic sounds of the Long Beach audience in the throes of its wild reactions to the *Body Snatchers* preview, but even as the noise was bouncing off the office walls Broidy hit the roof, out-screaming the Webcor, "What the hell did you think you were doing? Nobody gave you guys permission to take the film down there and run it!! We don't do sneak previews! *We make 'programmers,' exploitation pictures*—and what-in-hell is that *laughter* in there—!!" He ordered them out and evidently instructed his editors to remove virtually all the humorous nuances Siegel had—

with a little help—instilled in the picture to give it a little subtlety and sophistication.

McCarty: One of the myths surrounding the movie is legendary director Sam Peckinpah's allegedly having a hand in rewriting the script, which is disputed by his biographers. Did he?

McCarthy: Nonsense! Sam had no hand at all in rewriting the script. There was no rewriting going on; but he did have the script *"in hand"*: he was *the dialogue director,* the guy on the set who always has the script available in case of uncertainty about a word or a speech, etc. He also played the pod meter reader. Seemed like a decent guy. Had a little curve on what he had to say; but was otherwise fairly unassuming. Wore a small mustache.

McCarty: Was the the film all cast when you arrived in L.A.?

McCarthy: Guess so . . . I just came out, found myself a hotel somewhere, and showed up for work. I can recall so clearly coming off the TWA plane after a seven-hour flight and spotting my director standing there in the night air at the foot of the steps, Don of the twinkling eyes and crooked smile. He greeted me with the line, "Well, kiddo, what about it? Do you think we can pull this off?" Instantly my identity became clear. I was a spore that had just descended from space with a mission to perform, landing here next to an entity designated as a Mr. Don Siegel, which entity which could surely use my extraterrestrial or heaven-sent talents, so I said simply, "I do."

McCarty: Thank goodness! What do you recall about Dana Wynter?

McCarthy: A paragraph of appreciative adjectives for her! A delicious, delightful, adorable lady; humorous, bright; very composed. She was so attractive, just luscious and princessly, you might say. She had a sedateness to her and a reserve. You didn't make any passes, or moves, or remarks, or you didn't get out of line with Dana Wynter. I don't think we ever even had a meal together, or any kind of an et cetera. . . . God, no!—gol' darn it! . . . But I wasn't unaware of her glamorous femininity—hell, no! . . . And was lucky enough to kiss those luscious lips. Inside all the while the melancholy McCarthy was reeking with wishful desire for a closer relationship with the heroine, but Dana wasn't up for grabs—no invitational flirt ever lurked behind her lovely eyes. She was cool, but never cold . . . and yet . . . ah! . . . and yet! Whew! Am I inventing all this, now? Isn't it likely that I did experience beastly male inclinations toward that goddess and kept them hidden? I do keep a lot hidden; even now while I'm in this revealing modality with you, sir.

McCarty: Let go! C'mon! Let go, Kevin!

McCarthy: All right! *Now* I can safely speak the unspoken desire, "Yes! yes! yes! I want you! Dana be mine! Or let me be yours! Either way is *okay!* [he sings] "Love I Bring You My Heart! If You Would Take This Gift I Bring You—Tell Me Tonight! Etc." and then some! I made another film with Dana (*and* Raymond St. Jacques), *If He Hollers, Let Him Go* [Charles Martin, 1968] but found myself at sea, "Without a Song!"

McCarty: How about King Donovan and Carolyn Jones, who plays his wife, Teddy Belicec?

McCarthy: Same thing; didn't *really* get to know either of them very well. We were just people busy working. But

I had a friend on the set for a week or so: Larry Gates, who was playing the little town's psychiatrist, Danny Kaufman, the guy who turns out to be the mouthpiece for the virtues of being a pod.

McCarty: Did you get together to reminisce while you were making the film?

McCarthy: Not much; dear Larry and I maybe shared a couple of coffee breaks.

McCarty: Were you antisocial?

McCarthy: Maybe I didn't eat!

McCarty: *You* had to—you were working like a truck horse, kiddo—in your jitney for maybe a total of no more than ninety seconds of screen time—yet stirring your stumps madly for the other eighty minutes or so.

McCarthy: Remind me not. Any time I jump out of my bed at night, to stamp out a damn charley horse, takes me back to those 1955 shindigs. I *see myself* in some of those shots loping around Santa Mira with *roped calfs!* No absorbine stops to be found. But the toughest day for me was staggering up those long, interminable stairs (still there) on that steep flank of Beachwood Canyon and then across and down the rugged landscape that falls away to Bronson Canyon. The crew had rigged a gizmo out of block and tackle and so forth so the camera could dolly upwards but be looking downwards to study Dana and me (for half a day) as we tried to escape the pursuing throng of vegetables. We made it to the crest! Half-hour lunch break. Then we started down the other side of the hill into Bronson Canyon, fighting our way through wild brush, the terrain, rough and moguly. Then Dana took her spill and I carried her into the cave where we hid under those boards. Rigorous going.

McCarty: There's a shot where the foot of one of the pod people who pursues you into the cave slips between the boards, but the camera cuts away just before he falls.

McCarthy: Oooh—yes! I remember that happening; we couldn't move—two people glued together in that space in the dirt, under the deafening pounding of our pursuers' feet on the bouncing boards six inches above our heads and then—that foot ripped in at us!! The incident was accidental but the camera caught it and Don was glad to have another tortuous turn of the screw.

McCarty: One of the strengths of the film, what makes it so chillingly effective, is its everyday look, the *believability* of the locations. How much of the film was shot on sound stages?

McCarthy: Most of it was filmed on low-key natural locations, but there were some scenes in the studio, too. The challenge for the production designer, Ted Haworth, was to match the soundstage stuff with the real locales in terms of naturalness and authenticity, and that he did and did well. For example, all the scenes taking place in my office were produced in convincing style, in our Sunset Studios. There is talent galore in the various craft divisions. However, the glimpses one gets of the fictional town of Santa Mira were all extracted from spots within the limits of this metropolis of millions of inhabitants (that doesn't include those pods still lying low). The scene where you see the seed pods being unloaded from the farm trucks for distribution to parts unknown? A [P.O.V.] shot made of the town square of Sierra Madre not far from Pasadena. The interiors of the house where Becky lives and her father [Kenneth Patterson] plants her poisonous pod in their cellar? Made in some rented residence on a pleasant street near the studio and the deserted cocktail lounge, where, early in the film, I order the dry martini—that I never get to drink—the Real McCoy.

McCarty: That scene is one of the film's creepier touches, at least in retrospect, because it really sets up the whole disturbing idea of what it's like to be a pod: no emotion, no passion, no real interest except survival. The guy's business is off because nobody is going out anymore to enjoy themselves. There's no need for it. But the scene in the Belicecs' house where that weird blob spread out on the pool table, already a halfway materialized "Belicec pod," that later begins to come awake is, for me, *the film's creepiest high point*.

McCarthy: There is still, no doubt, on a quiet street up near Lake Hollywood, a now legendary dwelling where we dealt with that horrific interlude. But the greenhouse ("podding shed?") next door to Miles's house, where the pods for the four of us are stashed and waiting to "morph" to life was soundstage work. Hell, yes, had to be done in the studio, because there were so many elements that needed to be controlled (and I'm not talking about the talent!): the bursting open of the pod casings, the inflation of the pods themselves, the foaming bubbles that gradually reveal our likenesses. Rubber casts were made of each of us: Dana, King Donovan, Carolyn Jones, and the Kevin person.

McCarty: How was that done?

McCarthy: We were sent to a nondescript Melrose Avenue joint in Hollywood, that was in the plaster-cast business, I guess. We stripped to our respective gender "essentials" before getting into the casting tubs. . . . ("Now, now! one to a tub! Hop out of there, Mr. McCarthy, no monkey business in the vichyssoise, please!")

McCarty: Wouldn't I love to have been over there that day with my paid-up "Peeping John" card.

McCarthy: Once in your own special tub it was filled with slurpy, plaster goop until you were completely immersed—not underwater, but worse—totally under the goop and as the stuff hardens and heats up at the same time, *you discover you are imprisoned and immobile and breathing only through a soda straw in some anonymous sadist's cockamamie kiln*. Yes! my big head (don't say it, JM!) got in the gunk, too; naturally so: when the pod that contains my duplicate opens and you see its ghastly contents—that spooky creature has got to be a very vivid, damn good copy of me—same for Dana—or the show don't go on!

McCarty: Some guys have all the fun, Kevin. Maybe you are one of the last of the Good Time Charlies.

McCarthy: Hang on, John! We are getting to the crux of the conflict between *Body Snatchers* and the *Defenders of the Faith in Humanity*. But let's move along, folks! United Parcel has delivered the goods. The inflatable rubber pods made from our plaster casts have been signed for, and at this point in our account, are done and good—and the various orifices of the pods are well-connected to the hoses of the Allied Artist's Special Effects Department. All right! I must ask you to imagine us, now, on our Studio soundstage, in the haunted greenhouse—where the director, camera team, and crew are getting set to photograph the action between the pods and the four palpitating actors tensely waiting to confront their nemeses. "Okay! On to *the big moment*!" Last minute instructions from Mr. Siegel. "Listen folks!" says Don. "We've got a two-bit operation going on here—no cost overruns possible—no duplicates to fall back on!! 'Twarn't in the budget. If something goes cockeyed—such as, God help us—Mr. McCarthy's pod having a goddamn flat or a blowout before the crucial moment—well, that would be doomsday for the pivotal scene in this flick! So let's give it no further thought—upward and onward with arts! Now, here's the way we'll shoot this thing. The camera will see the pods popping open and your "duplicates" flop out and expand until they're life-size; Miss Wynter's twin, a vision of glistening beauty, apparently just emerging from a bubble bath, in her life-size peapod shell, should take stage first, and then, Whoopee!—Kevila McPod in all *his* virile pulchritude should come gliding in—or burbling in—or plopping in, beside the delectable Becky-pod. Camera then sees *you*, Kevin, in a closer shot—pitchfork in hand, observing this whole horrific event; next, a series of shots—Very Close on "Miles"—I'll want to see your pitchfork coming up into the shot just beside your right shoulder, and then you should start making a couple of small "aiming" moves downward as if preparing to strike. Earlier in the shot, I will have had a glimpse of those terrifying long, sharp tines of your pitchfork gleaming beside your head as you are looking down at that gorgeous McCarthy puss which you are about to stab." "But Don," says I, "what if I smack this rubber version of me and instead of piercing the darn thing, the fork just sorta pricks it and bounces off??? Don barks, "Don't just *hope* to pierce it, you prick, stab your alter self right in the puss! Your puss—you'll recognize your own face I assume, eh?"

McCarty: Hold on! Was there an NC-17 category in those days? *The kids!* . . . Huh?

McCarthy: (Eliminate the negative, McCart!) "For God's sake, Miles, stab it, don't just pierce it, and don't miss! We've only got one of you. *Also, for God's sake, if you're not sure of hitting the pod puss, the target, so to speak, then stop!* If you miss and you end up puncturing your rubber self—outside the area the camera lens is focused on—*we'll have no shot!* What we'll have is a flat Bennell pod and a flatter McCarthy because I'll be knocking you on your ass!"

McCarty: One of the scenes that has always bothered me is the one where you come back to the cave and discover that Becky has become a pod.

McCarthy: Because it gives the impression that Becky herself has actually *turned into a pod.* Bingo! Just like that! Which, we know, is not how takeovers occur. Don gives the audience no time to be speculating about it, by having them riveted to *what Miles may discover up on the hillside.* It needs to be realized that the film's point of view, primarily, is "what Miles sees." Watching this key sequence in the film, I have the impression that Miles hasn't been out of the cave for more than a minute or two; nonetheless the magic of Becky's transformation in the cave is sprung on us, no explanation! Two minutes to ten minutes, whatever—*they* got her and the show must go on! (A good time could be had by hearing or reading possible scenarios for The Happening.) Of course, by that time in the film "pod power" has been so prevalent and ubiquitous and the audience so brainwashed that Becky's transformation slides into place without a "Wait a second, Don, what happened in the cave that we weren't able to see?" And thus the audience goes with whatever Miles discovers, which, as we find out, ain't good. Alarmed to find Becky apparently dozing, he seizes her—embraces her. But loses his footing as he desperately tries to pull her from the cave and the deadly inhuman sleep, he tumbles down into the mud. Still, he attempts to awaken her with a feverish kiss, only to realize he's embracing a pod bod and his lips are smushing pod lips!! Oh, N-o-o-o! Becky isn't Becky anymore!

McCarty: Becky's loss is a rather bleak turn of events.

McCarthy: To put it mildly, and the way the film originally ended was even bleaker. Miles out on the night highway—in the headlights of streams of traffic, trying to stop someone—screaming to the motorists for help, "Get outa there, you bum!" but no one would heed him—and the final shot, the image on which the (O.V.) picture ends, was of Miles looking dead into the camera in a last spasm of horror and screaming that desperate warning, "They're coming! You're next!" But the studio, specifically Steve Broidy, got cold feet. He said, "That ending is too downbeat." Broidy insisted on shooting a prologue and epilogue, where my character is brought to a skeptical psychiatrist [Whit Bissell] who eventually believes me when he learns about a truck carrying these strange, huge seed pods that was involved in an accident, and calls the FBI. Some narration was added as well to tie the prologue and epilogue together, and that's how the film went out and is still shown today.

McCarty: Did Daniel Mainwaring write those added scenes?

McCarthy: I think either he convinced Don, or the other way around, that if the scenes *had* to be done, *they* should do them rather than some hack. So, maybe six months after the picture wrapped, when I was in South Africa shooting the pilot for a proposed TV series that never came to pass, I got a call from Don asking me to come back; I did the narration and he directed the prologue and epilogue with me, Whit Bissell, and Richard Deacon. We shot them on a soundstage in what is now KCET Television, the public television station out here.

McCarty: In a way, the added scenes solve nothing, for while the menace has been exposed, it hasn't been eradicated.

McCarthy: Yes, but you get the impression that it *will* be eradicated, which is the upbeat note Broidy wanted to end on. But who knows, maybe Broidy saved us all, because the film turned out to be a big hit, although it took a long time coming. At first the picture just disappeared. There was evidently some tiny little notice in the *New York Times*, which tends to review all films when they first open. But I was totally unaware the picture had legs until I was doing a play called *Brecht on Brecht* in New York some time later. After the show, we'd all go over to the White Horse Tavern to unwind, and I well recall hearing some of the regulars saying, "Hey, Kev, we're going up to 42nd Street tomorrow. It's coming back!" The picture kept reappearing, and then I heard from Don that people like the future director Francois Truffaut, who was a movie critic at the time, had raved about the film, even in its tampered form, in the French magazine *Cahiers du Cinema.* Don hated that prologue and epilogue, though, and the narration just bugged the hell out of him. He thought the original ending was so much more frightening, even if it was bleak, which was true. But I think Ted Haworth, the production designer, was even more upset. Ted wrote a letter to Broidy telling him he was destroying the picture. Ted had worked with Alfred Hitchcock, as had Wanger, and he said Hitchcock would have given his eyeteeth to have made a picture as frightening as this. I still have a copy of that letter. Ted thought the film was a masterpiece.

McCarty: Do you?

McCarthy: It's got some masterful things in it. It's undeniably a classic, that's for sure. Here we are still talking about it forty years later.

McCarty: And one of the things most often talked about is the film's meaning. Most people today accept that the film was intended as an attack on the communist witch-hunt mentality of the 1950s. Would you agree with that particular interpretation?

McCarthy: I wouldn't dispute it, although there was never any talk of it among any of us when we were making the film.

McCarty: What did you think it was about?

McCarthy: I viewed it as an attack on or satire of Madison Avenue attitudes. *The whole idea of programming us*

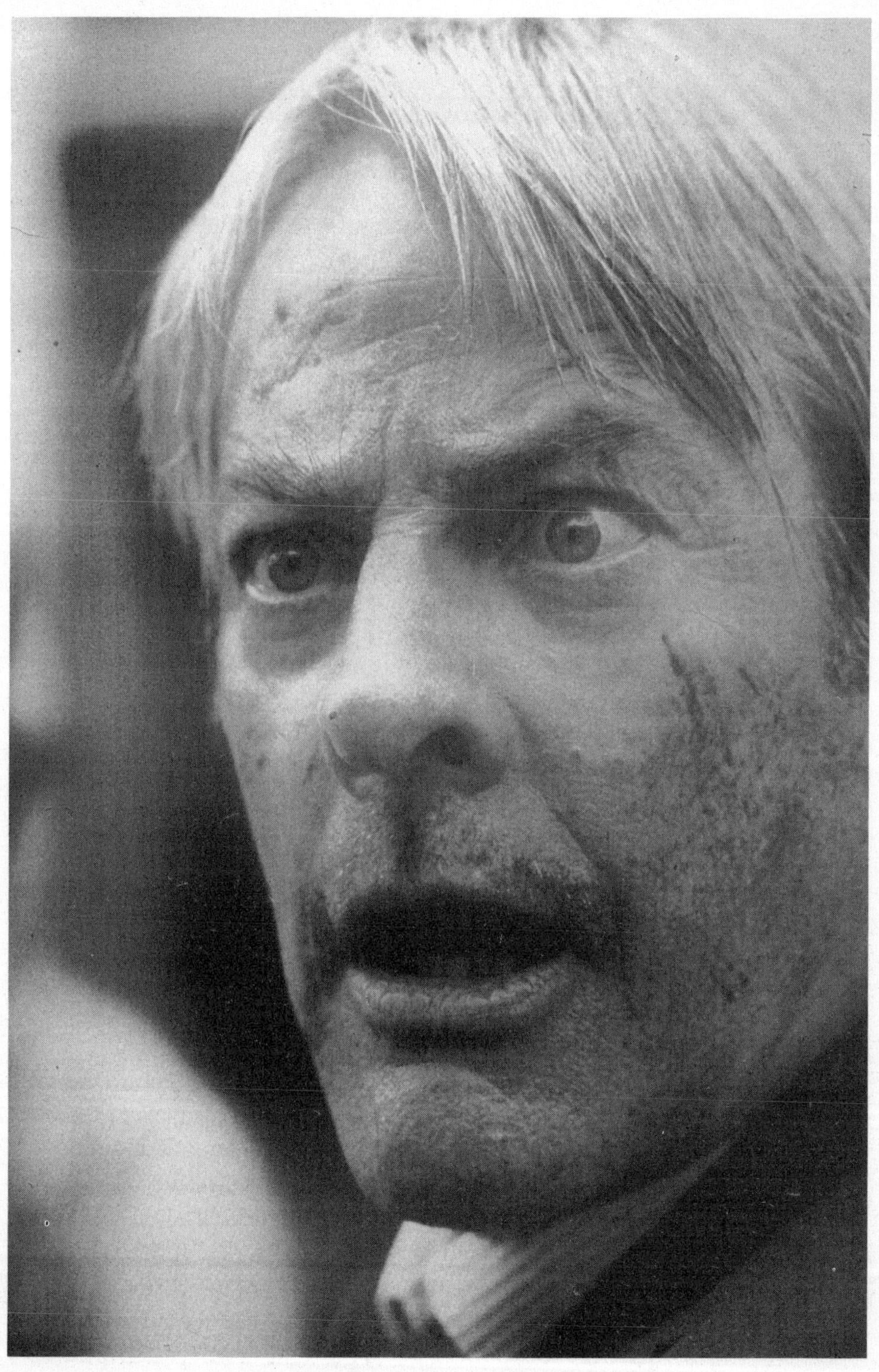

Kevin McCarthy, star of the original *Body Snatchers* classic, in the 1993 remake. Photo from *Invasion of the Body Snatchers* courtesy of Republic Entertainment, Inc.

to eat the same foods, drink the same beverages, conform to certain modes of behavior.

McCarty: Vance Packard's *The Hidden Persuaders* and the "man in the gray flannel suit" sort of thing.

McCarthy: Yes, though I can see where it resonates with the political witch-hunt theme, too.

McCarty: Especially these days, where the "us versus them" mentality is polarizing every aspect of America's social and political life, it seems. The witch-hunt theme was even more pointed in the 1978 remake directed by Phil Kaufman in which you had a cameo. How did that come about?

McCarthy: I was calling on James B. Harris, Stanley Kubrick's old partner, at MGM. He was considering me for a project that never bore fruit. Don Siegel was also at MGM that day either making, preparing to make, or just having made a film called *Telefon* [1977], which Harris produced. Harris told me Don was on the lot so I looked him up, and he introduced me to Phil Kaufman, who was doing the remake of *Invasion* for MGM in which Don had a cameo as a pod cab driver. So, Kaufman asked me if I would make an appearance in the remake, too. I said, "Sure. Why not?" I went up to San Francisco and shot the cameo in a day, but the producer, Robert H. Solo, didn't want to pay me anything except my expenses for airfare, meals, and a hotel. He said, "We just want you to make a contribution." I said, "Listen, I'm a working stiff. I can't just make a contribution." He said, "Well, Don's doing his cameo for free." And I said, "Well, Don's getting about $250,000 a picture, and I think it's great that he's giving you a freebie. Would he give you a day's worth of his directorial talent "on the house," so to speak. "At least pay me scale," which he finally agreed to do. Don Sutherland played my part in the picture and Brooke Adams was Becky. They almost run me over in their car when I race into their path like a lunatic. It was the idea of the screenwriter, W. D. Richter, to have me bang on the hood shouting the exact same lines I'd used in the original, "They're coming! You're next!" It was as if the epilogue hadn't been tacked on and here I was, twenty years later, still running all over the place, trying to convince people of the pod menace. I liked the "time warp" idea of that and enjoyed doing it.

McCarty: How do feel about your performance in the original?

McCarthy: Less is more didn't seem to be my strong suit in those days. It seems strong—almost painfully so, and yet very real. I feel somewhat uneasy about the intensity of certain scenes, but maybe that gives the picture its extra measure of credibility. I forget it's me and feel, "Wow, that character really has his back up against the wall, doesn't he?"

McCarty: Right after you did *Body Snatchers,* you did a film called *Nightmare* [Maxwell Shane, 1956], based on a Cornell Woolrich story, in which you played a guy who is also pretty stressed out.

McCarthy: I played a musician who becomes convinced he had committed murder while under hypnosis. Virginia Christine was in that. She was also in *Body Snatchers.* It was a remake of *Fear in the Night* [1947], which was directed by the same man. *Star Trek*'s DeForest Kelley played my part in the original, which I've never seen. I don't remember any incident or any anecdote about *Nightmare*. I just remember doing it and being excited about playing in the same film, being on the same soundstage, with Edward G. Robinson.

McCarty: What was he like?

McCarthy: Amiable, friendly. Just another hard-working guy.

McCarty: Why didn't you ever work with Don Siegel again after *Body Snatchers?*

McCarthy: I always wanted to work with him again, but it just didn't happen, though we stayed friends and saw a lot of each other. I was working in something at Universal when he appeared one day. He kidded with me, then looked at me and said, "No, you've got the wrong smile. Your gums show." I guess he decided I wasn't right for something he was doing, though what it was I never found out. It was about the time he was making *The Killers* [1964], I think.

McCarty: Given the sheer number of things you've done on stage and screen, do you ever resent the dominant emphasis people place on *Invasion of the Body Snatchers* in discussing your career?

McCarthy: Hell, no! I don't find myself resenting that attention. Can't think why I should mind getting a boost from that sector, and in the end, I'm damn thankful. What I'm finding out is that as time goes by there are not as many major opportunities for me on the screen or the tube as I would like; but, even as this becomes apparent, the Body Snatcher "factor" in my life is burgeoning with startling strength. Besides, I do get a chance to talk about other things when I do seminars and speak before groups about the business, the acting life, just as you and I are doing. I get asked about "Long Live Walter Jameson" [1960], an episode I did for Rod Serling's *Twilight Zone* [CBS, 1959–1964], almost as much as *Body Snatchers*.

McCarty: In it, you played a thousand-year-old man with the gift of immortality. You get found out by your umpteenth future father-in-law [Edgar Stehli], who shoots you to keep you from marrying his young daughter, and you finally turn to dust.

McCarthy: [laughs] Almost a mirror of real events, except for the ending. My second wife, Katie, is also much younger than I am. In fact, I'm older than my father-in-law.

McCarty: How did you get the part in that episode?

McCarthy: It may have had to do with the fact that I was a New York actor and had experience playing all kinds of parts. A lot of very talented people have had very successful careers playing essentially their own personalities. The *Twilight Zone* people seemed to prefer using actors who could call on something else.

McCarty: Plus you had also worked in what is now known as the Golden Age of Television, during which Rod Serling also made his mark. Did you know him?

McCarthy: Never met him. I mainly dealt with Buck Houghton [the producer] and Anton Leader [the director] when I did that show. Them and the makeup man, William Tuttle, and cameraman, George Clemens. Clemens had worked on *Dr. Jekyll and Mr. Hyde* [Rouben Mamoulian, 1931] and used the same photographic trick to reveal the initial stages of my aging process before your eyes that he had used to turn Freddy March into Mr. Hyde, but at a fraction of the budget, he told me. Lines were drawn on my face in different-colored greasepaint to suggest deep wrinkles and creases. They were gradually revealed by removing similar color filters from the camera lens. The rest was done with masks, ending with just my dust on the floor. Some cuts were made to that show over the years. There was a scene where a photographer snaps a picture of me that later appears in a newspaper—the picture that leads this old woman played by Estelle Winwood, a great old gal, to recognize me as the husband who walked away from her forty years ago. In some versions of the show, you don't see the picture-taking process, though it doesn't seem to matter.

McCarty: Why do you think that episode endures?

McCarthy: It's amazing, isn't it? People still find it unforgettable. There's some power in there that I don't quite understand. I'd like to think it's the intensity of the fact that the audience really believes it's happening, that I'm really undergoing that situation. I flatter myself to think that could be it. Many other episodes that are just as well done don't seem to sustain that kind of interest, but this one does. Maybe it was the writer.

McCarty: Charles Beaumont. Did you meet him?

McCarthy: Yes, I did. He was interested in automobiles, especially racing cars. He wrote quite a few of the *Twilight Zone* shows.

McCarty: What about Anton Leader? Do you recall anything about him? He seems to have just vanished.

McCarthy: He was a director who had worked in the New York television scene. I think I may have worked for him in one or another of the various things I appeared in on television in New York. I've done so much stuff, I've forgotten a lot of it.

McCarty: You never appeared in another episode of the *Twilight Zone.*

McCarthy: No, that was the only one [laughs]. They just used me once and threw me away.

McCarty: But you did appear in the segment Joe Dante directed for *Twilight Zone—The Movie* [1983], the segment based on another of the *Zone*'s most memorable episodes, "It's a Good Life" [1960] written by Rod Serling from a story by Jerome Bixby. How did that come about?

McCarthy: Joe came up with the idea because I'd already worked with him several times. I got started with him on *Piranha* (1978), the picture he did for Roger Corman—Joe's first big break, if you can call it that. It was a variation on *Jaws* [Steven Spielberg, 1975], but funnier.

McCarty: Even Steven Spielberg liked it.

McCarthy: Yes, I think that's why Spielberg asked Joe to direct *Gremlins* [1984], which I was not in. Anyway, I had a good time doing my own stunts in *Piranha,* like jumping into the river to be eaten by my own nice little piranhas. I had a lot of chances to act up a storm in that film, which I enjoyed. Joe is the kind of person who will use somebody again and again. He used me in his next film, *The Howling* [1981] and five or six times after that. There were also a couple of times when he wanted to use me, but it didn't work out, and other instances like *The 'Burbs* [1989], a film Joe did with Tom Hanks, where I wound up on the cutting room floor.

McCarty: In your segment for *Twilight Zone—The Movie*, you played Uncle Walt, a character that wasn't in the original TV episode.

McCarthy: I was supposed to play the father. Joe sent me the script. It was all very hush-hush. Steven Spielberg was producing and he exerts a lot of control over who gets to play what. He said, "Do you want to play the father?" I said, "No, I want to play the uncle, the guy who pulls the rabbits out of the hat." So he said okay, and William Schallert, another Joe Dante regular, was cast as the father.

McCarty: Apart from the rabbit trick, what was it that appealed to you about Uncle Walt rather than the father character?

McCarthy: I thought the father was, well, just a father, whereas Uncle Walt had special qualities. He was kind of a bum, a down-and-out hanger-on. I found a lot of things to do with him. A big part of the pleasure I get in creating a character is trying to find stuff that's interesting, amusing—some piece of business—to give a character, and Uncle Walt presented a lot of opportunities for that. Joe would say, "Well, there was certainly a riot [during the showing of your rushes] in the screening room today. Thank you very much, Mr. McCarthy." I'd say, "But how much of [what I did] can you use?" And he would laugh and say, "Not much."

McCarty: The segment is about a kid who exerts complete control over all the adults in his life, and, in the end, makes them all vanish because they displease him.

McCarthy: Yes, he decides that everybody's got to go, so they all start disappearing right and left. When it was my turn to vanish, Joe said, "Go over and throw yourself down in that big old armchair surrounded by all those magazines and comic books you've been reading over the years, and we'll zap you there." I suggested having a flask hidden under the cushion, which I would take a swig from just as the end comes, and Joe said okay. Right before I get the kibosh, before the boom gets lowered, before I get this atomic swat out of existence by the kid, I turned to the camera, raised the flask to my lips, and ad-libbed, "This really is the last of Walter Jameson!" Joe cracked up. But something apparently went wrong in the lab—at least that's what Joe *told* me—and my exit line couldn't be used. We couldn't go back and do it again because they had started shooting the next segment of the film, the one directed by John Landis that resulted in that terrible accident where Vic Morrow and those two children were killed.

McCarty: The next film you made with Honest Joe Dante was *Innerspace* [1987], wasn't it? Also produced by Spielberg.

McCarthy: Right. Playing in that film and with those delightful and strikingly talented actors and the nutty but necessary special effects was a favorite entertainment experience for me. I'd like to work early and often with that very dear Meg Ryan and that fabulous clown prince of comic personalities, Martin Short; that's a life I hunger for! And to be a part of the zany—somehow credible, humorous inventions of my favorite maestro, Mr. Dante! And who is finding fault with provocative locations in San Francisco? Do you recall how the very rich guy I played, Victor Scrimshaw, was desperate to acquire the worldwide rights to a secret miniaturization process and would do anything to get them? I marvel at all the things that came to pass because of that one man's greed. It led us up some very imaginative avenues! One day, Mr. Spielberg appeared to observe a goofy scene we were about to shoot in the Botanical Gardens set that was being used as my "breakfast space." Fiona Lewis, my aide in villainy, and Robert Picardo, a thief, were involved with my guy, Victor Scrimshaw, in a quite comical yet horrifying, extremely bizarre scene—but an early morning plane bringing Fiona from Los Angeles was delayed. Precious shooting time was being lost! So to get some part of the action on film, Joe improvised an alternate occupant for Fiona's chair beside me at the table for this weird breakfast interlude. When the cameras rolled and Joe called, "Action!", my snow-white Alaskan hound was sitting there as my breakfast companion, in place of Fiona; but the dog assumed a begging position when a poached egg and toast were set before him. It was a riot, and I imagine I was gurgling with delight at this behavior, but Maestro Joe asked for a more imperious attitude from Scrimshaw and tossed in an ad-lib for me—to be uttered to my canine in a stern and commanding tone; "Never Beg!!!" [Laughs] Then, still *no Fiona*, so the *next* ten minutes were passed with another gag, but *no cameras rolled*. Joe had hidden a giant Body Snatcherish pod among the Botanical greenery and waited for Miles/me to spot it! But, perhaps I was preoccupied with studying the thespic possibilities in the scene where my man Scrimshaw finds himself and his poisonous aide, Margaret Canker, miniaturized—and ensconced among bras and panties and spicy honeymoon doodads in Meg Ryan's locked-up suitcase! With me being preoccupied with figuring out the possibilities of that titillating scene it was up to one of Mr. Dante's shills to fake a fearful scream: *Pod!!!* and pretend to discover the *awful vegetable!* Much laughter and *snapshots* were had by all.

McCarty: Did you get to know Spielberg very well during the making of those films?

McCarthy: On *Twilight Zone—The Movie,* he didn't show up all that much for our episode. The same with *Innerspace.* He appeared on the set once in a while, as just mentioned. Not so long ago I did see the man again when I was making a brief appearance in *Just Cause* [1995]. The cast (which included Larry Fishbourne, Ed Harris, Ruby Dee, Hope Lange, Blair Underwood, Dan Travanti, and costarred a very attractive young actress, Kate Capshaw) were all staying at a Marriott hotel in Naples, Florida, near some of the film's locations. Producer-director Arne Glimcher had a small get-acquainted party for the cast the night before shooting was to begin, and *I* found myself sitting next to Kate C. In the film, she is married to Sean Connery, and I was going to be playing her Dad; which meant I was playing Sean Connery's father-in-law. . . .

McCarty: How about that! Are you going to play age as successfully as you have done youth?

McCarthy: I didn't know Miss Capshaw, but was aware that she had a very good reputation as an actress. I don't think I had seen any of her work; however, she was so friendly and natural and charming, as we sat chatting, that I was thrilled to be kin to her in the film. Anyway, while shooting the breeze during that "warm-up" cocktail, I asked her where she came from: Missouri was the reply. I had been playing Missouri's most famous favorite son, President Harry Truman, in the one-man show, *Give 'Em Hell, Harry!"* for more than a few years, so I advertised myself somewhat just to keep my luster in play. Hah! My enchanting actress-companion also disclosed she had two or three children. I, no doubt, cited the fact of having five bairn myself—but in parallel-time, I was thinking: "This girl is marvelous! Managing to carry on a life 'in the business,' while bringing up kids, is *no easy task*. How in the world does this admirable lady meet her budget—arrange child care—make the rounds—cut the mustard, or *whatever?"* Of course, I thought, she might have a working helpmate: Anyway, I asked her, "Is your husband in our game?" Also thinking the while, "the poor thing *may* be a single mother!" But I didn't get a chance to use the sympathy that was rising in my breast, somewhat prematurely (I am, obviously, a spendthrift "emotional reactor"), for with a delicious laugh, Miss Capshaw said, "My husband is Steven Spielberg." Whoa, Nellie! I bounced into a different time warp for a few minutes.

McCarty: You are turning *me* into an "emotional reactor." What can one take for that?

McCarthy: Actually, I bet she was pleased that I didn't know the fact of that relationship and wasn't talking to her just because she was *his missus*. A few days later, during the running of the *Just Cause* dailies (the *rushes* of the previous day's footage), Steven showed up in the hotel's makeshift screening room to look at the scenes, and as the lights were dimming down, I heard, "Hi, Kevin! It's Steven." I'm saying, "Huh?" *"Steven Spielberg!"*, enunciated he, quite clearly, just as the screen came to life with images of my *fictional* daughter, Mrs. S. herself! I guess he got this odd story from Kate. Haven't run into the man since wishful thinking has me imagining that I am a vagrant blip that drifts ceaselessly on this creative wizard's recirculating stream of consciousness, and any moment now "blip-*Kevin*" will sparkle up into a prime holding sector of the genial genius's bubbling think tank and an intriguing assignment *may be* on its way to this life-size actor—the *Body Snatcher* catcher.

McCarty: It now appears to me that you are a cock-eyed optimist as well as a spendthrift E.R. You were also in *Matinee* [1993], Joe Dante's delightful homage to the giant bug movies of the 1950s.

McCarthy: Yes, I was—in the movie-within-the-movie sequences, the matinee that's being shown, called *Mant!*

McCarty: "Half Man, Half Ant, All Terror!" as the ads exclaimed outside the theater in typical fifties fashion.

McCarthy: Joe populated the cast of the *Mant!* sequences with a host of veterans of fifties sci-fi, such as Robert Cornthwaite [*The Thing from Another World*] and Bill Shallert [Jack Arnold's *The Incredible Shrinking Man,* 1957, et al]. I played the five-star general. Remember the saphead who postpones using his atomic bomb against the Mant threat, when a brainstorm notion hits the galoot's "half-star" imagination and we see him trying to seduce the mammoth bug down from its perch up on the building with a cup of sugar? I put my wits to work on that grueling task in a five-hour one-night stand—proud of myself and of the Dante for casting me so "on the nose" for that challenging venture where I could use myself to the full, deploying my not-so-small army of talents at Universal Studios, Florida 32801.

McCarty: The whole picture was enjoyable, but the *Mant!* sequences are the ones you really come away remembering because they are so dead-on accurate and hysterically funny, though not in a put-down sort of way.

McCarthy: Word is that they're Joe's tribute; the man loves those films.

McCarty: What is it you enjoy about working with Joe Dante?

McCarthy: Well, he's easy, he's friendly, and obviously, the fact that he hires you is a compliment to your work. You feel good that he esteems you. He's quixotic, sardonic like Don Siegel, and inventive. Nothing seems to daunt him.

McCarty: Because he's also a film buff, Dante has a penchant for putting in-jokes into his films for other buffs' appreciation. For example, in *The Howling*, many of the characters were named after notable horror, science fiction, and fantasy film directors. Your character was Fred Francis, after Freddie Francis, the British horror film director with whom you subsequently worked.

McCarthy: Was not aware of that; thankee. Yes, Mr. Francis was at the helm of the jinxed *Dark Tower* [1987], a ghost story we shot in a little studio in Barcelona, Spain. The ghost failed to walk—but we, Michael Moriarty, Jenny Agutter, Theo Bikel, and yours truly, got paid and that was in the right spirit.

McCarty: You last teamed with Joe Dante on a cable TV movie for HBO, *The Second Civil War*.

McCarthy: A super piece of work done on a low budget and limited resources, well disguised by "magic" Joe. It moves like a wild and crazy comedy until the last seven or eight minutes, when suddenly the shooting begins and it turns very gripping. Beau Bridges plays the governor of Idaho. The late Phil Hartman, a fabulously talented guy and dear man, was the president of the United States. James Coburn, his PR guy. I play Hartman's chief of staff, who stocks his place at the cabinet table beside the prez with an array of Alka-Seltzer, Rolaids, Tums, etc. As stress in the "hot room" thickens, my man can be detected nursing himself with succulent slugs from his nippled Pepto-Bismol bottle. Dante's comment might well have been, "Grow up!"

McCarty: On stage, you've been touring the country as Harry Truman in *Give 'Em Hell, Harry!* for a good many years now. How many is it?

McCarthy: Twenty. Have appeared in more than 350 venues in that time. My first performance? At Penn State University in April of '78: got the go sign from a seven hundred–strong student and faculty audience after a one-performance tryout. Since then, in hitting *forty-eight* of our United States, I've done a hell of a lot more whistle-stops than Harry himself ever did. Two goals yet to be kicked: South Dakota and Alaska. Back in 1992, I played our *thirty-third* for *five straight weeks* at the Coconut Grove Playhouse in Florida just after Hurricane Andrew slammed through the area and just as our forty-second President, the venturesome Bill Clinton, was getting acquainted with the dicey, touch-and-go, sticky-wicket atmosphere of the Oval Office. My forty-in-a-row Coconut Grove performances in the Truman Oval Office meant two hours of dynamic vital giving 'em hell, not all hell, of course, but with the same amount of energy. I *did wonder* about the wear and tear of it; musta been nourishing—after each performance felt the better for it.

McCarty: It's almost become your signature role. How did you come to start doing it? *Give 'Em Hell, Harry!*

McCarthy: Jimmy Whitmore originated the role and was enormously successful in it, but he gave it up after six months on the road—don't know why. Another good actor replaced him but, I suspect, limited stage experience stymied him and he asked out. So, producer/playwright Sam Gallu decided to go in another direction and get someone who had a variety of stage work behind him. Some theaterwise New Yorker tipped him off to nail me, which he did, although my physical resemblance to our thirty-third president is almost nil. I told Sam, "I voted for the guy, sure, but look at me. You've got the wrong man." But he'd found something he wanted and talked me into giving it a whack. It took time to "get over" the physical thing but I took the job and have had a great experience *playing* that homespun original. And trying to stay close to his many admirable qualities (in my personal life, as well) has enriched me. Delightful, gutsy, salty, peppery, and funny and strong; and such a very caring person—that's Harry S. Truman.

McCarty: What was the worst review of your performance?

McCarthy: [laughs] Well after a boisterous reception at the curtain and lavish kudos from the local TV personnel backstage in Portland, Oregon, nineteen years ago, I found this in the next morning's newspaper: the reviewer wrote, "Mr. McCarthy seemed to be somewhere else last night. We certainly didn't feel he was with us in Portland."

McCarty: Your best review?

McCarthy: Harry Truman's daughter, Margaret, came to see the show on Saturday, May 8, 1982. It was a benefit performance in Kansas City for the Truman Foundation, or whatever, on the occasion of the late president's ninety-eighth birthday. I was a trifle nervous about it. I'd bumped into her at the Truman Library the day before the show. Said I, after mutual greetings, "I hope you won't lower the boom on me." Her comeback? "No, no, no, I wouldn't dream of doing that." Well, the next night an extremely distinguished audience was in attendance as the lights came up on the very first scene of the play to reveal me as Truman sitting at the president's desk in the Oval Office penning a letter to his dear daughter, and the first thing you hear is my voice saying, "And so, Margaret, to be a good president, I fear, a man cannot be, etc.," and as I looked up, scratching my ear or some damn thing, seemingly thinking of the next phrase, *there, before my eyes, in the front row not ten feet away,* sat the genuine article, Margaret Truman Daniel looking intently at her fictional "Dad." The *front row!* A very discombobulating thing for the not-so-self-confident "mummer" playing Papa, too close for comfort except possibly Southern Comfort and branch water; yet the show must go on, eh? The next morning, Sam Gallu called me from New York and asked me how it went over with Margaret. I told him I had no idea. She seemed friendly to me as she accepted the huzzahs from the audience, but nary a word did she say. She is a very lovely, modest person. Sam said he'd be having lunch with her soon and find out. "Maybe she'll say something we can use," he told me as he hung up. About a week later, I got a letter from Margaret. It read: "Dear Kevin, Sam said you could probably use something for your promotion of the play, and so here is a quote from me if you want it. 'Kevin McCarthy is *superb* as my father in *Give 'Em Hell, Harry!*, Margaret Truman.' "

McCarty: Say, I'm glad I ran into you! Do you prefer theater or movies?

McCarthy: Theater! Oh, sure! It's usually a *much* broader and deeper experience for an actor than most of what you get to do in films or television.

McCarty: Haven't we been talking about some pretty broad and deep experiences with some of the movies you've been in?

McCarthy: Migod. Yes! You have tipped me off to something I have *never* considered closely: It is true you won't find yourself getting much deeper—or ranging much beyond the higher limits of dramatic intensity in theater, than what's called for in the *Death of a Salesman* film or in the *Invasion of the Body Snatchers* movie. But on a more prosaic level—may I inquire of you, Sir John, do you suppose, that at the sci-fi Annual Award ceremonies my 'Lifetime Achievement Award' will be a giant golden pod?

McCarty: You betcha: you are *the* guy who saved the world! What do you feel about your film career overall?

McCarthy: It's no great shakes.

McCarty: Why do you say that?

McCarthy: There are hundreds of admirable achievements in theater and film and television, aren't there? *If* some pieces of my work make it into that honorable registry that would be a pleasant surprise but—damnation—if truth be told, there are too many parts of my makeup, too many deposits in my memory bank that are "bedizened by sin."

McCarty: You, a sinner? What are you gassing about, Goody Two-Shoes?

McCarthy: Envy! The "effing," abrasive *deadly* sin of envy!

McCarty: Is St. Kevin of Glenalough, County Cork confessing?

McCarthy: Hell yes—envy; the Deadly Sin of Envy—about all the parts that didn't come—and aren't coming his way, at the moment. [Interesting sidelight: Dana Wynter our "Becky Weckio" is a longtime resident of Glendalough; hangs her bonnet very nearby to the the hallowed ground of the ancient St. Kevin's Kitchen where the saint hung his "halo" between miracles.] I guess it would have taken a miracle to have made the *Seinfeld Follies*. . . . Wouldn't my appearance as Dr. Miles Bennell (Ret.) toting a punctured pod—a pod with a flat needing a patch, let's say—have made for a wild and crazy scene with Kramer or George Costanza? That's typical of the kind of notions that churn through my upper-story as I wend my diurnal way through the Valley of Dissatisfaction or do a lap around the Reservoir of Lost Opportunities. Surely that'll give you an idea why I'm a mite dissatisfied with my career in film and/or TV. Theater was better: a wider variety of parts to play and ways to use oneself: high drama; tragedy; *daffy* comedy (such as the nutty, forthcoming *Addams Family Reunion* film, wherein I play opposite that intriguing and hilarious Estelle Harris—yes, George Costanza's mother!). She and I are Gomez Addams's grandparents. Oh, Lordy! (That dizzy five weeks as Gramps Addams has sparked my inner ever-ready rabbit to start banging out a bulletin to me inside my echo chamber of a skull: "Kevin! You are really ready to roll now . . . c'mon, man! Let the career come full flower!" Very well, message received. Our voice-mail and fax are standing by.) Seriously, I'm grateful for the warm regard I've gotten for my work from my fellow professionals—it feels damn good. And the public's response all over the place *or the globe* is invigorating. It seems *Invasion of the Body Snatchers* can now be experienced everywhere—from Turkestan to Timbuktu to Tacoma. Great jumping jehoshaphat!—*wherever I get to*—it's been there. Astonishing, isn't it? I'm certainly not reticent with my gratitude and I mostly enjoy the rambunctious give and take that can go on—the "public" feels like my extended family. Yet, all the while, I'm convinced I am being mistaken for someone else—some celebrated luminary or other; so, I'm busy doing double duty: saying thanks for me *and* for the guy I'm thought to be!

McCarty: In thinking about this project, I catch myself becoming aware of an intriguing factor about roles you have played on screen and stage that have a common denominator; two "ordinary" men, with no special endowments, as President Truman said of himself. Yet Harry S. Truman (in real life) and Miles Bennell (in fiction) were able to rise above the ordinary or "average" when called upon; and each, in his own way, overcame enormous odds. And both figures continue to have a unique and powerful influence on life as we know it. I'm glad to have been present at the creation of this memoir about the man who had the good fortune to play those two characters: (1) Mr. Truman, *on stage*, in the one-man show *Give 'Em Hell, Harry!*, and (2) Dr.

Miles Bennell, *on screen*, in the ever-enduring, may I say "gripping," never-to-be-forgotten film we celebrate here, the *Invasion of the Body Snatchers*. Thank you.

McCarthy: Thanks to you, John McCarty.